THE BROKEN

VENGEANCE

A. L. FRANCES

Ruby Rose Publishing

Ruby Rose Publishing
Amazon PAPERBACK

A CIP catalogue record for this title is available from the American/British Library.

ISBN: 978-0-9601051-6-8 (paperback)
ISBN 978-0-9601051-7-5 (ebook)

Amazon is an imprint of
Ruby Rose Publishing House.
Morrisville, PA
www.RubyRosePublishingHouse.com

First Published in 2020
Amazon
Printed & Bound in United States of America

Author's Note

Seeing as this is my final author's note, I would like to make the following statement:

Young people are the very core of purity and innocence.

Young people do not create childhood trauma.

Adult corruption does.

Do not let anyone tell you any different.

It does not matter what role or stance they believe they have in *your life*.

You will always be the innocent one in my eyes.

Dedication

I wrote this for you…

A. L. Frances

Contents

Prologue

Life, the one thing that has the residents of the world wound uptight. Some individuals believe their lives are much more valuable than others. They walk around with their heads held high, as though superior to the rest of the world, doing as they please with seemingly no repercussions, their power and authority over other people having gone to their heads. And where does this notion come from? Generations of history teaching us about hierarchy.

When you read books in school, you learn about your place on the planet and who is untouchable, and get the distinct feeling that you are not. You feel as though your low ranking in this life has left you open to all sorts of abuse by others. After all, who is going to listen to you with your tiny voice?

Let me ask you this, have you ever been aggrieved so badly that you held the firm belief that you were the only person on the planet who could truly get justice for the wrongdoing against you? You are filled with hate, anger and frustration, and deep down you know the legal system isn't powerful enough to dispense justice to the one who mistreated you. The punishment of prison would be too kind, given the level of poison they have injected into your mind, causing you unspeakable pain. The aftermath of this disgusting individual's actions has left you feeling as though they have wrapped their hands around your throat. And with every second, they're squeezing tighter and tighter, slowly draining the life from your body. You're consumed by an overpowering sense of suffocation. Anxiety and fear have set in. Just knowing that this individual is walking around free and could strike again at any moment has you locked away. A prisoner inside your own mind. You know, this person believes they are exempt when it comes to the law of the land. Well, not anymore! *You* have officially had enough. A decision has been made. You want vengeance upon their soul. You want to know that they are going to suffer just like you have. You want justice!

Now, with this newfound strength, you begin to ask yourself just how far you are willing to go, in order to take control of your life and seek the revenge you so desperately crave. Questions circulate at a rapid rate. Are you willing to bare your soul and potentially leave behind the life you have built for yourself? Huh, maybe you *do* want to go to the lengths of committing the ultimate sin and take the last breath from their body… maybe, just maybe, the scars run so deep that you wish to crush them with every part of your existence?

And just like that, once you begin to consider committing the ultimate sin, you can no longer stop yourself from obsessing and visualising the process. A process which thrills you immensely. You take great pleasure as you see yourself smothering the repulsive person with the same evil that they have suffocated you with for so many years. You get them whilst they're sleeping peacefully in their bed at night. Finally, you're winning. Overpowering them by placing your knees upon their shoulders, you then begin pressing with such force that you know they stand no chance of freeing themselves from the destiny you have chosen for them. Once you have reigned supreme over the situation, you become their fate as you place your bare hands around their neck. And, as your fingers feel the warmth of their skin, you begin to squeeze. You squeeze so tightly, you can feel every thud from their pulse. It's gone from rushing like a racehorse competing against its biggest rival, to the slow tempo of a snail trying to move its way across the stone-cold path. With every second that passes, their pulse grows weaker and a rush of ecstasy surges through your veins. You see the life beginning to drain from their body as their eyes roll back and turn bloodshot from the pressure, and you savour every sweet moment for its beauty.

Finally, they've gone quiet. They're no longer pleading for you to spare them their life. No longer pleading for you to let them go and forgive them for the evil which they have inflicted upon you. Instead, they've gone limp and their pulse is no more. They're dead, and it's all because of you. A pure toxic substance is now racing throughout your body and the power feels orgasmic and real. You throw yourself back as you rejoice in the righteousness you have just received. Closing your eyes, you smile because you've won the hierarchy war. You've taken the most precious thing away from them: their life.

Then, as you open your eyes and wake in your bed, you realise it was only a dream. You lay gazing at the ceiling, confused, pondering whether the dream is merely a fantasy that lives inside of you, or is it something more sinister and real? You begin questioning your abilities – is the power truly within you to take the life of another?

As your sadness grows deeper, you hang your head in shame and admit defeat. This vision is, in fact, nothing more than a fantasy. You hold back for one very valid reason. You might have poison surging through your veins for that one individual, but you are not them. You don't have the power within you to take the action required to complete such a toxic task. Not only this, you feel the legal system will be too kind to them and yet highly stressful for you, so you don't even try to reach out and get justice by way of the law. You sit quietly and try to live your life with the pain held deep inside you, as hard as that may be.

Unlike you, Matthew Honey *is* prepared to do anything he can to get the justice he believes he deserves. Even if this results in his own death. A man on a mission, Matthew is ready to take vengeance upon the individual who has stolen his daughter's soul. His time is now! And he's ready to commit the ultimate sin by any means possible. And yet, the question remains: will Matthew live to see the day, or will the evil lurking amongst us devour his soul before he can complete his purpose? Well, there's only one way to find out. It's time for Matthew to meet his daughter's captor. And let it be known: there can only be one victor.

CHAPTER ONE

"What is Happening to Me?"

"Please, no, not again..." Eve whispers tiredly.

Alone, exhausted and surrounded by energies unknown, Eve is standing completely still. Her eyes are the only part of her that are moving. As far as her sight can stretch, she sees nothing but a blanket of black. Desperate to break free from the entrapment that she has once again been very cunningly thrown into, Eve shouts, "Hello?"

A brief silence. Then a quiet repetitive reply travels through her eardrums. Unfortunately for Eve, this reply is not from another person, it's the echo of her own voice. Taking a deep breath and rolling her eyes, she is about to shout again when a bright beam of green light appears from a great distance above her head. Peering up, Eve places her hands above her brow and squints. An instant stabbing pain shoots through her eyeballs as the light permeates through. It's so vibrant it's impossible for Eve to look directly at it. Quickly accepting defeat, she looks away.

The light casts a green tinge on Eve's hair, which is dark brown, bone straight and hangs heavy past her hips. Her feet are bare and grubby looking, as if she had just ran through the depths of a forest with no shoes on. She looks down and sees she's wearing an unfamiliar long, discoloured white cotton gown, which is also tinted green by the light. Frills have been neatly sown around the neck, wrists and hemline. She touches the gown and her fingertips become sensitive as a wet, sticky substance squelches and begins to absorb into her skin. Confused, she looks at her hands and is horrified as they now appear to be covered in a thick, gloopy, bloody substance. Jumping back, Eve gasps. She has no clue where the blood has come from. Checking her body, Eve sees that she isn't the wounded one, and so this can mean one thing! The blood on her hands must belong to someone else. Tears form in her eyes as she whispers to herself, "What have I done?"

Panicked, Eve desperately tries to wipe the blood off her hands onto the gown. She wipes harder and harder, until her hands feel raw, but the bloody substance is getting thicker and is now staining her skin. The more she wipes, the stodgier it becomes. Holding out her hands and watching it develop at a rapid rate, Eve's eyes widen with panic. The substance, which hangs heavy from her fingers, has the consistency of slime. It gradually drips onto her bare feet. Looking around once more, Eve again sees nothing and no one.

"Please, someone help me," she whispers.

She is caught off guard by a swirling sensation, and her head becomes fuzzy, her sight hazy. An intense, gut-wrenching pain rips through the centre of her chest, directly into her heart. Eve falls to the ground. She lies on her side, her mouth wide. The pain is real. She tries to scream out loud, but she cannot. She closes her eyes as tears stream down her face and fluid gushes from her nose. Feeling as though someone is standing over her pouring litres of acid directly onto her chest, Eve curls up into the foetal position and begins rocking back and forth. Resembling a small child, Eve desperately tries to soothe herself. Deep rips tear their way through her chest. The pain becomes unbearable. Eve opens her eyes. "I'll do anything. Please," she mouths.

Eve glances down at her body. The gown is soaked in deep red blood. As the seconds pass, the bloodstains turn black. Her pleas not met, Eve's hands shake as she is filled with apprehension and fear. Gently pulling the frills on the collar of the gown, Eve peers underneath it at her naked body. A wound gapes between her breasts. Layers of skin, muscle and bone have peeled back to expose her heart, and with every thud it pumps out an immense amount of the thick substance. This vital organ is becoming tired. Each thump gets slower than the last one. Nauseous, faint and highly panicked, Eve attempts to shout for help once more. "Help. Please, somebody help me." But again, no sound leaves her mouth. Releasing the gown, Eve curls back into the foetal position.

Her face is bright red and the veins on her forehead begin popping through. Her energy levels are depleting rapidly.

"I'm sorry," she mimes, as her eyes drift closed.

Eve lies flat on her back with her arms spread out either side of her body. She has made the mental transition and has surrendered to the torments. Her consciousness has detached itself from her physical form, and Eve's soul is now floating outside of her body. The sight is horrific. Her white gown is covered in blood and her skin is turning pale. A tinge of grey takes over her once pink lips. Drifting down and kneeling at the side of her own head, Eve attempts to stroke her hair. Seeing her body lie still, she doesn't know whether to feel relieved that she is no longer suffering the cruel torments that continue to tease her daily or to fight for her life.

Then she hears the innocent giggle of her daughter. "Mama."

Stunned, Eve's soul looks around. "Honey, where are you?"

"Mama."

"My baby, where are you?" She looks back at her lifeless body. "No, it can't end like this. Eve, wake up! Your daughter needs you," she cries, desperately attempting to shake her own her body to bring herself back to life. "You can't just quit like this. Please, Eve, you have to wake up!"

But, yet again, her body doesn't so much as flinch. Looking up high, Eve begs, "Please, you have to let me return to my body. Please, it's not our time yet. Please, let me return. I'll do anything you want!"

A sudden force drags Eve back into her physical form. Coughing, she thankfully opens her eyes and pushes her upper body up using what small amount of strength she has. Looking straight ahead, Eve searches for her daughter in the darkness. Her breathing is heavy and she feels as if, at any moment, her ability to expand her lungs will once again be no more. Gasping for air, with her hand to her throat, Eve whispers, “Honey. Where. Are.” She takes a deep inhale of oxygen and continues, “You?” Her head slumps to the ground.

Crawling towards her, wearing a cream-coloured onesie, with a full head of golden-tipped curly brown hair and brown eyes, is her beautiful, bonny, nine-month-old daughter, Honey. Tears fill her eyes. She looks on in admiration as her daughter places one hand and one knee in front of the other. Smiling, Eve doesn’t feel the pain that is ripping its way through her chest. She doesn’t see the blood gushing from her body. In this moment, she’s connected with her one true love, her daughter, and that is all. Reaching out her arms, still fighting for her life, Eve whispers, “Come here, my darling.”

Arriving with a cheeky grin upon her face, Honey nestles her way into her mother’s bloody chest. Embracing her daughter’s love, Eve wraps her arms around her. The thick black substance smears all over Honey’s clothes and body. Not caring about this, Eve savours her daughter’s touch. The pair close their eyes. There is now nothing or no one in sight. No blood, no pain, no measurement of time, just a blanket of black and peace.

“I love you,” Eve whispers.

Content with her daughter’s affection, Eve is ready to submit herself to the entrapment and be devoured by the dark abyss. But she is suddenly woken by multiple voices whispering at a fast frequency. Looking into her arms, she sees her daughter sleeping peacefully, as if not affected by the noise, yet for her, the continuous sound is becoming louder and louder. Covering her ears and closing her eyes once more, Eve realises that she’s powerless. The persistent whispering transitions into an almighty ringing, which travels directly through her eardrum. On top of this sound, Eve hears every mother’s nightmare: her daughter screaming at the top of her lungs. Opening her eyes, Eve is horrified to see a tall, grey, shadowy figure dragging Honey by her legs.

Reaching out, Eve screams “Nooooo!” as she helplessly watches her daughter disappear into the darkness.

She attempts to stand, but is immediately thrown back to the ground by an invisible force.

"Stop! Please, just stop. I'll do anything. Take me, I don't care, just please do not hurt my daughter."

The ringing stops immediately, and in its place is a whisper from an unknown, yet familiar female voice, "Eve, is that you, darling?"

A pause.

"Eve… darling, is it you?"

Eve squints up at the elegant woman hovering above her face. Like an angel, she's radiating a golden glow. Eve sees her smile and it makes her feel warm inside. There is something familiar about her.

The woman tilts her head as she whispers, "Shh." She places her arms around Eve.

An overwhelming warming sensation takes over, and in that slight moment in time, Eve feels safe.

"But my daughter. Please. Help. Me..." Eve whispers.

There is a loud bang and a blinding flash of vibrant green light.

Chapter Two

"The Man"

Eve throws herself forward, desperately gasping for air. It feels like she has been strangled. She touches her chest and her hand becomes moist; her silk blouse is soaking wet. Her senses on high alert and her heart beating uncontrollably, she peers down her blouse at her chest. Sighing with relief, she sees it is nothing more than her own sweat.

She's wearing a knee-length, navy-blue pencil skirt and tanned tights. Her attention is drawn to the huge ladder down her left leg, stretching from her knee to her ankle. One of the buckles on her brand-new shoes has come loose and is hanging on by a thread.

Eve moves a long strand of hair off her face and tucks it behind her ear. Grazing her fingers across her temples, she whispers, "Argh."

Her skin is boiling hot and feels overly sensitive to her touch. Enormous beads of sweat form on her forehead, roll down her skin and drip onto her already saturated blouse. Slowly looking around, Eve sees that she's alone and is sitting on the black and white tiled kitchen floor inside the staff room of the school where she works as a teacher's assistant. At the side of her body, the dark oak chair she had sat on just moments ago is now lying flat. Sharp splinters are exposed from the broken piece of wood that was once a sturdy chair leg.

The ambience is eerie and cold. There is a swift shift in the vibrational energy, and Eve gets the distinct feeling that she's no longer alone. She tries to gulp down the lump in her throat. Closing her eyes, she takes a deep breath in. Upon exhaling, Eve opens her eyes and pulls herself up using the support of the table. Dusting herself off, she stumbles back as the blood rushes to her head. She regains her composure, but her legs feel somewhat wobbly, and so she takes tiny steps over to the sink. Turning the cold-water tap on, she places her hands either side of it and hangs her head. Desperate to feel normal again, Eve cups her hands together and begins aggressively splashing the freezing cold water in her face.

The modern décor room which Eve stands inside caters for all sixty-two staff members at Grange Park Kindergarten and Elementary, situated in the homely, quaint little village of Morrisville in Bucks County, Pennsylvania.

Grange Park provides education for five hundred and seventy-seven children ranging from six months to eleven years in age. Amongst these children are the school's brand-new intake of students: Freddie, Terence, Rupert, Hope and Honey, along with fifty other children from the local newly built orphanage across the way. The same orphanage that is run by Grange Park's very own, brand-new Principal – Principal Jesiah.

Wiping the excess water off her face using a raggedy looking kitchen towel, Eve turns and picks up the broken chair leg. As she places it on the table, she wonders how on earth this could have happened. Touching her scalp, Eve feels an almighty surge of pain through her skull. Distracted by this, Eve's is caught off guard when she hears a creak from the wooden door.

Eve is relieved to see it's her colleague, Mrs Galinsky. Her bright blue eyes glow through the lenses of her leopard-print-framed glasses, which are perched up on her slight freckled nose. Mrs Galinsky is forty-eight and yet she doesn't look a day over thirty. She has short, coarse, red hair and a fringe. Seeing the broken chair on the floor, Mrs Galinsky rushes over to Eve. "Oh, Mrs Parkinson, are you okay?" she says in her over-the-top New York accent. "I've been looking everywhere for you."

"Yeah, sure. Sorry, I'm fine," Eve replies. She walks across to the broken chair, picks it up and rests it against the wall. Pulling out another chair from under the table, she sits down and rests her elbows on the tabletop as she puts her head in her hands.

"How did that happen?" Mrs Galinsky asks as she sits down. "Did you hurt yourself?"

"Not really," Eve replies. "I've got a slight bump on my head, but that's it. If anything, I've just ruined a perfectly good pair of shoes and tights."

Glancing at Mrs Galinsky through the gap in her hands, Eve is filled with sadness. She would love nothing more than to share the burden and tell her colleague what's been happening to her. After all, she and Mrs Galinsky have become quite close in the three months that Eve has been working there. It would be a great relief to have someone whom she can confide in outside of her network, yet the sad reality is, she knows she can't. The secret must remain with her. A burden she must carry. Her blackouts are becoming more and more frequent, and Eve is getting worried herself. The severity of the visions is the greatest concern, and she's struggling to ignore the potential message being given to each one.

"You can tell me anything. I promise I won't tell a single soul. You have my word."

Smiling, as she knows Mrs Galinsky is one of the most genuine women at the school, Eve replies, "I know you wouldn't and I promise, it's probably nothing."

"Have you eaten today?"

Just as Eve goes to answer the question, a sudden crackle blasts through the speaker of the tannoy. A distorted, strong British male voice radiates loudly throughout the school. "All students and staff report to the main sports hall immediately!"

A worried look crosses Mrs Galinsky's face. "That's Principal Jesiah. Oh my, Mrs Parkinson. Here, reach out, you can lean on me." She puts out her hand.

"It's okay, I will be fine to walk alone," Eve replies.

"We can't be late or he'll notice and we'll be in for it."

Standing up, Eve says, "Honestly, I will be fine. You go ahead."

Eve walks across the room and opens the door. Without looking back, Mrs Galinsky rushes out. Feeling an icy blow down her ear, Eve turns. Baffled, she sees there's nothing and no one there. Shaking her head, Eve again steps forward to make her way to the hall, but this time she becomes frozen stiff as the sudden chill travels down her spine and locks her bones tight. Frightened, Eve shouts down the corridor, "Mrs Galinsky, help!"

Unluckily for Eve, her colleague has already disappeared. Eve's senses are back on high alert. She once again doesn't feel alone. The chill develops, taking over the whole room. It circulates around her ankles and travels up her body. As it reaches her face, Eve hears a whisper, "*Prohibere.*"

Eve screams as an intense pins and needles sensation shoots round her body. The hairs on her arms stand to attention and tiny pimples appear on her skin. Again, she hears a whisper: "Beware, Eve."

Unable to move the middle part of her body, Eve slowly turns her head and scans the empty room behind her. Not a soul can be seen. The energy is dense, and the oxygen surrounding her has been tainted, suffocating her from the inside. Desperate to stay in control, Eve closes her eyes and concentrates on breathing deeply.

"One." She breathes in.

"Two." She breathes out.

Five long, deep breaths later, Eve opens her eyes. Something in the far corner of the room piques her interest. A tall wooden bookcase rests against one of the walls. Each shelf is filled with books, all of which have been arranged in alphabetical order. Some are old with tatty covers and spines. Others are new and remain in pristine condition.

Around the lower part of the bookcase a thick grey mist is insinuating its way into the room, bringing with it an icy breeze. This same mist has become all too familiar to Eve. As it continues to spread, it creates icicles on everything it touches. Eve is unable to look away. The mist is almost hypnotic. Her eyes travel up the bookcase. There is a seven-foot gap between this sturdy piece of furniture and the ceiling. Suddenly her eyes widen. On top of the bookcase is a man lying on his back, his legs dangling down over the edge. His hair is jet-black, his skin a tone that belongs only to the afterlife. Wearing a white T-shirt and pair of white trousers, he's got his hands behind his head and is gazing at the ceiling, humming to himself. Without lifting his head, he stops what he's doing and whispers, "I release you."

With a *crack* and a *twinge*, Eve's spine unlocks itself. Relieved that she can once again move her whole body, Eve slowly turns.

"Hello," she says cautiously.

Eve gets no reply.

"Erm, excuse me, you can't be up there."

Again, the man doesn't reply.

Placing one foot in front of the other, Eve carefully makes her way towards the bookcase. Every *thud* of her beating heart can be heard and felt as she takes one nerve-wracking step after another. She knows that this male's appearance cannot be a coincidence. Wanting answers, Eve approaches the bookcase. She doesn't want to scare him off and so, as she reaches the wooden structure, she gently places her hand on one of the shelves and pulls herself up, standing on her tippy toes.

"What's your name?" she says with a sympathetic tone, her heart now beating at a dramatic rate.

The man turns his head and sniggers slightly. "Well, wouldn't you like to know."

Eve is confused. The man appears to be around the same age as her and he has a distinctive British accent much like her own.

"Well, yes, I would, as a matter of fact. So come on then, what's your name? Did she send you?"

He says nothing.

Frustrated, Eve says, "Fine then, I'll start the introductions. My name is—"

"Evelyn Jade," he interrupts. "I know who you are. And I know that they all call you Mrs Parkinson here, but that's not your real name." He laughs.

Taken aback, Eve replies, "What do you mean not my real name?"

"You know, the one you were given when you were born."

"Oh really? Well, if you actually knew me, then you would know that I was created in this form and not born into it."

"That's what she wants you to believe."

"What?"

"You're Evelyn Jade Honey and you were born into this world and you better start believing it because he's coming for you."

"Wait, who's coming for me?"

The man doesn't respond.

"Why are you talking in riddles?"

"I'm telling you what you already know deep down. She just has it all locked away."

"Oh really, now, and how is it you know so much about me?"

No reply.

"See, you can't even answer the question because it's a load of nonsense and you know it."

Lifting himself up, he leans on his right hand as he stares at Eve, smiling slightly. "I know all of the children here say that you're the friendly teacher. If only they knew your real intentions, aye? Tut, tut, tut, Mrs Parkinson."

"You know nothing. And if you did, you'd have no issue telling me your name."

The man goes quiet.

"What's wrong, cat got your tongue?"

Silence.

"Look, I don't mean to be rude. Just tell me something about yourself. Did you go to school here when you were younger or something?" Looking to the ground, Eve knows this can't possibly be the connection as he knows what her name was before she married Lewis.

"Are you from Moycullen?" she asks warily.

"You know something, Evelyn Jade, even with my unfortunate fate, you did a pretty good job of making them happy during your time with them."

"Making who happy? The children…?"

"You healed their pain and brought them back together. I think you did better than I ever could have. You know what I mean?"

"No, I do not know what you mean because you're talking in riddles."

"Well, as much as it pains me to say this, you certainly were the correct chosen one."

Now even more confused than before, Eve replies, "Bringing who back together? Chosen one? Right, what are you talking about?"

Laying back on the bookcase, he continues with his ramblings, "If only you knew Evelyn Jade. If only you knew."

Placing both her hands on to one of the shelves Eve attempts to pull herself up even more. Deciding against prying too much, she simply asks, "Okay, I believe you do know things about me that others do not. Now can you at least tell me your name?"

A slight pause. The male then turns his head.

As Eve makes eye contact with him she gently says, "Please, just tell me who you are?"

"You really don't remember me, do you?" the man asks.

"Should I remember you?"

"I have never forgotten you."

"Well, maybe if you told me your name it might help me to remember who you are."

"You don't need to know my name," he replies abruptly. "All you need to know is I'm your—"

"Mrs Parkinson, get yourself to the main sports hall now!" Principal Jesiah's voice bellows out over the tannoy.

Eve's heart begins to race.

"I have to..." Eve stops herself. The man has disappeared and the mist has also vanished. Looking around the kitchen, Eve doesn't know if what just happened was real or part of a deeper hallucination. Panicked, she decides against trying to work this out now, as she rushes to the door and heads straight out into the corridor.

She passes rows of dark green personalised lockers on either side. The lights flicker above and the energy remains eerie. The only sound that can be heard are the thumping of the heels of Eve's shoes and the clinking from the broken buckle as she stomps her feet against the hard vinyl floor. In a fluster, Eve's aware she's going to get an icy reception from Principal Jesiah.

"Just breathe deep and hold your head high. You have done nothing wrong," she tells herself.

Twiddling her fingers, she picks up the pace. The strong oak wooden doors leading to the hall are now in sight and her palms are getting sweaty.

"It's going to be okay. Just breathe."

Slowing down, Eve takes her own advice and breathes deep as she places her hand on the cold metal handle.

"Okay, no going back now. Just creep in and keep your head down," she whispers to herself. "Okay. One. Two. Three."

Eve gently pulls the door open in a desperate bid to make as little noise as possible. Unluckily for Eve, the assembly hasn't started yet. Every single head turns and stares at her. As her face goes bright red Eve looks to the ground.

"Oh, so glad you could find the time to join us, Mrs Parkinson," says Principal Jesiah.

Standing in the centre of the sports hall, he has a very stern look upon his face. His dark brown eyes appear almost black. Even with his slightly aged face, it's clear to see his steely expression is one that demands respect. Dressed in a mint green shirt, mint green tartan tie, black blazer and black trousers, Principal Jesiah has a thick head of brown hair and stylish stubble upon his face. Standing six feet, six inches tall, his shoulders are wide and his back is straight. Principal Jesiah runs a tight ship. He has full control over all staff members and children at Grange Park.

Eve slightly raises her hand as she says, "Yes, I'm sorry, Principal. I'm here now."

"Oh, you're here now. So I suppose we should all be thankful that you've found time to finally arrive after keeping us waiting for ten minutes. Please, do tell what was so important?"

"Principal, please, I said I'm sorry. It won't happen again."

"That is not an answer to my question," Principal Jesiah responds in his highly intimidating tone as he steps towards Eve.

Putting her head down once more, Eve chooses not to reply.

Appearing furious, Principal Jesiah bellows, "Report to my office as soon as I have finished!"

"Of course, Principal."

"Now everyone has arrived, let us begin."

Standing next to Principal Jesiah shaking her head, with a smirk spread across her face, is Vice Principal Elisabeth. Principal Jesiah's personal pet. Eve ignores her glare, and her mind begins drifting off. Principal Jesiah's voice becomes a distant sound. Gently placing her head on the wall behind her, Eve glances across the space. Her colleagues are all standing to attention, staring intently at Principal Jesiah. They're spread out around the edges of the hall. Either side are rows of benches, each one filled with children arranged in age order. Eve's eyes eventually lock with her husband's. Lewis has an overly concerned expression upon his face. "Are you okay?" he mouths.

"I'm fine," Eve mouths back with a smile upon her face.

Feeling a tap on her shoulder, Eve jumps. She looks to the side and sees the man from the bookcase. Knocking into her colleague, Eve instantly turns and apologises. When she turns back, the man has once again disappeared. Nervous in case Principal Jesiah has noticed her disturbance, Eve looks in his direction. Thankfully, he hasn't noticed her outburst. He is pacing the length of the hall with his back to her, speaking in his very animated tone.

"Isn't he dreamy?" Eve hears from at her side.

Smirking at Mrs Violet's innocent, and yet way off the chart, comment, Eve replies, "Huh, if only you knew what I know."

Ignoring Eve's words, Mrs Violet continues to stare at Principal Jesiah with her bold green eyes and her hand to her chest. She has a true schoolgirl crush expression.

"Your souls are mine!" echoes throughout the hall.

The shutters on the windows slam down, the doors all lock and the lights go off. The hall is now pitch black.

CHAPTER THREE

"Gehenna."

Across the globe, people are embracing all that is festive. Twinkling lights in an array of different colours brighten the darkness. Delightful looking decorations are displayed both inside and out, mesmerizing all who see them. Fires are aglow and stockings hang from mantelpieces, just waiting to be filled with treats. Accepting the challenge, families wrap an extensive number of gifts for loved ones near and far, whilst drinking mulled wine and listening to Christmas music. Some love-smitten couples even have a cheeky snippet of mistletoe or two dangling from their doorframes. What an incredible time to be alive. Most of the population are celebrating, sharing their love and appreciation for one another. And why not? After all, *'Tis the season to be jolly.*

But sometimes, just sometimes, there isn't an awful lot to be jolly about, and there's one home in the south of England where the mood is most definitely the opposite of festive. The Honey residence sits upon the cold, dark, crisp winter seafront without a single fragment of this festive time of year showcased upon it. Indeed, the only light that can be seen is from the lamppost on the street front, which is flickering on and off. With each flash of golden light, a thin layer of fog is revealed, and it is developing at a rhythmic pace. Icicles form on everything it grazes. Jack Frost has begun his reign of supremacy. The house and grounds are neglected and unattractive. The overgrown bushes, dead plants and brown grass are coated with a thin layer of frost. And the interior decor isn't any brighter. There's not a single strand of vibrant tinsel. Not a glisten from any twinkling lights. No personalised, embroidered stocking hanging from the fireplace. Nor a snippet of bright green, crunchy mistletoe dangling from a single doorway. There isn't even a tree with a giant star on top. Nope, not a single item present inside the Honey residence to indicate that Father Christmas is soon to arrive. The central heating system is turned to maximum and the fire is lit, so at least the temperature inside the house is cosy.

Matthew Honey enters the dayroom and sees Phil Parkinson sitting in his usual spot by the window looking extremely pleased with himself, staring at his phone.

"Right, come on, who are you texting with that goofy smile on your face?" Matthew asks.

"No one," Phil responds, with a rather sheepish expression on his face. He attempts to cover his phone.

"As if it's no one… For the past two weeks you've been looking at your phone every minute of the day like you've got a schoolboy crush. Spill – who is it that's making you blush every five minutes?"

"Erm, mate, it's no one. Honest." Phil awkwardly squeezes his phone inside the rather tight front pocket of his jeans.

"What are you being ridiculous for? Just tell me who it is."

"There's nothing to tell."

"So, just to be clear, you expect me to believe that there's nothing to tell when you've had that thing glued to your hand, hip or ear for the past two weeks? And not only that, but you're giggling like a child and having what you think are secret whispered conversations in your room at night. Oh yeah, you think I can't hear ya."

Phil says nothing.

"Okay, fine, be that way. I'm going upstairs to do some work." As he leaves the dayroom in somewhat of a huff, Matthew mumbles to himself, "I'm not sure what the bloody big deal is anyway."

He shakes his head as he climbs the spiral staircase. As is his usual ritual, he stops by Eve's bedroom door, places his forehead and his hands on the wood and breathes deeply. As he exhales, he gently whispers, "I love you."

Smiling, with deep sorrow in his eyes, Matthew kisses the wood and walks away. The pain he feels is just as strong today as it was the day his daughter was cruelly taken. Wiping the small tear that has fallen from his eye and clearing his sniffling nose, Matthew quickly composes himself. Putting his hand inside his trouser pocket, he retrieves a golden key. Fiddling with this as he reaches the door to his office, Matthew gently graces his fingertips over the golden **Creation Station** plaque. Once again, tears form in the corners of his eyes. No matter how much time passes, the grief he feels for the loss of the only two women in his life consumes him with every memory. Closing his eyes and shaking his head, he snaps back into reality. He turns the key and enters the room. Restored to its previous organised manner, the office has become the headquarters for their mission to get their children back.

The walls are plastered with what can only be described as an investigation storyline. There are images and possible links and leads to the whereabouts of the children. Matthew lets out a huge sigh at the thought of the overwhelming amount of work still left to do. Seating himself at his desk, he lifts the top of his laptop and switches the device on. While he waits for it to fire up, Matthew picks up a framed image of Eve, the last known photo of her, taken from her social media account. He places his two forefingers to his lips and kisses them softly. Touching the glass where Eve's forehead is on the image, he says, "I will find you and bring you home, my darling. You have my word. I will search the ends of the earth to bring you home where you belong, make no mistake about that."

Placing the picture back in its perfect spot, Matthew opens the top drawer of the desk, rummages around and takes out the crucifix that Reverend Andrew gave to him. "Hmm, I'm yet to find out how you fit into the puzzle."

The door creaks and Matthew jumps.

"Sorry, mate. Didn't mean to scare ya," says Phil.

"No, don't worry about it. I was just—"

"Look," Phil butts in, "before you continue, I just want to say I'm sorry about what happened a moment ago. It's just, well, you know, a sensitive subject."

"Phil, what you have to understand is I've come to learn that everyone deals with grief differently. Some have the ability to move on quicker than others. And to be honest, I see this as a blessing because they get to find some form of new peace in life. Others hold guilt and are unable to move forward with their lives. The guilt that I have will not permit me happiness whilst my Lauren no longer breathes. Will this last for all eternity? Probably, because my Lauren ain't ever coming back." Matthew shakes his head and smiles ironically as he continues, "And then look at what happened. When I slowly started to accept that moving on was a possibility for me, I brought a path of devastation upon our family in the worst possible way. I lost the one person I promised I would keep safe. I mean—"

"Matthew, please, you don't have to—"

"Phil, it's fine. I'm fine."

"Fine? You know what fine means, right?"

Grinning slightly, Matthew says, "Yes. Fucked up. Insecure. Neurotic. Emotional."

"See, so how can I not be concerned about your reaction?"

"Phil, if you can process the loss of Alice and move on, then I hold no ill feelings and wish nothing but happiness for you. If you have found someone who can ease your pain and make you smile again, then please don't feel as if you have to hide it from me. You are my friend and I will always want what's best for you. I mean, don't get me wrong, on a personal level, I won't understand it because of my own shit and the burden that I carry, but know that I would never begrudge you happiness." Fumbling with the crucifix in his hand, Matthew sighs. "All I ask is that you promise you'll keep your head in the game."

"Of course, mate, that goes without saying."

"Well, as long as you don't lose sight of the real mission, I will wish you all the best. You have my word."

"I don't know what to say." Phil smiles. "Erm, thank you, I suppose, for being so accepting. And please know, finding our children and returning them all home safely is, and always will be, my priority. Believe me, this wasn't an easy thing to do. At first, of course I was nervous because of what happened to you. But I just had to let go of that because, really, what else has anyone got to take from me? I've already lost my wife and our children. There's nothing left. My life has already been taken. So why not take the risk? I mean, I just think, come on, give me your best shot, because it can't get much worse than this, can it?"

"Very true, my friend."

Phil hangs his head and begins twiddling his fingers. "It gets really lonely and depressing at times, especially as I'm still in recovery and want to pick up a bottle at least once or twice a day. I suppose Selena helps ease the pain. She's really great at talking me down off the ledge in my darkest moments."

"Oh, Selena. So we've gone from nothing and no one to a name now. Aw, that's truly great. Seriously, I'm happy for you. Come on then, how did you guys meet?" Placing the crucifix on the desk, Matthew gets comfy in his chair, ready to hear the gossip.

Scratching the back of his head, Phil looks hesitant.

"Just spit it out. What do you think I'm gonna do?"

"I know, I'm just…"

"Phil, just tell me how you guys met."

Taking a deep breath in, Phil says, "Okay, well, it was before I got sober. Remember that time when I was late for the meeting at Scotland Yard with Terry when he told us he wanted to help us an all that?"

"Yeah."

"Well, that day when you knew I was in the pub and you told me I better sort myself out, sober up and get my arse to the meeting, well, Selena was in the pub and she was the only person who gave enough of a shit to try and help me. Even when she thought I was married, because I was wearing my wedding ring, she said that she didn't want me to go home to my wife in the state I was in."

"Wait, so you've been chatting to each other for that long?"

"No, no, no, no. I mean she gave me her number, but I never reached out. Then about two weeks ago I saw her standing in the hairdressers when I was walking to get something to eat. She looked at me through the window and she just gave this massive smile when she saw me. I waved and she came running out and gave me a huge hug and asked me why I'd never text her? So I told her I'd been busy and she grabbed my phone and rang herself from it so she had my number. And from that point on, we've been texting back and forth and have been chatting on the phone pretty much daily."

"Aw, I'm happy for you Phil. I really am."

"Matthew. Please know that she will never replace my Alice." Phil hangs his head as he plays with the wedding band, which he now wears on his right hand. "No one will ever replace her. She will always be my angel and much like you, I will stop at nothing to make sure that I get all our beautiful children back where they belong, even if I have to die trying. It's the least I could do – after all, I was the one who, you know, left them all."

Matthew smiles a sympathetic smile. "I understand."

"Thank you. That means a lot. I suppose it's just nice to have some female attention at times. Stops me feeling like a worthless piece of shit."

"Phil, honestly, I know. It's all good."

The pair sit in silence.

Tapping Phil on the knee, Matthew turns to face his laptop and opens the web browser. He types Gehenna in the search bar and hits enter. Phil pulls up a chair next to Matthew.

"What's this you're searching?" Phil says as he leans in close.

"Just looking into a hunch I have."

"What do you mean?"

"Well, last night I had a very vivid nightmare."

"You haven't had one of them for a while now."

"I know, and this one was horrifying. Sort of like a lucid dream."

"Oh, what was it about?"

Pausing for a moment as a shiver travels rapidly down his spine, Matthew turns to face Phil. "It was so scary and felt real. I was trapped in a graveyard and I couldn't find any way of escaping. It was pitch black everywhere. Even the sky didn't have the moon or a single star in it. I could literally feel and hear every beat from my heart as it was racing. I remember frantically searching for an exit, but one never appeared. I could see headstone after headstone, and it was terrifying because I knew I was standing on ground that had decaying bodies underneath it. I could smell the rotting corpses. And if I'm totally honest, I couldn't help but think one of them was gonna come back to life, reach out of the ground and grab my ankle or something."

"Ew, mate, that sounds grim."

"That's not the freakiest bit." Matthew says as he scratches his head. "The centre of the cemetery suddenly became all misty. And then it was like as soon as it appeared and I noticed it, it began drifting away. Once it disappeared, I could see in its place a table set up for two people. I mean, this table looked immaculate – white tablecloth, red rose in the centre, glowing candlelight, prestige silverware and thick, expensive looking napkins in the shape of a heart. There were two wooden chairs facing one another, and the scene just felt, familiar, and I didn't know why. I turned to see if there was anyone behind me, and when I turned back around I could see myself sat at the table with a glass of wine in my hand laughing. But it wasn't me as I am now, I was like an illusion of sorts. How can I explain it…? I sort of looked like a ghost version of myself."

Scratching his head, Phil replies, "That's weird."

"Well, when I got closer, I noticed I wasn't alone."

"Huh, who was sat with you?"

"You'll never guess. It was that evil bitch – Jess. She was sat at the table with me and she was laughing, too."

"What? The real—"

"I swear, Phil, I got so mad. I charged at her… and ran right through her and came out the other side. I fell flat on my face on top of a grave. I jumped up, but she hadn't so much as flinched. I lifted myself up and suddenly realised that this was a moment in time that I knew. A moment that I'd once belonged to. It was in fact my second dinner date with her."

"How did you know that?"

Matthew's expression becomes animated as he explains. The pieces are beginning to fall into place as he relives the nightmare. "It all became clear when I saw Daniela. He was our waiter that night and I could see him pouring our wine. We were talking amongst ourselves and laughing but I couldn't hear any words. And then, all of a sudden, as clear as day, I heard her say, 'I'm from Gehenna'. And just like that, I woke up."

"Mate, that's freaky."

"Surely that can't be a coincidence, right?"

"No mate, I think there's defo something in that. Where is Gehenna? I've never heard of it."

"Well, when I woke up, I instantly remembered that date. And I remembered asking her where Gehenna was as I'd never heard of it myself and she'd said that I never will. Mate, I think if we go where she's from we might discover something that could possibly lead us to a way to get rid of her once and for all and get our children back."

"Yeah, but is it even a real place?"

"Let's find out."

Matthew scrolls through the search results. He stops when his attention is drawn to an image of what can only be described as the human mind's true vision of hell. Burning bodies upon burning bodies. They lie on the ground in a heap, surrounded by fire. Leaning closer to the screen, Matthew realises that the burning bodies are children.

"Mate, what in the Lord's name is this?" Phil asks.

Ignoring his question, Matthew reluctantly guides the cursor of the mouse and clicks the image. As he takes a deep breath in, a full article about Gehenna loads on the screen. In bold letters, the headline reads, Gehenna, the Tainted Valley of Hinnom in Jerusalem. Looking at Phil he says, "Well, here goes nothing."

And so, the article reads:

Gehenna, the Tainted Valley of Hinnom in Jerusalem

The things they will never tell you

Written by Hermon Shimai

Gehenna, what a tangled web you weave. The desolate land of sacrificed individuals. A tragic place on earth where tiny lost souls remain, aimlessly wandering the grounds without a place to go. Sad, right? Well, here is an alarming fact I thought I'd share with you: it is said that when the moon is at its full capacity the screams of the young can still be heard for miles. Yes, terrifying screams from once vulnerable young people.

Upon the land of the living is the devastating aftermath of a hideous event that took place many years ago. Those who know the tales of this land will think I have lost my mind for documenting this; however, I feel it is my necessary duty to warn the world of what I have witnessed in my mind's eye, what I have learned and how the curse upon the Valley of Hinnom is real.

If you do not know anything about Gehenna, and this is your first time coming across such an article, then brace yourself, because you are in for a rude awakening. I'm cautious that it is my duty to warn you in before I deliver the harsh truth. Gehenna, in Jerusalem, which is my family heritage home, is positioned just eight or so kilometres away from where Jesus was born. Yes, yet again, you read right! Our Christ Saviour came into holy grounds and graced the world with his arrival on earth. Blessed, surrounded by love and cradled with care, our little Lord Jesus was embracing his new surroundings. And yet, he was blissfully unaware of the unholy acts that would one day take place not too far away. Acts of sin that would be committed in one of the valleys of Gehenna. A valley that would hold one of the darkest secrets.

Are you still interested?

Well, not to seem too abrupt, but it gets worse. Cursed and positioned south of Mount Zion, this unloved location witnessed events that would torment the living for all eternity. Yet we are never taught about this distressing period. People wince and go silent when questioned about what they might know on the subject. Tight-lipped and afraid of the repercussions, those who live in Jerusalem do not wish to discuss the events that unfolded in the tainted Valley of Hinnom. And, unlike most myths that seem to dwindle away over time as life goes on, this one has stuck. Those who live in Jerusalem stay as far away as possible from the tainted Valley of Hinnom. Not a single living soul exists upon this land. So, I'm guessing you want to know the true reason for the hostility towards the Valley of Hinnom. Well, I will not disappoint you. And yes, this is indeed the part where you need to brace yourself.

Some years ago, the Kings of Judah sacrificed their flesh and blood, their children, to gain a path to righteousness and wealth. Yep, you read right again. These hideous, selfish kings would stand by and watch as their children burned at the stake, praying and worshiping to the false gods that their desires and wishes would come true by gifting them with the souls of their very own flesh and blood.

I may be a modern-day man; however, I cannot even begin to contemplate how one stands by and watches their own child burn to death in the hope of pleasing a false god. I mean, think about it, they'd be watching as their children screamed and begged for their lives to be spared. And yet no such wish was met. This cruel act indeed backfired as the land became unholy. As the Lord stated in the verse the Smashing of the Clay Pot: Jeremiah 19:2-5: ***"Say, 'Listen to God's Word, you kings of Judah and people of Jerusalem! This is the Message from God-of-the-Angel-Armies, the God of Israel. I am about to bring doom crashing down on this place. Oh, and will ears ever ring! Doom—because they have walked off and left me, and made this place strange by worshiping strange gods, gods never heard of by them, their parents, or the old kings of Judah. Doom—because they have massacred innocent people. Doom—because they've built altars to that no-god Baal, and burned their own children alive in the fire as offerings to Baal, an atrocity I never ordered, never so much as hinted at!"***

Upon this dark order from the Lord, a curse was born. And low and behold, the land was claimed by a demon. But not just any demon; this particular entity vowed to take revenge on mankind on behalf of the souls of the young who had been tortured and killed at the hands of the people who should have been their protectors. Formed from pure hatred towards families, she is the Dark Empress and devastating families and taking her full reign over this world and the whole universe is her aim. And how will she do this, you might ask? By using the souls and bodies of the young as her army. Possessing them in their dreams. Luring them into her universe and vowing to protect them. Which she will, but at what cost? I'll tell you what cost. It's the cost of their family life.

People of the world, I believe her time is now! I believe this entity has started to strike and the world as we know it will soon be no more, for

I have visited this land in my own mind's eye and I have seen things that would keep you up at night. With more power than the average demon, this one will not pass if you call out her name. No, she was created wiser than that. There is only one sure way to defeat this entity and the truth lies here, in Jerusalem.

Please, people of the world, let us pray that I am wrong.

"Erm, what the fuck have we just read?" Phil says, looking stunned.

Sitting back, Matthew remains speechless.

"Mate, what do we do with this information?"

"I, Phil, I don't know…"

With his hand to his mouth, Matthew tries to process the information he has just read. He never expected to find an article that would speak such truths based on a nightmare he had.

"Matthew, do you think we should contact the person who wrote it?"

Matthew scans the page. "Herman Shimai. He's left an email address."

He types out a quick message:

Sent: MatthewHoney@honeyproductions.com
To: Hermon.Shimai@historicinvestigations.com
Subject: We Need Your Help!

Dear Hermon,

I came across your article online about the land of Gehenna the Tainted Valley of Hinnom and I had to reach out to you. You are right! The entity you speak of, The Dark Empress, or Jezebel, which is her name, she is here! And I know this for a fact because she has taken my daughter. Hermon, she has not only taken my daughter, but she has taken my friend Phil's five children and that of fifty other children from an orphanage in

> Ireland. Phil and I have been trying to track her down for some time. We have no clue where she has gone. We lost her trail back in July when they left Ireland and we have been desperately trying to find her and our children again ever since. The reason why we are desperately reaching out to you, is that in your article you stated that you are aware of how this entity can be defeated. We really need this information because when we do find her, which we will, we want to be ready. Please can you disclose this and any other information you might have about her to us so that we can finally take her down once and for all and claim back our children and prevent the world from becoming unholy land? Please Hermon, we are down on our knees begging you.
>
> Kindest regards
> Two very desperate fathers
> Matthew Honey and Phil Parkinson

Hitting the send button, Matthew looks to Phil and says, “Let’s see if he gets back to us.”

“Mate, I have a good feeling about this,” Phil responds with a big smile on his face.

“Me too.”

Chapter Four

"Father, say it isn't true."

Alannah stares out of the window of her new home, a fifth-floor apartment at The Verona on sixty-fourth street between Madison and Park Avenue South, in New York City. She is no longer in her religious attire. Her tiny frame is accentuated by tight dark denim jeans, complemented by a white silk blouse with a loosely tied bow at the neckline. Her hair is scraped back into a neat bun. She sits back in the comfy leather chair in the study, locked in a trance. The morning light highlights the flecks of green in her hazel eyes.

Heightened emotions circulate in her mind – guilt and deep sorrow at the memories of the life she left behind. The view outside her window confirms daily that she is no longer a sister at the Moycullen Nunnery. Although there's the odd tree positioned outside every apartment building, at present they are all bare without a single leaf. Tall, dark brown trees with extended branches layered in frost. The view is quite the opposite of what she had become accustomed to over the years. Outside of her window is tall brick building upon tall brick building, as far as the eye can see. They have been built by professional architects, but in her eyes, this isn't the true beauty of nature. No, this is mankind's version of beauty. Simply put, how to make money and suppress the way God intended the world to look. And the traffic is worse than anything she's seen – a never-ending queue of yellow cabs and delivery trucks generating non-stop noise pollution. However, one thing puts a slight smile on her face: Christmas time in New York is magical and she had always wanted to experience this first-hand.

Festive decorations take over the streets along with thick layers of snow, and tourists from across the globe travel to New York to embrace the beauty of this magnificent city. And yet, as stunning as the decorations and the snow looks, this seasonal change is far from practical for those who live here and for the commuters who must travel into the city for work. Even now, Alannah can see people from all walks of life on the sidewalks attempting to navigate the sludge and snow. Slipping and sliding on the pavement, they cling to everything and everyone within their reach. Alannah looks away from the window before she sees someone fall flat on the ground.

Gazing at her hand, Alannah admires her simplistic white-gold wedding band. Taking a deep breath, she scans the room. She has settled into her new marital home quite contentedly. With that being said, at times heartache overcomes her as she cannot help but miss her family, along with the solitude and privacy that Moycullen Forest had to offer.

Pondering the sin of leaving her sisters behind and going against her devotion to give her life to the Lord and to Moycullen, Alannah is surmounted by a strong sense of guilt. Tears form in her eyes. She misses her sisters. She misses the children terribly. As she remains deep in thought, Alannah hears her husband's voice.

"Alannah, baby, where did you put my wallet?"

Turning towards the door, Alannah smiles as she sees Brennan's handsome face as he enters the room. He is wearing trendy dark denim jeans, a navy-blue t-shirt and thick black rimmed glasses. Looking as if he's in somewhat of a hurry, Brennan says, "Hey, baby, I'm going to brave the cold. I need to call at the store for a few things. Where did you put my wallet?"

"It's in my bag," Alannah responds as she gets up from her seat. Walking towards her husband, Alannah puts out her arms and hugs him. She then kisses him on his perfectly plump lips and says, "Lord knows how much I'm in love with you."

Smiling back with a look of admiration in his eyes, Brennan replies, "Aw, I'm in love with you too, baby."

Content with his response, Alannah releases him from her arms and makes her way to their bedroom. The room is lit beautifully by the rising sun. The interior design is gleaming. An impeccable, romantic room, for an adorable newlywed couple. Walking to her side of the bed, Alannah collects her handbag from off the floor.

"Are you okay?" Brennan queries as he follows her into the room.

"Yeah, why?"

"You just seem distracted today. You've been quiet in the study for hours now."

"Yeah, I'm all good. Don't worry about me. I'll be fine," Alannah replies as she retrieves his wallet from her handbag and passes it to him.

"Come on, you can tell me. What's ticking away in that brain of yours?" Brennan says as he holds his wife in his arms and kisses her on the top of her head.

"I… erm…" A slight pause. "I'm sure you don't want to hear this."

"And why wouldn't I want to hear what's bugging my beautiful." He kisses her. "Kind." He kisses her again. "Funny." He kisses her a final time. "Wife. Huh?"

Smiling, Alannah looks deep into his eyes. "Because you've heard it all before."

"It's okay. I don't mind, and if it's still bugging you, just tell me. And hey, who knows, I might actually be able to cheer you up."

Laughing slightly, Alannah responds, "That you always do, my baby. That you always do."

"See, so tell me what's on your mind."

"Okay," Alannah says as she slumps onto the bed and looks to the ceiling, twiddling her fingers. "I suppose I just still feel immensely guilty for having left them all behind like I did without saying goodbye. I didn't say goodbye to any of my sisters or the children. They were my family. The only family who truly loved me for who I was. They took care of me and looked after me, which is more than

I could have ever said for the people who were biologically related to me and should have taken care of me regardless. And how did I repay them for that act of kindness? Huh? I walked out on them all. Some sister I turned out to be."

"Oh, my baby, it's okay," Brennan says as he sits next to Alannah on the bed and puts his arm around her shoulders. "Look, there's no rule against contacting the nunnery and checking in on everyone. Why don't you just give them a call?"

"Well, I just don't know if I can after the way I left and the amount of time that has passed."

"Baby, look at me." Brennan places his hands on her shoulders and turns her to face him. "I'm sure they'll find it in their hearts to forgive you. After all, isn't that what you guys preach all the time? Forgiveness and all that jazz?"

"But what if they scream at me. I just don't—"

"Baby, please, you're going to make yourself ill. Do you want me to call? Maybe I could speak to them first and just tell them it was all on me?"

Smiling at her husband's desire to protect and take care of her, Alannah replies, "No, it's okay. I will face the music and call myself."

"Okay, well look, I'm just heading to the store two blocks down, I won't be long." He giggles. "Huh, that's if I don't slip on my butt and die of embarrassment. Have you seen some of the sights out there this morning?"

"Yes, I've decided to contain myself and not laugh so karma doesn't bite me on the ass the next time I go out."

"Well, that's me definitely falling flat on my back, then. I've not stopped laughing all morning."

Tapping him on the arm in a playful manner, Alannah says, "Now that's just cruel."

"What?" he replies innocently with his hands in the air.

"I'm sure our Lord will forgive you for your sins and will make sure that you're okay on your travels." She kisses him gently on his lips. Every time his lips are in reaching distance, a strong urge to kiss them takes over. His desirable, soft lips are just one of the many things that drives her crazy about her husband.

"Hmm, I love it when you kiss me," Brennan says.

"Oh, you do, do you?"

"Uh huh."

"Well, why don't we continue this kissing session?"

"What, so you can get out of calling the nunnery?"

"Nooo..." she replies with a seductive smirk upon her face.

"Ouch, I feel so used," Brennan jokes.

"Aw, my baby, you should never feel used."

The pair share a passionate kiss.

"Right, missy, I've got to get to the store, and you've got a call to make."

"I know." Apprehension is running throughout her mind. The unknown reaction and possible rejection from her sisters scares her greatly.

Stroking her hair, Brennan says, "Okay, well, I'll make you a deal: wait for me to get back from the store and I'll hold your hand and be on standby for kisses and general moral support while you make the call."

"Aw, you really are the best husband a girl could ever wish for." She kisses him. "I am." She kisses him again. "So blessed." She stares deeply into his eyes. Stroking the back of his head, she gently grips his hair with her fingers. "Honestly, I'll be okay. You go to the store. I'll be brave and give them a call while you're out."

"Are you sure?"

"Yes. I'm a big girl. I promise, I'll be fine." Looking over his shoulder to the clock on the wall above the doorframe, she works out the five-hour time difference in her head. "So, it's… currently three fifteen in the afternoon there, they should be back from after lunch prayer by now. I'll call the office. I'm sure Sister Marie will be around." She smiles. "I can't wait to hear her voice again."

With a sincere grin on his face, Brennan says, "Well, as long as you're going to be okay?"

"I'll be a-o-kay. You just make sure of one thing…?"

"Hmm, and what's that, then?"

With a slight giggle in her tone she replies, "You just promise me that if you do fall flat on your back you do it in front of someone with a camera."

"Hey, cheeky."

"I'm not even sorry." She continues to laugh. "Honestly, I'll be fine. Go. Go to the store and bring your wife back some chocolate and potato chips."

"Okay, well as long as you're sure. I can't promise someone will have their camera at the ready, but I can promise that I'll bring you back your favourite chips and chocolate."

"You're the best."

"I won't be long." Brennan kisses her on the forehead and walks out of the bedroom.

"I won't be long, baby!" she hears him call out. The door clicks shut behind him.

Now alone with her thoughts, Alannah whispers to herself, "Okay, it's time to face the music."

Back in the study, her hands tremble as she dials the number for the Moycullen Nunnery. A *bleep* sounds in her ear and a message is repeated: "This number is no longer in service. Please redial and try again."

Alannah does just that, this time cautiously watching every digit as she presses it. Yet again, the same *bleep* and message. Believing that she might have remembered the number incorrectly, Alannah reaches for the keyboard on her computer and types *Moycullen Nunnery Ireland contact number* into the internet search bar. The details of the Moycullen Nunnery come up and underneath them it says 'closed' in red letters. Scrolling down, Alannah's eyes widen as her attention is drawn to the headline: Who Killed the Nuns of Moycullen and Where Did the Children Go?

Alannah frantically dials the number of Father McDoyle. Thankfully the number is in service. The line *rings* and *rings*. What could this mean? She clicks on the article and an image pops up. It comes with a warning. As clear as day, she can see the Moycullen Nunnery. And on the grounds of the nunnery there is a line-up of what appears to be a gathering of sisters deceased on the floor with their faces blurred out.

"Father McDoyle speaking, how can I assist you today?"

Alannah is relieved to hear the familiar strong Irish accent. "Father McDoyle, it's Sister Alannah. Please, what has happened at Moycullen?"

"Sister Alannah? Where are you?" he asks urgently.

"Father, I am in America. What has happened to my sisters?"

"America? Is Sister Elisabeth with you? Are you both safe? Oh, good Lord thank you. Thank you." Father McDoyle sounds tearful.

"No, Father. Why would Sister Elisabeth be with me?"

"You were the only two missing sisters. We thought that you were either snatched or that you had both decided to leave the convent before – well, you know."

"No, Father, I don't know. Please, tell me what has happened to my sisters."

Silence.

"Please, I really need you to tell me what is on the internet is not true. Please just say it's another cruel internet rumour."

Again, there is nothing but a deadly silence.

"Father, are you still there? Can you hear me?"

A moment or so passes before Father McDoyle speaks. "Yes, Sister Alannah, I am here. I really don't know how to tell you this. The things you have read online are true."

Alannah breaks down crying. "No, why?"

"We don't fully know. The children have been taken and your sisters have unfortunately passed. The Lord was looking over you and Sister Elisabeth when you both left the convent. Had either of you stayed your fate would have more than likely been the same."

"I just…" Alannah's jaw has dropped. She never in a million years believed this would be the response she would receive when she made the call home. Tears slowly descend her cheeks. "I just don't understand how this could have happened."

"I know, Sister, we are all very much in shock ourselves. It is believed that a dark spirit had somehow gained entry into the nunnery. We don't know when and we don't know how, but what we do know is that it had one sole purpose and it succeeded."

"How do you know this?"

"When I received the call from the police to say that an incident had taken place at Moycullen, I had no idea what it could be. I panicked and immediately made my way there. Please believe me, Sister, I wasn't prepared for the horrors that lay ahead and I won't go into any details with you. I believe it is my duty to spare you. Upon my arrival, I was met by a young gent called Matthew. He was the one who found your sisters and he had stayed behind with the police to give them all the information he knew."

Alannah tries desperately to muffle the sound of her sobs with her hand.

"It would appear that a dark spirit of sorts is capturing souls of the young and is killing the adults who hold legal rights over the children so that they do not get in the way of their possession and bring alarm or attention to their plans."

"What? Why?"

"What do all bad spirits arrive on earth for?"

"You mean…"

"Yes, I believe this one is more powerful than ever. We even know her name. And she is showing no signs of slowing down. It is rather concerning and quite frightful indeed. I have been praying for us all."

Alanna wipes her face and takes a big sip of water from the glass on her desk. Grabbing a pen and notepad she continues, "Father, what was the full name of the man who knew this information?"

"Erm, it was Honey something."

Alannah can hear Father McDoyle fumbling around with some papers.

"Ah, Matthew Honey, that's it. His daughter, Evelyn Jade Honey, has been taken by this entity already. He had another gent with him by the name of Phil and I believe his five children have also been taken. Erm, I can't quite remember their names off the top of my head."

"Not Sister Eve," Alannah whispers to herself as she's taking notes.

"Sorry, what was that? I didn't quite hear you."

Stopping her scribbling, Alannah says, "Were the other children called Freddie, Terrence, Rupert and Hope?"

"Yes, yes, I do believe those were their names, and there was an older boy. I don't fully recall his name. Levi something."

"Do you mean Lewis?"

"Yes, yes, that's it, Lewis."

Alannah writes the list of names on the notepad.

"Well, they were the other gent's children and this dark spirit has taken possession of those little ones, too. And all the children from the nunnery. I had to identify all the bodies and the only missing members of the convent were the children along with you and Sister Elisabeth. We were all so worried that the entity may have taken you both."

"Now that I think about it, Sister Elisabeth wasn't herself at all. She was acting strange for weeks before I left. She'd even managed to get herself ostracized and locked away by the sisters as we thought it was going to be the best thing for her own safety and for the protection of the convent so that she didn't get us shut down." Sitting back in her seat in shock, Alannah continues, "I remember she was ranting about strange happenings. She'd been locked inside her room for weeks. Something inside her changed. Oh my goodness, Father, what did we do? She was trying to warn us the whole time, wasn't she?"

"Quite possibly."

"And we just left her." Alannah gasps at the realisation. "It all makes sense now."

"When was the last time you saw Sister Elisabeth?"

"The last time I saw my sister was just as I was leaving the convent with Brennan. I remember her standing at the top of the stairway and questioning me about where I was heading. It was weird, like she already knew what I was doing before I had a chance to do it. But she never stopped me. Do you think she may have been influenced by this entity?"

"It would appear to be the case. If you say she was left vulnerable and alone, then yes, I believe we may have to start thinking of this as a potential outcome for her."

"Do you have any leads on where they could have taken Sister Elisabeth and the children?"

"No, we have no clue as to their whereabouts and I'm not sure if we ever will."

"Well, do you have a contact number for Matthew Honey?" Alannah asks as she leans forward, pen at the ready.

"I don't. They were with a Detective… erm… his name was Terry something. He left me his card. One moment, I'll get the details for you."

Alannah waits anxiously, overwhelmed by the information she has just received. There is scuffling as the receiver is picked up at the other end. Alannah is relieved to hear Father McDoyle's voice. "Okay, so his name is Detective Chief Superintendent John Terry and he's based within the Metropolitan Police in London."

Father McDoyle reads out the contact details, and she writes them down.

"Thank you so much, Father, that's all the information I need."

"Sister Alannah, you must know that the Lord and your sisters will never judge you or Sister Elisabeth. I believe if anything, the Lord was looking over you, especially as he was powerless to stop what happened at the convent. Yet I think he knew you would be the one who could help bring justice for all of your sisters and of course the children, wherever their blessed souls maybe."

Fidgeting in her seat, Alannah replies to his kind words, "Thank you, Father. However, I'm not sure that my betrayal will be taken as lightly as you may believe."

"Sister Alannah, you're certainly misreading the situation. I truly believe you and Sister Elisabeth have a much bigger role to play in this. Neither of you have betrayed our Lord, you have taken the path he had always set out for you."

"You really think that?" Alannah says.

"Yes, of course I do. You are courageous, you are dedicated, and you are strong. If anyone can bring back Sister Elisabeth and those beautiful children, it is you. You have such a huge heart and a fire in your tummy like no other."

Alannah is smiling through her tears at his kind words.

"I know our Lord chose you for this path because he knew he required a strong and heroic figure to end the suffering and rid the world of this entity. You are that chosen one."

"Thank you so much. Those words mean more to me right now than you'll ever understand."

"I speak the truth."

Sitting up straight, Alannah pulls herself together, wipes her face and says, "I will stop at nothing to get justice for my sisters and claim those children back. And you are right. I will rid the world of this dark spirit."

"I know you will. Goodbye, Sister. You will be in my prayers."

"Thank you, Father. Goodbye."

As she hangs up the phone, Alannah hears the door *bang* shut, and then her husband shouts, "Hey, baby, where are ya? Ha, karma missed me this time, the New Yorker pro that I am, didn't even slide. Oh, and you'll never believe what snacks I got you from the store."

Alannah runs out to him, her face swollen and blotchy and tears drenching her blouse. She jumps on her husband and wraps her arms tightly around his neck.

"Hey, hey, hey, what's happened? It can't have gone that badly."

Unable to speak as she begins hyperventilating, Alannah falls to the ground.

Quickly dropping the bags and kneeling by her side, Brennan holds her and says, "Alannah, please, talk to me."

Her head in her hands, Alannah says, "They're…"

"They're what?"

"They're…" Alannah chokes on her words, her breathing so erratic she feels as though her chest is going to explode.

"Baby, take deep breaths. Deep breaths. Copy me. In. And. Out."

Following her husband's breathing pattern, Alannah calms slightly. Eventually, she is able to speak. "They're dead, Brennan."

"What? Wait a minute, who are?"

"My sisters. They're dead. They were brutally murdered. All of them except the children, and Sister Elisabeth. I just spoke with Father McDoyle."

"What?"

"They're dead, Brennan!"

"How can they… oh my, baby. I am so, so, so sorry."

Alannah is now incapable of stopping the tears from falling. The traumatic news has made her eyes and her head heavy.

"Shh, shh, shh, oh, my baby. It's okay. Everything is going to be okay. I've got you. You're safe," Brennan says as he lifts her off the ground and guides her into the bedroom.

Sobbing uncontrollably, Alannah lies down on the bed. Through the tiny gap in her swollen eyes, she sees Brennan pull off his wellingtons and place his coat on the floor. Opening her arms once more, she whispers, "Hold me."

Brennan immediately crawls into her arms. As time passes, Alannah's sobs slow down. She feels safe and thankful to have her husband. And yet, the pain surging through her heart at her overwhelming loss is more real than ever. Wishing this was nothing more than a horrific nightmare, Alannah's eyes grow heavier and heavier as she tries to piece things together in her mind. In a desperate bid to ease the pain, she closes her eyes. Eventually, she falls silent.

"I'm so sorry for your loss, baby," Brennan whispers as he kisses her on the head.

The pair embrace one another as they fall asleep.

Chapter Five

"Collect their souls!"

It's just past three a.m. and the moon is at full capacity. Stars beam brightly as far as the eye can see, creating a blanket of beauty over the county of Morrisville. Lavish trucks and cars are parked on the driveways, which lead to enormous homes. Spread out one after the other on various plots of land, each house has its own character and unique take on Christmas decorations. And yet at present, they all have one thing in common – a singular light on the upper floor glaring out through a window. A desperate attempt to deter the predators of the night from entering.

The town is positioned behind the Delaware River, which is famous for the crossing of George Washington during the seventeenth century. The historic location is soon to gain another notch on its belt, and this time it will come in the form of notoriety.

Moycullen Orphanage stands undisturbed and alone in the murkiest depths of the woodland. A long, dark driveway leads towards it. There's not a single item present that would indicate Christmas time is upon us. A wicked and intimidating atmosphere surrounds the orphanage. It's so strong it keeps even the nocturnal and scavenging animals of the night away. It is hidden by the trees, which have grown to an impressive height. Out of sight, out of mind. And that's the way the owner of this eccentric establishment wants it to remain. It is widely said that behind every closed-door secrets are held – and this home is no exception. Hidden behind the oversized entrance, the most sinister of secrets lurk.

Oversized oil paintings with expensive, thick gold-trim frames hang upon the walls, displaying each resident proudly. And yet, these images are not the happy family image you would expect to see inside a home. Each child's expression is blank. Utterly emotionless. Appearing stiff in posture, they're all positioned in the exact same way. On the right, the girls all have their hair tied up high and wear white-collared shirts with grey knitted tank tops. On the left, the boys all have short hair and wear the same uniform. Not a shade of their natural colour is present in any of their eyes. They're all black and have dark rims around them. Their hands are placed upon their laps. And although they have youthful features, the children's eyes tell no lies. These youngsters have more stories to tell than most elderly people.

Inside the biggest room, where all the gatherings and the height of possessive activity take place, on the left of the central feature wall, hangs the painted portrait of Elisabeth. Below are the portraits of Freddie, Terence and Rupert. On the right-hand side of the wall hangs the portrait of Eve and Lewis cradling baby Honey. Now for the piece de resistance: the centre of the feature wall has an eccentric Victorian-themed fireplace, and in pride of place above this is a portrait of Principal Jesiah, with a stern expression upon his face, and Hope perched upon his hip. A man who is also known to those inside the orphanage as Jezebel, the Dark Empress.

Jezebel took great pleasure in retaining the name Moycullen as a trophy for her biggest collection of souls in one swoop to date, though this wasn't going to be any match for the number she is now ready to accumulate and the plan that lies ahead.

"Ring a' Ring o' Roses…" echoes throughout.

"Your souls are mine," follows.

The children levitate from their beds. The transition has begun. Their skin has turned grey, their eyes as black as the midnight sky. Deep cracks slowly form across their tiny bodies, oozing a thick, black sinister substance. They're all the mirror reflection of their owner. As she moves around the home, dragging her feet, Jezebel is embracing every tiny bit of their evolution. Slowly drifting back down to their beds, the children haul their bodies across their rooms and head out of the doorway and onto the landing space one by one. They wait for Jezebel to pass, and then follow her to the bottom of the staircase. Gaining a strong sense of pleasure that becomes orgasmic, Jezebel is thriving from the vision of all fifty children travelling in the same direction. They levitate slightly on their tiptoes, creating a scratching sound as their overgrown jagged grey nails grind against the wood.

"Ring a' Ring o' Roses…" continues to echo throughout.

The main room of the house is lit only by candlelight, along with the flames glowing from the fire. And true to form, these flames are no ordinary flames. They glow vibrant green, giving the room a wicked ambiance. As Jezebel enters the room, she sees Elisabeth, Eve, Lewis, Freddie, Terence and Rupert standing either side of the main focal point wall. Setting an example, their heads are low and they've all made the transition. Thick drops of the black substance drips from a great height and lands on the floor. A dulcet giggle then follows. Looking up high, Jezebel sees Hope, who appears to be enjoying herself as she crawls at a rapid rate across the ceiling. Now positioned in front of the Victorian fireplace, Jezebel glares out at the view before her. More powerful than ever, Jezebel is ready to enter the homes of the young using her army of children. She is content with their acceptance and transformation. The black substance drips from her mouth and flies across the room as she initiates the summonsing of the children.

"*Nunc est tempus nostrum.*" Raising her arms, she continues. "*Resurgemus mecum. Resurgemus mecum. Resurgemus mecum!*"

In single file, the children continue to enter the room. Gazing through the gap in her hair, Jezebel smirks as she continues to admire the sight before her. Her jet-black eyes are like gaping holes in her face. She has waited decades upon decades for this. As the last child enters the room, the door slams shut. Clicking her fingers, Jezebel summons Hope. The baby crawls down the wall and makes her way to her owner. Jezebel scoops her up and rests her on her hip. Using her coarse tongue, she licks the black substance from Hope's face and begins ingesting it.

"My greatest prodigy. You are so compliant."

Hope smiles, a thick dribble of the black substance hanging from her mouth. Appearing happy, she nestles into her owner's arms. Looking around the room, Jezebel is beyond satisfied. Her time is coming – fast. Soon she will reign supreme across this pathetic planet, and everyone will obey her command or face the consequence of a horrific death at their very own hands.

"*Liberi* – our time is now!" Dragging her feet, Jezebel gradually begins to make her way around the children. "We have worked the minds of the young throughout the day, and they are now ready to embrace us in the night. We will complete our mission in phases. Each of you will enter their homes in pairs. One will sedate the vile people those children call parents. And do not forget, it is imperative that you abide by the techniques which I have taught you. To recap, you will attain sedation by standing at the end of their bed. You will watch as the suffocating mist travels up their body to restrict their movements. Wait until this reaches their necks. At this point, you will repeat the following rhyme – 'Ring a' Ring o' Roses, their souls are ours. Ring a' Ring o' Roses, they belong to the dark side.' In doing this step, you are placing them into their worst nightmare. The nightmare I have set for them all inside the depths of the forgotten forest. It is your mission to have them filled with fear. You want them to beg for their release. Beg for their life. It is your responsibility to get them to submit to you. Taunt their soul."

Leaning down and grabbing young Rita by the chin, Jezebel turns her to face her, as she continues, "Scare them to their death." Through the slight gap in her hair, Jezebel can see her reflection in Rita's eyes. "Ensure that they're quivering in their skin. At this point, you will command *Temimi* – only then will they truly submit themselves to you. Be on guard, do not let them lie to you. They will try and trick you to let them go. You must not surrender. It is vital that this process is completed. We must control their minds, ready for when it is our time to rule." Letting go of Rita's chin, Jezebel steps forward once more. "Do I make myself clear?"

The children respond in unison, "Yes, Dark Empress."

Making her way back towards the central wall, Jezebel continues, "While you keep the parents sedated, your partner will take charge of all the children in the home. Our greatest assets. Treat them with care. Nurture them into our world. Lure them in with your words as you repeat the following rhyme – 'Ring a' Ring o' Roses, your soul is ours. Ring a' Ring o' Roses, you belong to the dark side.' And when the time is right and the implantation has been completed, you will capture an element of the child's soul. We will continue this ritual night after night until we have collected every piece of every child's soul and captured that of the parents. At this point, I will wake my sleepers throughout the globe. And then, we will strike!"

Looking around the room, Jezebel is content with her plan. No one is going to stop her, that she is certain of. As she turns to face Eve, a sinister smirk forms on her features.

"Where is that child of yours?" she says.

"Resting."

"Still not willing to submit her to me, aye?"

Eve doesn't respond.

Looking to Lewis, Jezebel says, "What about you? Wouldn't you like to have that daughter of yours come along for the midnight ride?"

"Erm, erm…" Lewis stutters.

There is a *bang* and *squawk* at the window.

"Looks like you've been saved by the bird."

Jezebel gives a quick twitch of her head, and the windows swing open abruptly. In flies a huge black raven with blood-red eyes. She circulates the room, her oversized glossy wings generating a powerful breeze. The green flames of the candles and the fire ignite even higher. The room looks sadistically magical.

"Ah, there you are, my precious. You have been gone for so long. I have missed you."

The raven *squawks* as she continues to fly around the room.

"Hmm, you have been a busy girl, haven't you? Well, my darling, welcome to our new home. Tell me, how are all my sleepers across the globe?"

Flapping her wings once more, the raven swoops down and lands upon Jezebel's shoulder. Appearing enthused by the raven's entrance, Hope bounces up and down as she crawls up Jezebel's body. She then cuddles the raven and crawls upon her back. The raven pecks at the black substance, leaving Hope's body and Hope giggles.

Stroking her glossy feathers, Jezebel says, "Such a good girl. It is almost our time to wake them. You must ensure that your flight time is as quick as it can possibly be. After all, if everything is to go according to my plan, it is imperative that they are all awakened at the same time before those despicable people have any time to communicate and warn one another."

The raven squawks again, then takes off and flies out of the window with Hope still perched on her back.

"Now, children, it is time! Go. Go in your pairs. Enter your designated houses. Travel amongst the town and wreak havoc. Enter their pretentious despicable homes and take what is ours. Take their souls. Get each of them to submit the most treasured possession they have to you. Do me proud." Ready to infect the whole of Morrisville, Jezebel raises her arms. "*Ad liberos meos*!"

Ecstasy surges throughout her body as she watches the children disappear one after the other before her eyes. The room is now empty. The only thing left is traces of the thick black substance, which is slowly being absorbed into the floor.

Jezebel peers through the gap in her hair at the couple in the bed who are peacefully sleeping, unaware of the evil intrusion into their home. Smiling, she edges closer to the bed. She has personally selected this home as one which she will take full reign over herself. Gazing in admiration at the infamous thick mist as it takes over the room, Jezebel whispers, "It is time."

Circulating up the bedframe, the mist moves onto the next phase. It elegantly travels around the bodies of those who are sleeping inside the bed. The parents of two very obedient twin boys who have taken a distinct liking to Principal Jesiah. Their names – Ashley and Kane Harrington. They have the potential to do destructive and great things within her universe, and so Jezebel has selected them to join the elite section of her empire. The boys will stand before her feet with Eve, Lewis, Elisabeth and the rest of her favoured captured souls. But first, she must deal with these two – their parents, Lisa and William Harrington. Closing her eyes, with her dulcet tone, Jezebel begins to chant her possession rhyme, "Ring a' Ring o' Roses – their souls are mine."

Lisa scrunches her nose as her eyelids begin to flutter. Her expression is pained. Her legs start to move rapidly. Physically fighting with the quilt, Lisa appears to be getting increasingly agitated with every second that ticks by. Jezebel knows this can only mean one thing: the possession is taking full control over her internally. And this is the part she enjoys the most. Aware that Lisa's mind and body are trying to alert her to the goings-on inside her bedroom and wake her up, Jezebel smiles deceitfully as she steps closer. Lisa is too far gone into the possession. She is now trapped and will be unable to wake herself until Jezebel is through with her. A feeling of euphoria travels around Jezebel's body as she drags her feet, one after the other. She perches on the edge of the bed, leans over and hovers her hand above Lisa's face.

"Ring a' Ring o' Roses – they belong to the dark side."

Lisa's eyes shoot open and her mouth widens as she attempts to scream. Laughing, Jezebel pushes her disturbing, wounded grey hand against Lisa's face and rapidly throws her into the nightmares of the forgotten forest. Watching her like a true predator, Jezebel is gaining strength from seeing Lisa so vulnerable in her tainted forest. Lisa's body is exposed as she only has a silk nightie on.

"William?" Lisa says.

There's nothing but deadly silence.

"William, please."

Stepping forward ever so slightly, Jezebel intentionally snaps twigs beneath her feet.

"William, this isn't funny. I think I've been sleep walking."

Again, silence.

"Help!" Lisa shouts.

Now standing behind one of the trees in close proximity to Lisa, Jezebel licks her lips. She is getting a thrill from watching Lisa panic.

"I must be dreaming. There's no way that this can be real. Lisa, wake up! Please wake up. Oh my God. I can't cope with this right now. Lisa, wake up, damn it." Tears set off streaming down her face.

"He can't save you," Jezebel says in her luring and yet frightening voice.

Lisa stops moving.

"Why so scared, Lisa?"

"Hello, who's there?" Lisa replies as she spins on the spot, scanning around her. "I said, who's there?"

"Don't fight it, Lisa. They were never yours to keep. Surrender to me and all will be right within your world."

Lisa says nothing.

"You know why I'm here."

"Please, I don't, I promise. What do you want?"

"Oh, lying already. Still making promises you can't keep. I see some things never change. You heard what I want. Deep down, you always knew they weren't yours to keep, just admit it. Anxiety-ridden mother scared to let them out of her sight. Claiming to have postpartum depression, but the opposite effect – crying as you won't let even their own father take them out for an hour alone. And they all thought you were a control freak. Ha. You knew those boys never belonged to you. You knew a predator was waiting in the wings to come and snatch them from you. And yet, everyone around you told you that you were crazy. Tried to get you to attend therapy to 'fix yourself' and your anxiety, but I must say, bravo, Lisa. You were the only one who sensed I would one day be on my way."

"My boys won't leave me for a monster like you."

"Ouch! If I had feelings, that might have hurt. You see, I am the Dark Empress. I always get what I want, and I am your worst nightmare. One day soon, those boys are going to walk out that door and leave you for good. Those boys are mine. They're not loyal to you and knowing that drives you insane."

"Just shut up!"

"Hit a nerve, have I? You can try and keep them right by your side all you want. I promise you, it will not work. And I always keep my promises. You see, they've already submitted to me. Precious little souls, Ashley and Kane are enjoying living on the dark side."

"Don't you dare talk about my boys, you know nothing about me or my family."

"I know that you and William are one happily married couple. I know that you two set yourself up as the role models of society with the perfect home, perfect careers, perfect marriage, and you had ambitions to be the perfect family, and yet this isn't quite true, is it?"

"I said. Shut. Up."

"Oh dear, I have hit a nerve, haven't I?" Edging closer, but still not in Lisa's sight, Jezebel continues. "No matter how hard you try, you've never quite managed to achieve the parenting. Hmm, I wonder why that might be…?"

"I said don't talk about my family."

"Ah, so you're not denying the things I say, which can only mean one thing – you know I speak the truth."

"No. Not at all."

"Lisa, I am going to say this just once: it would be wise of you to do as I say. If you do, I will let you live with them inside my universe in honour of your sixth sense ability. I will consider keeping you alive as my pet. You can kneel before my feet for the rest of your days. What do you say?"

"I'm done with you," Lisa replies as she closes her eyes and chants to herself. "It's just a nightmare. Any minute now you're going to wake up."

"Huh, that's what you think. I have been watching for a long, long time. This nightmare will not go away. I am now your reality. Your fears have manifested. And you only have yourself to blame. You have been talking about your boys being taken from the moment they were conceived. Did you not think someone was listening to your subliminal messages being sent out into the universe? Thoughts raiding through the ether, just waiting for someone to pick them up. You were probably thinking some righteous spirit was going to collect them and ease all your concerns and worries. Well, ha! You got the complete opposite. They were collected by me! I heard you loud and clear. We can all manifest our desires, and we can also manifest our deepest fears. Don't you know, there's always someone or something listening out there?"

Her eyes closed, Lisa continues to chant: "It's just a nightmare. It's just a nightmare."

"Let me put this very clearly. You have two choices: you can surrender to me and live alongside your boys in my empire, or you can face your death at your very own hands. Which one will you choose? It's up to you."

Lisa doesn't respond. Her lips are still moving, but her voice is faint.

"I'm permitting you to decide your own fate, which is more than I offer most. I suggest you pick one before I decide for you. Maybe I'll have those boys of mine turn on you. Hmm, choices choices…"

"I said don't talk about my boys."

"Tick tock. Tick tock."

"Why would I surrender to you? You're disgusting." Lisa spits on the ground.

"I'll give you one last chance to redeem yourself."

Lisa falls to the ground and places her head inside her hands. Her strength appears to be wearing thin.

"Let's play a game. You could win everything your heart desires, or you could lose your boys and your life."

"I don't want to play a game. Just tell me what it is that you want?"

"That was a very silly decision. I want what is rightfully mine."

Lisa turns. She is now facing the tree which Jezebel is standing behind. "And what might that be?"

"The children." As Jezebel says the words, she steps out into the forest.

With an expression of horror spread across her face, Lisa shouts, "Dear God, help! Somebody please help me!"

"You lose." Jezebel slowly drags her feet. "Ring a' Ring o' Roses, their souls are mine."

Frozen stiff on the ground, Lisa whispers, "What are you?" A single tear falls down her face.

"Ring a' Ring o' Roses – they belong to the dark side." Jezebel charges at Lisa, her mouth wide. Her razor-sharp grey teeth are ready for the bite, and the black substance is gushing down her chin.

Screaming, Lisa throws herself forward. She's soaking wet from head to toe and is gasping for air inside her bed. Staring at her from the darkest corner of the room, Jezebel is content with the evening's events and her implantation. Those boys are as good as hers already.

"I'll see you real soon, Lisa," she whispers.

Chapter Six

"You Were with My Daughter?"

Matthew, Phil and DCS Terry are in the middle of a deep discussion in the oversized airy meeting room on the tenth floor in Scotland Yard. Unable to contain himself and hyped from the breakthrough he has had thanks to the outspoken and brave Mr Hermon Shimai, Matthew is bouncing up and down on the edge of his seat.

"Terry, don't you see, this email means everything. This Hermon guy knows exactly how to get rid of that bitch once and for all. He said it here in his response – look." Matthew points to the screen on the laptop. "I'm telling you, we need to go and meet with him, and we need to go now."

Matthew pauses, expecting Terry to jump up and down with joy at this revelation. But Terry silently breaks eye contact with him and looks at the ground, his head low. Matthew bangs his fists on the table and throws himself back in his chair. His patience is wearing thin.

"Erm, earth to Terry, did you not hear what I just said?"

Terry's silence makes his blood boil.

"Right!" he shouts as he pushes his chair back and stands in protest. "Well, you've clearly got something on your mind that you wanna say, so do us a favour and just spit it out."

"Matthew, come on, sit down," Terry pleads.

"Why? Why should I?"

"Matthew, look..."

"Oh, don't 'Matthew, look' me."

"See what I mean? This is exactly why I can't speak to you sometimes. It's not all about you."

"Never said it was," Matthew says as he makes his way towards the door.

"Matthew, it's Christmas in four days. My wife is already pissed at me cause I'm in the office today, on a Sunday afternoon. There's just no way I can run off to Israel right now. I'm sorry, lad, it just can't be done."

Stopping in his tracks with his hand on the door handle, Matthew turns and says, "Feel better now you've rubbed that in my face?"

"Come on, Matthew, don't be like that. It ain't fair."

"And you?" Matthew says as he releases the door handle, folds his arms and looks to Phil, somewhat concerned by how quiet he's been. "Suppose you wanna stay here an' smooch up to your Mrs while you exchange presents as well?"

"Mate, don't be daft. You know I'm already on the plane. Ain't no doubt about it. I'm with you all the way."

As Phil's words sink in, Matthew takes a deep breath in and decides to stay. He walks back to his seat, feeling somewhat victorious. "Well, that's settled, then. Me and Phil will go to Israel, and we'll report back to you. What you think about that?"

Again, Terry is quiet. Matthew is no longer able to ignore the internal thoughts as they become louder.

"Wow, what is his problem? Why is he being so cagey? Does he know something we don't? I bet he does. Either that or he's about to bail out on us all together."

"Are you hiding something, Terry?" Matthew blurts out.

"What? Why would I be hiding something?"

"You seem, I don't know, distant."

Seeing him breathing deeply, Matthew's baffled as Terry once again returns to saying nothing and looks back towards the ground. And this time his head is hanging even heavier. Now really alarmed, Matthew puts his elbows on the table and his head in his hands.

"Right. Fuck. Him. We don't need him anyway. We've got a real lead here, a real shot at finding the children and not only bringing them home safely, but potentially saving the world from this sadistic bitch's clutches. If he doesn't wanna rave about this, then he can get to fuck. Let him keep his family life, he doesn't know what you're going through anyway. Like he said, rubbing it in your face because he has his wife and children at home for Christmas. Screw him, the dickhead."

Slowly, Matthew zones back into the room as he hears Terry calling his name.

"Oi, Matthew, did you just hear anything I said?"

Shaking his head, Matthew replies, "No. All I know is you're acting like we just got slapped in the face when we actually got a real lead here. You'd think with you being a detective constable or whatever your title is you'd recognise a lead when you see one." Sitting back in his chair and crossing his arms, Matthew continues, "Tell me, Terry, what's your real problem? Is it too much for me to want to have my family home for Christmas? You not think I'd rather be in your shoes than having to get a fuckin' plane to Israel, a country I had no plans to visit in my entire lifetime, let alone at Christmas? Huh, did you think about that when you were having a pop at me about your wife and her attitude? Oh dear, how selfish of me."

Holding his hands in the air in an "I surrender" gesture, Terry says, "I ain't got a problem, Matty lad. What I was saying, if you'd have listened to me when you zoned out the room, is that my only concern is…" Fidgeting in his seat slightly and clasping his hands together on the table, Terry continues with an air of caution about him. "Okay, so what my concern is, let's say you travel all the way to Israel and you do find this guy, this Hermon guy, and if by some miracle he tells you how to get rid of her, we're still no closer to finding her or the children—"

"I hear you," Matthew butts in. "But if we find her, and we don't have a single clue on how to get rid of her, then were chasing our fuckin' tail again, aren't we? I mean, what's the sense in that?"

"Okay, I get ya. Look, I'm just being honest. I'm trying to think outside the box, and I don't want you gettin' your hopes up with this guy and then he turns out to be some fraud and you're stuck in Israel."

"Terry, at the minute, this guy is the only hope we've got. I can't just ignore it. This information came to me for a reason, and I have got to see this through."

"Matthew, I hear ya. I really do. But it leads me onto the next issue. I'm at a loss as to how we're gonna find the children this time."

Rolling his eyes at Terry's problem-finding and solution-avoiding, Matthew says, "Well, maybe your ex-partner on the force is finally well enough to see us now. I mean, Maria was the one who helped us track 'em down at Moycullen through Alice. Can't you just speak to the staff on the ward again and ask if we can visit her quickly? Maybe just say it's a social Christmas call or something? Terry, communicating with Alice again may be our only hope."

"Maybe," Terry replies. "However, I've heard through the grapevine that Maria's somewhat—"

"Terry, look," Matthew snaps. "I don't need you to hold my hand throughout this whole journey, but what I do need is for you to keep the faith and not bail out on me now. We are close. I can tell."

Terry stays silent.

"What's the harm in calling the ward and just checking in on her? Me and Phil will do the rest. We don't have a problem with going to Israel, do we Phil?"

"No mate, not at all."

"See. You stay here and enjoy Christmas with your family and me and Phil will go and do the hunting. All you have to do is call the ward and be on standby for a phone call from us, that is it. Sound fair?"

Before Terry can reply, his phone begins lighting up and vibrating on the table.

"Hello, DCS Terry speaking."

Matthew hears a very distinctive female voice through the speaker.

"Sorry, can you just repeat that," Terry says as he places the phone on speaker mode and puts it on the table.

A young sounding woman with a sweet Irish accent introduces herself. "DCS Terry, my name is Sister— I mean Alannah, just Alannah. I was a sister at the Moycullen Nunnery and I have been given your number by Father McDoyle. He told me to reach out to you because you were the person in charge at the scene where all my sisters were murdered."

"That's correct, Alannah," Terry replies. "How is it I can help you?"

"Well… I… I don't actually know. I'm so confused. You see, I wasn't even aware that any of my sisters had died or that the children had been kidnaped. I… I just…" Alannah sobs.

"Please take a moment, there's no rush. I'm here to help. First things first, I am sorry for your huge loss. This must have come as a huge shock, and I can only begin to imagine how you must feel right now."

"My heart is completely broken in two," Alannah replies in between sobs. "I don't know where to begin, but I need answers."

"We're after the same thing," Terry replies. "Alannah, if you don't mind, I'd like to ask you a few questions. Is that okay? If not, we can do this another time."

Panicking that she might end the call, Matthew waves his arms in the air and mouths, "What you saying that for?"

Terry puts his finger to his lips.

"Sure. I'll answer some questions," Alannah whispers.

Feeling a huge sense of relief, Matthew closes his eyes.

Terry leans towards the phone as he continues, "Alannah, thank you. So, let's start with how you found out about what had happened at Moycullen. Did you say Father McDoyle informed you?"

Matthew's heart is racing as he waits for her to answer. He's sat on the edge of his seat with his ear as close to the speaker as he can possibly get. The seconds feel like minutes.

Looking at Matthew and raising his hand, Terry mouths, "Stay calm."

All eyes and ears inside the room are on the phone. Alannah blows her nose and clears her throat.

"Sorry, this has just been mortifying, and I still haven't got my head around it."

"It's okay, just take your time, Alannah," Terry says in his nurturing tone.

Alannah explains how she tried to call the nunnery and then came across the article online. "It… it said that they were dead." She goes silent, then her sobs resume.

Feeling her pain, Matthew closes his eyes, shakes his head and rests it on his hands.

"Alannah, I'm so sorry," Terry says.

Alannah blows her nose again. "That's the thing. As shocked as I was, a part of me didn't want to believe it. I honestly thought it was just another cruel rumour. You see, there were always so many of them floating around about us and so a part of me didn't think it would be true. I never thought that would be the fate of my sisters, nor the children. I decided to make contact with Father McDoyle and…" A brief pause. "Well, you know the rest. Father McDoyle told me all that he could about what had happened, he gave me your number and said I should reach out to you. So here I am – reaching out."

"Thank you for being brave and contacting me. I know this must be a hard time for you, but any information you have may be pertinent to helping us locate the children and apprehending the cruel individual who did these despicable things to your sisters and the children."

"Yes, sir, believe me, I want to help in any way that I can. They were my family."

"Of course. And thank you."

"I just feel so lost."

Coughing, Matthew gestures for Terry to introduce him and Phil.

Terry says, "Alannah, I just want to let you know that I'm currently in a meeting room at Scotland Yard Police Headquarters and I'm sitting with Matthew Honey and Phil Parkin—"

"Oh my," Alannah interrupts. "Matthew, Phil – I am so sorry for everything you have been through. If I knew Eve, Lewis and the rest of the children had been kidnapped and were being held against their will, I would have contacted the authorities immediately."

Matthew is stunned by what he's just heard. "Wait, you were at the nunnery when my daughter was there?"

"Yes."

"So, you were with my daughter? My Evelyn Jade?"

"Yes."

Instantly becoming teary-eyed, Matthew grabs the phone and pulls it towards him.

"Alannah, please, how is she? Please, tell me how she is?"

His heart is beating a million miles an hour, and the slight pause feels like an eternity.

"Matthew, I promise you, she's okay. Sister Eve is a real tough girl. You raised her very well. You should be proud."

Matthew puts his head on the table as he begins crying with relief.

"I hope it's a slight comfort to you. She appears to have adapted to life away from her family home extremely well. And I have seen first-hand how she has settled into married life and motherhood. She's doing a truly beautiful job. Commendable for a girl her age. And baby Honey is a darling, for sure."

"What did you just say?" Matthew sits back in disbelief.

"I'm sorry, which part?"

"Did you say my daughter is married and has a child?"

"Yes, she married Lewis on the grounds of the Chapel at the Nunnery, and she—"

"Eve and my son Lewis are married?" Phil chimes in.

"Yes, that is true. I should have attended as a witness to their promise to one another, but I didn't make the ceremony or the blessing of Honey. I was set to be her godmother. It was decided by the pair that they would get married after Eve had given birth to their daughter, Honey."

"Wait a minute… what the… so I'm a grandfather?" Matthew says in complete shock.

"And I'm a grandfather?" Phil says, uncertainty fast spreading upon his face.

Sat back in his chair, scratching his head, Terry says, "What on earth is happening here…?"

"I am so sorry," says Alannah. "You didn't need to find out this way. I'm sorry, I shouldn't have called."

"Alannah, wait!" Matthew shouts out. "No, please, I am so happy you have called. You are the last person to have seen our children. You have been with them and they're alive. Please, I'm just in shock. I haven't seen my daughter in so long. I had no clue she would be okay, let alone a mother and a wife. Honestly, it's just a surprise. Please, please don't hang up. I'm relieved that she's not being kept in a dungeon and drugged up against her own will."

"Oh no, I assure you she seemed more than okay to be there, that's why I never suspected a thing. None of us did."

Phil jumps in. "Alannah, what about my other children? Please, what about the boys, Freddie, Terrance and Rupert, and my baby girl, Hope? Are they okay?"

"They're all okay, Phil. They're all okay. You both have very beautiful children and they didn't appear to be in harm's way at all. Like I said, we all didn't have a clue that they were being held by…" Alannah pauses. "… by evil."

"Good lord. Thank you," Phil whispers as he begins sobbing into his hands.

Patting his friend on the back to give him some reassurance and moral support, Matthew breathes deeply and decides it's time to be strong. "Alannah, when did you leave?"

"I left back in July. Judging from what's been reported online, it would seem that I left moments, if not minutes before the tragedy happened."

"Why did you leave them? I know you said you didn't know they were being held by evil, but please tell me you didn't know what was going to happen to them and you decided to save yourself?"

"Oh, no, no, no, no, please, not for a millisecond did I have any idea. You have to believe me."

"Wait – did she send you?"

"Matthew," Terry warns.

"What?" Matthew turns to him. "We all know how sadistic that bitch really is. What if she sent one of her spies to make sure we don't catch up with her?"

"You're being paranoid and acting crazy, lad," Terry replies.

"Matthew, please, you have to believe me. I didn't have any inclination that anything untoward was going to happen. Please, whatever evil this is, it's very clever and highly manipulative. I just want to help get the children back and justice for my sisters. You have to believe me. Please."

Aware that he too was manipulated by the same evil individual, Matthew calms slightly. After all, he was blinded and has walked in her shoes. And right now, she's the only person who can tell him about his daughter as she is today.

"So, I have to ask – what was it?" Matthew asks. "Why did you survive and manage to break free just moments before my daughter was taken again?"

"Matthew, I'm so sorry for your loss, I really am, but I had no clue. I… I just fell in love with a man and decided to run away with him. It was against our beliefs and our promise to the convent and more importantly to our Lord to give your heart to another in a passionate way. I had committed the ultimate sin. I gave my heart to a man, and I took the sacred bond away between myself and our Lord. I could no longer live within the walls of the convent after such a betrayal. I thought it was best for everyone if I left discreetly. I didn't want to bring any hurt to my sisters, the children or the man I'd fallen in love with."

"Matthew, she seems genuine," Phil says.

"Alannah, where are you now?" Terry asks.

"I'm at my new home in New York. I live here with the man I ran away with. He's now my husband."

"Okay, so—" Terry begins.

"I think it's important that you come with us," Matthew butts in. We are heading to Israel to meet with someone who claims to know how to defeat the entity. I think it's best you come too, seeing as you were the last person to be in the physical presence of the entity and all of the children."

"When are you leaving?"

"Tomorrow," Matthew replies.

"Leave it with me."

Tying up his notes, Terry says, "Keep us posted. And, Alannah – thank you."

"Yeah, thank you, Alannah," Phil says.

"Yeah, thanks," Matthew says with a slight smile as he nods his head.

"You're welcome. We will find them, I'm sure of it."

"I will text you Matthew's number so you can stay in touch," Terry says.

"That would be great. Thank you."

"You're welcome. Goodbye, Alannah, speak soon."

"Speak soon."

Terry then hangs up the phone.

Looking at Phil and Terry, Matthew says, "What in the actual fuck was that?"

"Mate, we have a granddaughter," Phil says with a huge beaming smile plastered across his face.

Jumping from their seats, Matthew and Phil hug and begin patting each other on the back in celebration. His head leaning on his friend's shoulder, unable to hold it in anymore, Matthew breaks down. The tears keep falling as the relief he feels is real. A survivor from the nunnery who has been in the presence of his daughter has confirmed that she is doing okay.

"I just can't believe it." Matthew weeps.

"I know, mate. Don't worry, we will bring them all home. We're getting closer."

Composing himself, Matthew sits in his seat. Wiping his face, he throws his head back and looks to the ceiling. His hands begin to tremble.

"Happy Christmas, lads. What a great gift. A granddaughter that you both share."

Matthew smiles. "I just can't believe it. I have another little princess. A granddaughter. I swear, I never in my life thought I'd be on the hunt for my daughter and my granddaughter." Looking up high once more he says, "Lauren, my queen, I promise, I'm going to bring our girls home."

"Right," Terry says, clapping his hands and rubbing them together. "We'd best get these flights booked for you both, hadn't we?"

Matthew breathes deeply, then says, "Lads, let's do this!"

CHAPTER SEVEN

"Why Are You Following Me?"

The curtains are drawn in the bedroom that Eve and Lewis share with their daughter, the room lit only by candlelight. It's seven thirty in the evening, and the winter darkness has settled upon the Moycullen Orphanage. Honey lies peacefully inside her black wooden crib in the far corner of the room, opposite her parent's eccentric, gothic black four-poster bed. Wearing her navy-blue onesie and covered by her ivory silk comforter, Honey is dreaming. She is completely still on her back with her arms by her side. Her black curly locks rest on the ivory silk pillow. A tiny red bow that was clipped on one side of her hair has come loose. Even in the sinister surroundings and the dark energy circulating the premises, Honey looks nothing other than angelic.

Standing at the top of her daughter's crib, Eve is gently humming. Wearing a purple silk button-up blouse dress with a loose bow around the collar and black tights, Eve brushes the hair off her face and tucks it behind her ears. Gazing into the crib, she admires how sweet and innocent her daughter looks. Her rosy cheeks are blossoming while she sleeps, lighting up her face. Honey's long black eyelashes flutter in time with her eyelids as she dreams.

Feeling a warming sensation throughout her whole body, Eve smiles. She has never felt love like this before. And yet, this overbearing obsession she has when it comes to her daughter is causing deep internal conflict. She cannot bear to leave her side. She ponders how she could have created such a flawless and innocent little being when she is made up of such evil. Her mind once again sets off trying to justify how this could be so… The only possible explanation Eve can think of is that Honey must have solely inherited her daddy's genes. Mankind is clearly stronger than the forces of evil when it comes to creating life.

Determined to ensure that her daughter remains untainted, Eve refuses on an almost daily basis to submit her over to the dark side. Strong, fearless, and willing to take on anyone who attempts to capture her daughter's brand-new soul, Eve's relentless ability to protect her is the main reason why Jezebel has stayed away.

And even though Eve doesn't wholeheartedly believe in any other powers within the universe outside of that of her own, there's a minuscule part of Eve that hopes the blessing her daughter was given by the sisters at Moycullen has helped in ensuring Honey's soul remains untouchable.

She argues with herself daily. When times get tough, she eases her thoughts by recalling what Sister Jennifer would say to her: "Our Father loves everyone who has been blessed in his house" and "He is a man of forgiveness". This calms Eve's anxiety a little, particularly when she must leave Honey alone in the orphanage during the night whilst she conducts her duties.

Eve has no one to turn to without raising alarm bells, but she's resolute that she will do whatever she can if it means that her daughter can keep those rosy cheeks she's grown to love so much for as long as she can. And, until the time arises where she no longer has a choice, she has vowed to keep her daughter's precious little spirit protected and pure.

Eve whispers, "Baby girl, I know we don't follow any of the traditions practised on this planet, including Christmas, but my darling, you are the best early Christmas gift I could have ever wished for."

Kneeling on the floor and looking through the bars of the crib, Eve continues, "Honey Parkinson, you are the best thing that has ever happened to me."

Peering up at the oil-painted picture on the wall of her, Lewis and Honey, Eve smiles. "You, and of course your handsome daddy."

Reaching her fingers through the gaps, she strokes her daughter's tiny fingernails. Content with her touch, she closes her eyes and breathes in deeply. As she exhales, she hears, "She is truly beautiful."

Eve's eyes shoot open. Turning, she sees there is no one in the room but her and Honey.

"Hello…?"

"Forgot me already?" the male voice responds.

An instant warning sound sets off inside her head. She now recalls who this voice belongs to. Scanning the room, she soon sees the young male who was taunting her at school. He is wearing the same white outfit, sitting on the wicker rocking chair in the opposite corner of the room next to the bedroom door with a glowing smile on his face.

"You," she whispers.

"Yeah, it's me," he replies. His smile now appears somewhat enchanting.

"Who are you and why are you following me?"

Crossing his legs, he places one hand upon his knee and one under his chin. "Did you know that alongside evil there is good out there in the universe?"

Rolling her eyes, Eve responds, "There's no such thing. Believe me, the sisters at Moycullen tried to convert me many times. Judging from your know-it-all attitude, I'm guessing you are aware of their fate."

"Hmm, okay, so let me ask you this – who do you think is protecting your daughter's soul from your captor right now?"

"Captor? I think what you meant to say is my creator." Eve looks to her daughter and smiles before turning back to the irritating man. "And I'm not protecting her soul, I'm embracing her purity for a little while, that is all. I don't want her having to go out night after night, entering home after home. She is much too young to take on such a huge responsibility just yet. Not that it is any of your business, but let me assure you, Honey will be welcomed on the right side, the dark side, with her family when the time is right."

"Stop trying to kid yourself, Eve. I know you better than you know yourself. And I know that you have no intention of permitting this gorgeous little girl to join you." Sniggering he continues, "Nope, no siree. There isn't a single fraction of a millisecond in a day when you agree to submit her to the dark side. You want her to stay pure, sweet and innocent, like all the other children on the planet before you take over their souls in a hideous and cruel fashion."

"Hey!" Eve snaps. "I resent that comment. We are not cruel to any children."

"You take children away from their parents. I consider that cruel," he says as he crosses his arms and legs.

"What a naive and uneducated young man you are. You have no clue what we do. We do not remove them from their parents. We return them to their rightful owner," Eve snarls. "There is only one way to live upon all universes out there, and we are the ones who have that rightful passage. We are saving them from death."

Waving his hands and placing them on the armrests, the man says, "Word it however you would like. Believe the dribble coming out your mouth. I really don't care, because deep down I know that you're slowly recognising that all may not be as it seems."

"You know nothing."

"Well, I clearly know something you don't, or else why would I be here?"

"To annoy me…?"

Chuckling, he continues, "Good one. Well, I guess we're going to have to agree to disagree on the subject."

"Maybe I just don't care what you think. Ever thought about that one?"

"Oh, you will care if you don't already. You see, Eve, what I'm sensing is, and hear me out, the biggest issue you're currently facing is that you really do know deep down that your precious princess can't remain pure for much longer because your *captor*, not *creator*, has a different set of plans for this planet which are soon to come into effect and this factor confuses the internal hell out of you. So much so, that it eats you up inside pretty much every minute of the day. And, if you really want to get into it, it confuses not only you,"

He leans in closer. "But her daddy, too. He doesn't know why you won't just let her join you all and why you have to fight it so much. Believing in the Lord's protection while you worship and dance with evil, huh, what sort of hypocrite have you become? Tut, tut, tut, I swear, if it wasn't for the fact that you're being brainwashed, we might have actually disowned you by now."

Stunned by his level of awareness of her tormented thoughts and unsure on how he could possibly know this, Eve decides it's best to say nothing.

"Answer me this, Eve… Where do you think the souls of those who pass over on earth go?"

Again, Eve says nothing.

"Come on, you know the ones I'm talking about. Those innocent souls that aren't claimed by your so-called creator, however you want to describe her."

Still, Eve doesn't respond.

"Okay, let me put it in more brutal terms: the souls that she has zero interest in which she casts aside like that of a decaying carcass just waiting to be scavenged by wild animals. Huh, where do those people's souls go?"

Tired of the interrogation, Eve snaps, "Personally, I don't know, nor do I have any interest in what you're talking about." Getting up and dusting off her dress, Eve continues, "What do you want from me? And what's your name, or should I just call you 'annoying man'?" She sniggers at her insult.

Ignoring her question and keeping his legs crossed, the man places his thumb under his chin and his forefinger to his nose as he appears to be deep in thought. "Did you know that we are collected by the biggest angel up there?" He points in the direction of the window. "And, did you also know that if you die on this planet as a child, you get to pick what age you grow to in the spirit world? Even those babies that die before they ever get to take their first breath on this planet."

"No," Eve says. She crosses her arms in protest and stands tall at the side of her daughter's crib. "And like I said, I have no interest in any universe that may, or may not, exist outside of the one in which

I was created in and the one in which I belong. So, I'm afraid that you're talking to the wrong girl."

"I'm not talking to the wrong girl at all. You are very much the right girl for this job." He smiles. "Well, Eve, I'm going to give you some information about myself to bring us closer. I want to educate you a little about why I'm here. Sound fair?"

"Oh really, now you want to tell me… Well, I've only been asking you for that information repeatedly, but whatever."

"Fair enough. So, I'll tell you. You see, I was once one of those babies who never got to take their first breath. Referred to on this planet as a stillborn."

As a new mother herself, hearing the word stillborn makes Eve's insides curl up.

"And, I wasn't just any stillborn. I started out sharing my mother's womb with another. I was part of a set of twins, following the long line of genes from my mother's side. She was a twin, you know. She had an identical twin sister. Her name was Christina."

Humouring him, Eve smiles.

"Two little babies sharing the same woman's body at the same time. There is nothing more intimate than that. I had a beautiful twin sister. Magical, it was. We started our journey so closely together. You see, I can remember everything, as one of the perks of passing over is that you get to retain all knowledge of your time on earth. I remember everything down to the last detail. I can see us both sharing a sack, kicking one another, and I can always feel her presence next to me. It felt like we were in there together for an eternity. And then, with a *thud* and a *kick*, the water started to drain from around us, and somehow I just knew it was time to get the show on the road. I was getting ready to say hello to the world. My sister went first, and I wasn't too far behind. I was so ready to join the people behind the muffled voices I'd been hearing for as long as that sense had developed." He pauses and stares at Honey inside her crib.

"What happened?" Eve asks.

"Sadly, I never made it out alive. I died during labour. Complications with the cord. My sister lived. Fortunately for her."

An unexplainable strange lump begins developing at the back of Eve's throat. Swallowing, but unable to shift it, Eve whispers, "I'm sorry, I know it's really sad, but I'm struggling to see what this has got to do with me?"

Ignoring Eve's question, the man carries on with his story. "You see, when I was cradled by an elderly lady, I was just a crying baby. I had no clue I was a crying spirit baby and that this lady who had a huge glow surrounding her was my spirit mother and not my birth mother. I had no clue that the light which mirrored her and surrounded me was one that meant I wasn't a living being. And I had no clue where my sister had gone. I just felt a loss around me. I felt totally alone."

Eve's heart starts to race. She feels a deep internal sorrow.

Continuing with his ramblings, the man becomes animated. "Huh, ironic really. You see, the elderly lady would bring me to the home, to the place on earth where I was supposed to live out my childhood. I'd get excited to speak to my earth family. But I'd be distraught because they'd never answer me back."

"How sad," Eve says as tears well up in her eyes.

"I didn't know that they couldn't see me. All I knew was that I could see them so vividly. I suppose you're right – it is sad."

"It must have been hard for you."

"It was during one of these visits when it finally sunk in what I was. I spoke to my spirit mother and began accepting this over time, and then I decided that I wanted to get to know my sister. Strong-headed, fearless and loved by all, she was.

Eve smiles, as she sees all these qualities in her own daughter.

"A special girl with a big heart. And my, oh my, was she gifted. She had the most magical talent for all types of musical instruments. Our father and mother doted on her because they knew what it was to lose a child. Me. Never was I mentioned in my sister's life. My death became the dark secret amongst the family. I was the hidden taboo. Never to be discussed again."

"I can't imagine," Eve replies empathetically.

"Huh, they didn't want their precious surviving daughter to develop some sort of issue about the loss of her twin brother, and so life continued without me. I suppose, as sad as it was, watching the family continue like I never existed, helped me to learn over time how to create my own memories with them. Each year I'd help blow out the candles on the birthday cake. I'd get excited watching my big sister opening her presents on our birthday and at Christmas. I'd go hunting for eggs with her and watch as she stuffed chocolate in her mouth like it was going out of fashion on Easter. I even joined her at school on her first day and every day after that. I was a highly proud brother. Pretty cool really, isn't it?"

Slightly concerned where he's going with his story, Eve replies with an air of caution, "I suppose so – and honestly, I find your story quite moving, but what has this got to do with me?"

Appearing to be inside his own world, much to Eve's frustration, the man ignores her request once more and continues, "Did you know, I chose for my growth age to be twenty-one? I think that's also pretty cool, wouldn't you agree?"

Huffing and puffing, Eve replies, "Wouldn't know. I'm not there yet."

"Me either, but it looks pretty fun."

"Look, I'm getting fed up with this now. Tell me exactly who you are and what you want."

Smiling, he says, "You really haven't worked it out yet, have you?"

"Worked what out? That you're stalking me for no apparent reason? Yeah, I've worked that out."

"Ah, you see, that's not true. She had no use for me. I was a mistake. I wasn't supposed to catch on, but I did. There was only ever supposed to be one chosen one. Much easier when you're working alone to snatch one child unsuspectingly than two. Going against everything she believed in, she came to the conclusion that if I hadn't been born, no soul had been created, therefore no sacrifice of an innocent child had been made. And with that loophole she continued with the evil deed. Haunts me still. I can still feel the cord around my neck. It's as real today as it was back then. Like it's happening all over again."

"Right, I've had enough of this now. Who had no use for you? What are you on about? I'm about to get mad real fast. I'm sorry for your outcome, I honestly am, but what has this got to do with me? Either spit it out or leave me alone."

Smirking, he replies, "There's a real good reason why I'm here, and there's a real good reason why you are the only one who can see me after all these years. Evelyn Jade, I'm your twin brother."

Eve stiffens with shock. A gut-wrenching pain ploughs through her stomach and her palms become moist with sweat. "You're lying."

"I do not lie. My name is Thomas Noah Honey and I've been sent to tell you the truth and deliver the outcome of the path that you're on. It is time for you to know the reality of what is to come. It is time for you to understand that *you* out of all the people around you will be responsible for the outcome of the world's fate. You and only you. You are the chosen one. The fate of the world is in your hands. You will have to decide to either save humanity or destroy it. Eve, you must do the right thing. Evelyn Jade Honey is your rightful *birth* name – look it up, if you don't believe me. I am here to tell you that you're being—"

The door *creaks* open.

Peering his head into the room, Lewis says, "There you are."

Stood with her mouth slightly ajar, looking like a rabbit in headlights, Eve whispers, "Impossible."

Lewis glances behind the door at the empty wicker rocking chair that is moving back and forth ever so gently. "What's impossible?" With no reply from his wife, Lewis asks, "Baby, is everything okay?"

Blinking and shaking her head, Eve replies, "Erm, yes, yes, I'm fine. I'm okay. Yes. I was, erm, just making sure Honey was alright while she's sleeping, that's all. I'm fine. She's fine."

"O-kay… What do you say, shall we go for a walk while she's sleeping? Just me and you? Might be nice to have some alone time, huh? I'm sure Elisabeth will keep an eye on her for us."

"Have you lost your mind? You know I won't leave Honey. Especially with her."

"Aye. Aye. Aye." Lewis says with his hands in the air. "That's fine. I just haven't seen you all day, that's all. No need to get defensive."

Aware that she's snapping at him for a reason that is not his fault, Eve seats herself on the side of the bed. Twiddling her fingers, she says, "Lewis, what if I was born like you and not created?"

"Oh Eve, I thought we went over this a while ago?" Rolling his eyes, Lewis sighs as he says, "Where's this coming from again?"

"I know we did, but I just can't get it out of my head. Honey is pure, we know this to be true. Like, what if I am a tainted human too, and I just can't remember my captivity?"

"But you know that Jezebel created you. Why would you even begin to question that?"

"I don't know that. All I know is what she's told me. What if everything she has said has been a lie…?"

Looking around the room, Lewis says, "Shh, you know you cannot question her. She hears everything. Please, just let this go. I beg you. Come on, you're just tired and I think it's making you slightly delusional. Here, why don't you lie down," Lewis says as he makes his way to the bed and places her head on the pillow before he snuggles up next to her.

"I just—"

"Eve, please. If she hears you, we're in for. You're exhausted, end of discussion. Just go to sleep. You don't need to worry yourself about these things. Remember, soon everything we have been working for will come together. It doesn't matter how you got to this point, what matters is that you're right where you should be with the people who look out for you the most."

Eve breathes deeply and resumes staring intently at her sleeping daughter. Questions begin to circulate inside her mind.

'Is there is more to my existence than what I'm living? What if I am living a lie? What if Thomas is telling the truth? Is he really my brother? What if I have an actual human family? How can it be that the fate of the world lies solely with me? What if it is possible to save Honey's soul?'

Eve's head begins to pound.

"I love you."

Looking at her husband, Eve can see the fear inside his eyes. "I love you, too," she replies.

"We have a complete family. What's there to worry about? We are right where we should be."

Drained, and aware that she must leave in a few hours to conduct her nightly duties, Eve decides against pushing for answers. Instead, she's going to try and switch her thoughts off, block Thomas's visit from her mind and watch her daughter sleep while she embraces her husband's touch.

Chapter Eight

"Suspicious"

Locked away inside his room on the top floor of the orphanage, Principal Jesiah sits at his desk, completely focused on the task he has set himself. The space is lit only by candlelight and his shadow can barely be seen in the far corner of the five-thousand square foot bedroom. The room is bare but for a black queen-sized four-poster-bed layered with black silk sheets, a cracked oval mirror with gold trimming, which is the first thing your eyes are drawn to as you enter the room, and the black, wooden, gothic desk where Jesiah is sitting.

There is a sinister reason for the vast amount of empty space. The room is used to conduct sacred one-on-one sessions with the children to ensure that each one is aware of their infinite potential and unique possibilities. Their time is soon to arrive, and every bit of power and every skill is going to be required in order to secure the outcome of which the Dark Empress has dreamed for many centuries now.

Jesiah scribbles away on oversized pieces of discoloured cream paper using a thick black feather plucked from the infamous raven. He dips the black quill into a crystal inkpot filled with blue ink and continues writing ferociously. A man on a mission, he hasn't lifted his head in hours. Each cursive word sprawled upon the paper is unreadable to anyone who might attempt to decipher the contents on the pages. Not a single word is written in English, to ensure that this plan doesn't fall into the wrong hands. The Dark Empress wants the people on earth to be defenceless. This lengthy, well-thought-out document has a very sinister intention behind it and this language will soon be the only universal language spoken once their reign is complete.

He continues for sheet after sheet. As his writing pace picks up, the feather creates a slight breeze across his face. The intensity of the task can be felt in the energy circulating in the room. As he digs the feather deeper and deeper into the page, his expression and physical appearance slowly begin to change. Thick veins pulsate from his temples, turning black. They bulge through his skin like tree roots. With a mind of its own, his hand is focused on the insane scribbling and doesn't so much as lift as Jesiah throws back his head and closes his eyes. Letting out an orgasmic sound, he steadily brings his head forward and opens his eyes. They too are black and appear like gaping holes upon his face. Jezebel is pushing through. His head low, a smirk appears upon his features as the transition rapidly takes over. Jesiah is now Jezebel, and she is engulfed in power.

Hearing a *knock* on the bedroom door, Jezebel bellows, "*Intrabit.*"

The door creaks open, and the shadow of Elisabeth precedes her into the room. Her head is held low, her long dark hair hanging heavy past her pale face. Wearing a black long-sleeved woollen jumper, black trousers and black pumps, Elisabeth blends into the darkness. She doesn't make eye contact with her owner as she closes the door. Turning without hesitation, she makes her way to the middle of the empty space, falls to her knees, places her hand's palm up on her legs and rests her chin to her chest.

"So obedient," Jezebel says.

"Dark Empress, I am here to bring concerning news."

"Oh, and what may this be?"

Still, with her head low, Elisabeth responds, "I believe Eve may be communicating with another form."

Rising from the desk, Jezebel says nothing as she slowly drags each foot across the room towards Elisabeth.

Elisabeth's whole body begins shaking as she says, "Dark Empress, please forgive me. She is your greatest prodigy. I have misspoken. This is not my place."

Jezebel reaches out with a grey wounded finger, places it under Elisabeth's chin and brings her face to face. Staring into her eyes intently, Jezebel says, "What is it you are saying, Elisabeth?"

"I… I am sorry, Dark Empress, I thought I heard Eve speaking to another form. I… I… should have said nothing."

"Hmm, interesting. And, this betrayal you speak so boldly of – how have you attained this information?"

Elisabeth swallows deeply. "During my rounds of the premises, while I was checking each of the children in their rooms, I passed Eve's room. I could hear ramblings as I approached. She was speaking out of context to someone. And, Dark Empress, I honestly thought she was communicating with Lewis until I heard her say something about how her only interests lie with the universe she was created within. And so, I placed my ear to the door and began listening in. I could hear her talking occasionally. But I couldn't hear any other voice. It was as if she was talking to herself, but what she was saying made no sense at all. She was very clearly answering or communicating with another, but I couldn't hear who that person was."

"You heard her mention her universe which she is loyal to. I would hardly say that is betrayal, Elisabeth."

Appearing nervous, Elisabeth places her head back down.

"What other evidence do you have that my chosen one is a traitor?"

"I apologise, Dark Empress. I am wrong, she is not a traitor."

"You have interrupted me to tell me you were wrong, really?"

"No, I am sorry. It was just suspicious. I heard her ask this person who they were and what they wanted. And she mentioned something about being stalked. Then Lewis appeared and I quickly moved along. I knew then that she wasn't speaking to Lewis and, so, erm, I thought I must tell you, because it may be that someone or something out there is trying to take your chosen one, and that you should be made aware of the things that are taking place under your roof."

Jezebel turns and makes her way towards the window. Looking out at the darkened sky, she ponders what entity out there could possibly be trying to break down her army from inside her own layer. Who would be this brazen and brave?

"Keep this knowledge to yourself, Elisabeth."

"Of course. You have my word."

"I will keep my eye on my chosen one. Maybe it's time I pay her prize possession a little visit tonight while the nights events take place." She turns away. "You did good bringing this to my attention. Now you may leave."

Standing, Elisabeth bows her head and quickly leaves the room.

Heading towards the window, Jezebel stares at the sky. "Hmm, who is daring to try and stop me? Looks like I shall bring my plan forward. I own every universe, and nothing is going to stop me."

Walking back to the desk, Jezebel collects a blank sheet of paper and picks up the quill. She then dips it in the ink and inscribes the word "*Goeominaonpler*" in the middle of the paper in huge letters. A deceitful smile stretches across her face, exposing her razor-blade grey teeth. The thick black substance travels down her chin.

CHAPTER NINE

"You Belong to Me."

Stillness is upon the streets of Morrisville. However, this is far from the reality behind the oversized closed doors. Deceitful events are unfolding. Spread amongst the village, Jezebel and her accomplices are out in full force. They are capturing elements of the souls of the young whilst taunting those of the adults within their own homes, and it's feeding Jezebel an endless surging stream of orgasmic energy. More potent than ever, Jezebel believes that she is now untouchable. Soon her sleepers across the globe will wake and her time to reign will arrive. Ownership of the universe she has always craved is now within reach. And it's been worth the wait.

Having dealt with the despicable parents Lisa and William earlier as they were sleeping, Jezebel is now standing at the foot of Ashley and Kane's beds with her arms raised. Floating in mid-air, the boys are in the final stages of the night's possession. Their demonic appearance gives her nothing but true gratification. They are mini versions of her true existence. With the takeover of the boys complete, Jezebel lowers her arms. Ashley and Kane begin drifting back down as they return to their beds. Each of the boys now retain only a miniscule remnant of their souls. Proud of her selection, Jezebel is satisfied with the evening's events that have taken place within the Harrington household. She is ready to take charge of her next task. The mist surrounds her as she disappears.

Jezebel gazes through the gap in her hair at her target sleeping inside her crib. Licking her lips, she whispers, "*Amplius. Meus es tu. Serve meus es coram me. Sufficit. I hæreditate possidebunt te. Veni mecum.*"

To her surprise, Honey doesn't react to the words. She continues to sleep peacefully and doesn't move so much as an inch. Intrigued by the defiance of Honey's soul, Jezebel decides to investigate further. She drags one foot in front of the other, the black substance smearing across the floor behind her. Raising her arms, she shouts, "*Autem!*"

The thick mist seeps into the room through the cracks around the doorframe and intertwines as it travels towards the crib. It wraps around the wooden frame, ready to restrain its pray. Confident in the ability of her devious element, Jezebel watches from the side of the crib. But as soon as the mist grazes Honey's comforter, sparks fly. Instantly the mist retreats behind Jezebel. In disbelief, Jezebel is fast becoming furious. She always gets her way, and this soul is not going to remain off limits any longer.

Standing over Honey's crib, Jezebel reaches in to remove her. A strong unexpected force awakens around Honey and throws Jezebel across the room. Outraged, Jezebel jumps up off the ground and charges at the crib. She grabs it and throws it into the air. Flying out of the crib, Honey is tossed across the room. Smiling, Jezebel raises her arms, ready to summon the mist to capture her defiant one. But before she can, Eve appears inside the room. She grabs her daughter as she descends from mid-air. Landing in a bundle on the floor by the foot of the bed, Eve stares at Honey.

The black substance gushes from Eve's mouth as she screams, "What are you doing?"

Holding Honey to her chest, Eve begins to transition back into human form. Appearing totally unfazed by the events that have taken place, Honey is alert and giggling.

"It's okay, darling. Mummy is here," Eve says.

Staring at her through the gap in her hair, Jezebel is far from pleased. "How dare you? Conspiring against me, are you?"

"Jess, what are you talking about?"

"You will call me Dark Empress!" Jezebel barks.

Putting her head down, Eve says nothing.

Dragging one foot in front of the other towards Eve, Jezebel replies, "It will be wise of you to remember that I created you and I can just as easily tear you down."

Cradling her daughter, Eve again stays quiet.

"What enchantment have you had placed over her?"

"Nothing, Dark Empress," Eve replies quietly.

"Enough of this nonsense! Her time is running out. I will capture her soul. You will hand it over to me when our time arises or I will crush you, do you understand?"

Eve gently nods her head.

"Good. And whatever it is that you have placed over her, you will have it removed immediately."

"I—"

"I don't want to hear it!" Jezebel bellows. "Remove whatever it is and submit her to me. Your time is running out. I suggest you pick where your loyalties lie and fast. I can easily eliminate those around you." Now just a stone's throw away from Eve, she continues with her threats, "Grown fond of Lewis, have we?"

Eve says nothing.

"Thought as much. You want this disgusting family unit you've created to survive; you will fall in line like everyone else." Now standing in front of Eve, Jezebel bends and grabs Eve by her chin. Staring at her directly in the eye, she continues: "The clock is ticking. Choose wisely. It would be a shame to waste my greatest prodigy. You were created by me. You are my chosen one and you will obey me or face the consequences."

Turning, Jezebel walks to the door. As she opens it, she glances back at Eve and says, "Whoever you are communicating with outside of this universe, it stops now." She walks out of the room and closes the door behind her.

Chapter Ten

"Acting Crazy."

"You don't understand, I have to help them." Alannah stands inside the walk-in closet, wearing a black velour tracksuit with her hair tied up high into a scruffy bun. She is hurriedly loading an oversized, worn-looking brown leather bag with various items of clothing, reciting the list of things she may need for her emergency trip to Israel. Alannah isn't thinking rationally at all. It's six in the morning and she's on a mission. Her mind is focused solely on packing, getting a cab to the airport and boarding the first flight to Israel.

"They're grown men, Alannah. Please, listen to me. I'm sure they can handle this without you. Stay here with me, where I know you are safe." Brennan's standing in the doorway looking exhausted with dark rims around his eyes.

Alannah stops in her tracks. She is fast becoming sick of her husband's lack of support. "We spoke about this all day yesterday after my conversations with DCS Terry, Matthew and Phil. You said I should sleep on it, which I did, and I've woke up this morning and have decided that I must go."

Clasping his hands together in a prayer position, Brennan continues, "Okay, baby, please, you need to hear yourself right now. You need to hear how odd this sounds. And please, no disrespect, but if you think I'm going to let you board a flight and travel all the way to Israel, which is twelve-hours away at least, to meet up with two guys who you've never met and have only spoken with, two, maybe three times, max, on the phone for a matter of minutes at a time, then you're very mistaken."

Alannah folds her arms, her expression stern. "Wait a minute, you think you have to let me go? Brennan, I don't need your permission to go on this trip. I am a grown woman, and I can make my own decisions. Not a chance am I going to live any more of my life with someone telling me what I can and cannot do. No way."

Brennan puts his head in his hands. He rubs his face and wipes his tired eyes. "Look, that's not what I'm saying. I know you don't need my permission. Please, I didn't mean it like that. What I meant was what sort of husband would I be to not even question this or at least try and stop you, because it just doesn't feel right. Alannah, what if something terrible happens and I just let you walk out that door without a question or concern in sight? Please, I don't want to fight with you."

"Then it's simple – come with me."

"Alannah, baby, it's three days until Christmas. Please, just stay home with me."

Alannah grabs a handful of colourful garments from one of the drawers and stuffs them into the bag. She is not giving in to her husband's tactics.

"Alannah, please."

"They're landing there today! I have to get to the airport now if I'm going to stand any chance of getting on a flight. I'm not going to be the one holding them back."

"Look, Alannah, I..." Walking across the room to her, he puts his hands on her shoulders and turns her to face him. "Baby, I can't say that this is okay. I am so sorry for what happened to your sisters and the children, but flying all the way across the world to meet two guys you don't even know on some witch hunt just doesn't sound very safe to me."

As the words begin sinking in, Alannah looks to the ground and replies, "Brennan, I don't—"

"No, Alannah, you have to listen to me," Brennan says, shaking her slightly. "This is a sad situation, granted. I get it. You're confused, upset and you feel guilty. Who wouldn't? You're my wife. When you hurt, I hurt. But please, you have to listen to me, this is not safe. Nothing about this set-up is safe." Looking into her eyes, he continues, "Just please, see how alarming this is. You might have lost your sisters and the children, but Alannah I can't lose you. I… you know I… I can't lose another person in my life."

She drops the bag, reaches up and places her hands on her husband's face. Gazing at his exhausted expression, she remains silent for a brief moment. Breathing deeply, she takes in his low energy and desperation. The worry, the fear and the anxiety oozes from every pore on his body and it's hurting her heart to see him this way.

Wrapped in her own selfishness, Alannah's very aware that she hadn't even considered her husband and the trauma he has been through. She didn't even think about how her disappearance might have impacted him. Placing her forehead onto his, Alannah knows her husband's right. Travelling across the world at Christmas – and not just any Christmas but their first Christmas together – to meet with two strangers on a mission that has a limited chance of success is crazy. Actually, she knows it's beyond crazy, it's borderline insane. And yet, there's a huge pull inside of her that isn't permitting her to accept the thought of sitting back and doing nothing. This just seems more inconceivable to her than taking this risk and travelling to Israel.

She has endured the heartache of taunting visions every minute of the day since she found out the tragic news. The thought of the children being lost in the world somewhere suffering at the hands of God's only knows who is eating her up inside. She'd happily sacrifice herself and her happiness right now if it means saving the children from those horrors.

Suddenly she smiles as she hears Sister Kathryn's voice in her head. "You're stuck between a rock and a hard place, my dear." A quote she would often repeat to her during her times of trouble at Moycullen.

Alannah's thoughts are racing. In a desperate bid to shut them up, she throws her arms around Brennan's neck and holds him tight.

"It's going to be okay," Brennan says as he tucks his head into her and holds her close.

Pressing her lips against his ear, Alannah whispers, "I know this sounds crazy."

"Really…?" Brennan says gently. "Because I was starting to think that you'd forgotten what common sense was."

Alannah chuckles.

Tears gradually trickle down her cheeks as the realisation of the dilemma she faces sinks in. Wiping her tears, she lets go of Brennan and makes her way into their bedroom. Sitting on the edge of the bed, she grabs the box of tissues from the bedside cabinet and cleans her face. She taps the empty spot beside her and says, "Please, come sit with me."

Brennan seats himself next to his wife. Looking her in the eye, he whispers, "I love you so much. You are the bravest woman I know, but baby, I can't risk losing you. You know I just cannot go through any more loss. I don't want to lose another person in my life and I don't know what I'd do. First Jannie and then—"

"Shh, you don't have to," Alannah interrupts. She might regret this decision, but it is one she has to make for her present life, her husband, the man who has supported her throughout and has given her the life that she had dreamed about for so many years from behind the walls of the convent. Grabbing his hands, she says, "I'm not going to Israel."

"What? You really mean that?"

"Yes. I mean it. How can I leave you in this state? Huh. Maybe Matthew and Phil can travel here once they have finished with their search in Israel. I'll ask them, and if not, then after Christmas maybe I could fly to England and meet with them there."

Brennan sobs into his hands. "I was so worried I was going to lose you. I haven't slept all night. Thank you so much for not leaving me. You really don't know how much this means to me."

Alannah's guilt hangs heavy. She feels terrible at the pain she has caused her husband. Taking him into her arms she cradles him.

"Shh, I am so sorry. I will never leave you. Please know that I love you. You're my life and I will put you first always." She wipes the tears from his face. "Look, I'm going to text Matthew now and tell him I won't be flying to Israel."

She takes her phone out of the pocket on her jacket and fires off a message to Matthew. Immediately, her phone begins to ring. Seeing her husband's expression, Alannah says, "Don't panic, I got this." She then answers the call.

"Hello, Matthew."

"Alannah, what's going on? I thought you were flying out and meeting us there."

"Yeah, I'm sorry, this just isn't great timing for me to be getting on a flight." Alannah smiles as she sees the relief on Brennan's face. "Erm, I can't meet you there, but if you like, when you and Phil have finished up in Israel, you're more than welcome to fly into New York and we can discuss any information you may have found out during your trip?"

In the background, Alannah can hear the announcements of departing flights and gate numbers.

"Matthew?"

"Yes, I'm still here."

Hearing the disappointment in Matthew's voice, Alannah feels a slight sense of guilt. "I'm sorry. I just can't…"

"It's fine." Matthew coughs. "A bit of a setback, but it's fine. Erm, look, Alannah. You were a nun, yeah?"

"Yes, I was a sister at Moycullen."

"So you would have studied the Bible?"

"To some extent, yes," Alannah says, confusion fast spreading on her face.

"Do you know anything about the Smashing of the Clay Pot verse?"

"Vaguely, yes. But nothing of any relevance. Why?"

"Well, this Hermon guy that we are going to meet has said that this is how the entity was created from that specific time and from the curse that was placed upon the land as a result of the events that happened. Can you do some digging and research as best you can on your end and then we can possibly reconvene on our return from Israel?"

Relieved that she can at least help in some way, Alannah jumps at the chance. "Yes. Yes. Of course, I will. It would be my honour to help. This is not a problem at all."

"Thank you. Also, maybe try and dig into your own memory from during your time at the nunnery with them. See if you can think of any conversations that might lead us to where they are today."

"I'll get on it right away. I'll go to the library here in New York and do as much research as I can."

"Look, I have to go, our flight is boarding. Let's agree to stay in touch and keep each other updated."

"Yes. For sure. You have my word. Safe flight."

Putting the phone on the side, she looks to Brennan and says, "All sorted. You can rest easy now. I'm not going anywhere other than the New York library. Why don't you go to sleep for a while?"

"Honestly, you don't know how much it means to me," Brennan says. "What you have just done is huge and I cannot thank you enough."

Smiling, Alannah replies, "Aw, my baby, you don't have to thank me. Remember, we're a team." She kisses him on the head. "Come, lie down for a little while. Do you need anything before I head to the library?"

"No, baby. I'm just going to rest. But thank you."

"You're welcome. I'll have my phone with me. Call me if you need me."

"Will do."

With that, Alannah tucks Brennan in and kisses him on the head once more. His temperature has risen and he feels boiling hot. Stroking his hair back, she whispers, "Sleep well, handsome."

Alannah then leaves the room.

CHAPTER ELEVEN

"More Bad News."

Matthew and Phil wait anxiously in line to board their flight after an agonisingly slow passage through the annoying airport security process. They want nothing more than to take off and land on Israel soil. Feeling his phone vibrating, Matthew awkwardly retrieves it while trying to juggle his backpack and pass the check-in lady his boarding pass and passport.

"Hey, Terry, I can't talk right now. I'm just boarding my flight. Erm, can I call you back in a minute when my hands are free and I'm in my seat?"

A stern voice comes back through the speaker, "Make sure you do."

Confused at his tone, Matthew replies, "Sure."

The call ends.

Staring at his phone, Matthew hears a sweet feminine voice at the side of him say, "Thank you, Mr Honey."

Saying nothing, Matthew nods as he receives his documents back.

"Enjoy your flight."

Again, Matthew says nothing.

Following his fellow passengers, Matthew walks through the narrow corridor. There is a sea of people, old and young, everywhere. The vast majority of them are not speaking English.

"What did Terry want?" Phil asks.

"I'm not sure but he sounds really serious and I'm a little alarmed," Matthew replies.

"He gonna call you back?"

"No, I'm gonna call him. If we ever get on this frickin' plane," Matthew shouts as he sees the next sea of people he has to queue behind.

After standing in the samc spot inside the tunnel connected to the plane for around ten minutes, Matthew's temper is surfacing. The incessant crying of babies, whining of children and chit-chat around him is grating on his last nerve. And now the signal on his phone is down, so he can't call Terry back to find out what the issue is. He wafts his ticket in his face in a desperate bid to cool himself down. Matthew's heart sinks as he wonders what could possibly have gone wrong now. First Alannah bailed and now Terry's got what sounds like more bad news coming his way.

"Told ya. Did you really think that this was going to go your way? Ha. Matthew, you do amuse me. He's ringing to tell you he's out, too. Alannah knows you're crazy and now Terry knows you're crazy. Going all the way to Israel to speak to some guy who recites biblical verses. What a moron."

"Shut up!" Matthew barks. "Will this goddamn line move?"

Phil's jaw drops.

Matthew's face turns a shade of bright red, partly with irritation and partly with the embarrassment he's now feeling like all eyes in the tunnel are glaring at him. Dying inside, he decides to copy his friend and put his head down. If he can't see them, then they're not there.

"Mate, chill out. It's going to be okay," Phil whispers.

"I just want to get in my seat."

"I know. I do, too, but you don't have to start yelling at everyone."

Then, to Matthew's delight, the line starts moving. As they get closer to the door, Matthew sees a tiny blonde male flight attendant.

His smile is gleaming from the reflection of the sun through the window, almost blinding them.

"Boarding passes, please."

Passing him his ticket, Matthew smiles.

Smiling back, the flight attendant says, "Welcome to your flight, Mr Honey. Please make your way down the aisle here. Your seat is to your right. A member of the crew will be along to take your drink and food order shortly."

"Thank you…"

"Enjoy your flight."

As soon as Matthew and Phil have taken their seats, Matthew pulls out his phone. Two bars. It might just be enough. He hits the call button and Terry answers within one ring.

"Terry, I've not got long, I keep losing my signal, and it's gonna go again any minute. What's wrong?"

"Look, you know that I wasn't supposed to be working today?"

"Yeah."

"Well, I just thought I'd check something."

"Okay." Matthew says, his heart now pounding out of his chest.

"You got me thinking about what we gonna do when you get this information if this guy is legit. Like, how we gonna find her again… So, I rang the hospital to see if I could speak with Maria on the phone or try to book a visit next month for us. I told them I wanted to wish her a merry Christmas and bring her a small gift. Well, it turns out that she's… erm… she's…."

Sitting up bolt right in his seat, Matthew feels sick to his stomach. "She's…"

"Well, Matthew, I erm…"

"Terry, spit it out. She's what?"

"She's gone."

"What, she's been discharged?" Matthew sinks back into his seat with relief. "That's not a bad thing. At least she can come with us now. So, did they give you her forwarding address?"

"No, Matthew, she's gone, gone."

"What do you mean gone, gone? Like untraceable gone?"

"No. She's dead."

"What?" Matthew's jaw drops. He can't believe what he's just heard.

"She appeared to be getting better and so they gave her more freeway or alone time. It turns out she wasn't as stable as they thought. She snuck into an unoccupied resident room and used the sheets on the bed to hang herself."

Matthew puts his hand to his mouth. A tear falls down his cheek. "Oh. Terry. I'm so sorry."

"I know. It hit me hard. At first, they were reluctant to tell me anything, but she'd left a suicide note and it was specifically to tell me that she was sorry."

"I… don't know what to say… Terry, this is horrible news. Just horrible."

"Look, I just wanted to tell you because now I really don't know how we're going to find the children and I thought you should be aware."

Tucking his head in his hands, Matthew feels sick. Another death. "No. No. That's, erm… Yeah. Thank you for calling. I'm just so sorry, mate. I know how fond you were of her, and you took her under your wing."

"It's just such a waste. She had such talent and promise. I should never have tried to take her under my wing. It's my fault, I was the one who requested she pair up with me. Matthew, I feel so guilty."

"Terry, I'm so sorry. Please, just go be with your family. Don't worry about what we're up to. I'll think of something, I'm sure."

There's a slight pause. "Thank you," Terry replies.

"Anytime. Look, I'm going to have to go. I'll let you know when we land."

"Okay. Please do. Safe flight."

Staring at his phone Matthew shakes his head. Another person he'd grown fond of has died. He has no clue why this trail of death and destruction is continuing to follow him. Feeling cursed, sad and muddled, Matthew releases a heavy sigh. Placing his phone on the table next to him, he looks at Phil.

"What did Terry want?"

"Maria's dead."

"What?" Phil says, his eyes wide.

"Yep, took her own life."

"When?"

"Not sure. Just know she's gone and she ain't coming back."

"Oh shit, mate. How's Terry?"

"He ain't good, as you can imagine."

"Shit, that's sad, man."

Matthew takes a deep breath. "Now we return to the drawing board to try and figure out how we're going to track 'em all down."

"Mate, we'll think of something. Wow, I'm just shocked. Another poor taunted woman. Tragic."

Looking up, Matthew says, "You wanna give me a break yet?" Talking to God is the last resort for him.

"Good morning, Mr Honey, have you looked at our drinks and food menu today?"

Matthew puts in his order and gets his notebook out. As sad as the news is, he's determined not to let the death of Maria set them back. He begins jotting down various ideas. With nothing left other than pure belief and faith, he's hopeful that his new contacts will help him on this journey. A journey to bring his daughter and his brand-new granddaughter Honey home where they belong. He scribbles away, compiling a list of questions in readiness for his meeting with Hermon.

"Good morning, everyone…"

Matthew jumps as the captain's announcement commences. It's almost time to start the seven-hour flight.

"Well, here goes nothing," he says to Phil.

Saying nothing, Phil smiles back. Yet Matthew sees that his smile isn't of the happy kind. His friend has sadness in his eyes.

Chapter Twelve

"Research."

Alannah can see the breath as it leaves her body. Hands in her pockets, she is walking past Bryant Park at a rather daring pace. Frost and slush are spread across the path. Not wanting to slip and land flat on her butt, Alannah tries her best to dodge any slippery spots.

She's wrapped up from head to toe. Over her velour tracksuit, she's wearing her ruby red winter jacket, black beanie hat, black silk scarf with gold detailing, and ankle height welly boots. Resting on her shoulder is her pride and joy, an oversized designer black leather handbag with a red silk interior. Having lived in her robes and habit for much of her life, if there is one thing Alannah has personally fallen in love with, it's the fashion district of New York.

Peering to her left as she waits for the lights to change at a crossing, she sees the festivities and commotion going on inside Bryant Park and smiles. Gone are the days when she and Brennan would sit outside enjoying the sunshine and five-star dining together as newlyweds. And yet, even with the cold weather, this vibrant location remains just as busy now as it was back then, with people from all walks of life. A huge ice-skating rink is centre stage. Everyone is chuckling with the person next to them as they desperately holding onto one another to travel the distance around the rink as successfully and embarrassment free as they possibly can. Winter isn't going to take the outdoor fun and joy away from the city that never sleeps.

The cars come to a halt and the lights change. With a skip and a jump, she crosses the road and finally arrives at the New York Public Library. After walking the twenty-three blocks to get there, Alannah is now somewhat hot and bothered. Releasing the scarf from around her neck, she instantly feels the cold breeze blowing against her skin. It's soothing and yet slightly orgasmic.

Looking, as she always does, Alannah is once again in absolute awe of this magnificent building. It doesn't matter how many times she visits this venue, every trip is just as magical as the last. One thing being locked away in the Moycullen Nunnery for so long has taught her, is to always stop and smell the roses. Gone are the days of dreaming about visiting places such as this. Beaming a smile as bright as the stars, Alannah is mesmerised by the matching grey-stone twin lion statues in pride of place at the front of the building by the steps.

She bounces her way up the stairs, panting as she makes it to the top. She opens her bag for the short lady behind the security desk, who scans the contents and waves Alannah in. "Thank you, Ma'am. Have a great day and welcome back to New York Library."

"Thank you, Lara," Alannah replies.

She makes her way towards the staircase through a sea of people, many of them taking pictures posing alongside the grand architecture. New York Public Library is breath-taking. Alannah feels very blessed to have it within walking distance. She glances up at the immaculately designed marble ceiling. It's like walking through a fairy-tale book. History, romance and knowledge from all walks of life are waiting for her, like treasure to be found. And no expense has been spared with the Christmas decorations. Extravagant lighting is intertwined throughout. Standing at least twenty feet tall, the Christmas trees are decorated with white and gold. The building is glowing and looks angelic.

She heads to the Stephen Schwarzman Building in the General Research Division. Unsure of what it is she's looking for, Alannah decides this is her best starting point. She finds an empty table, sets down her bag and puts her jacket on the back of the chair.

She spots a friendly-looking woman across the way. "Pardon me. Sorry to interrupt, but can I ask, are you a regular here?"

The mousey brunette puts down her novel and whispers, "Yes. I'm familiar with the library." With a friendly expression, she continues, "It's my place of sanctuary. I just love being surrounded by so many great love stories. I'm a sucker for romance. What about you? I love your accent, by the way."

"Oh, thank you. That's too kind," Alannah says as she seats herself. "I haven't been in New York for long. But I have been here a few times. I'm not an expert like you, though. I am yet to unlock all the knowledge that lies within these enchanting walls."

"Yes, it is quite a project." The girl chuckles.

"By any chance, do you think you could help me? I'm looking for a specific genre."

"For sure, I can certainly try. What is it?"

"Erm, okay, so do you think you could help me locate the historic religious book section?"

"Oh, your best bet for that sort of material would be the Rose Main Reading Room. Not a lot of people know this, but up high there are books that remain untouchable to the public. Those shelves house some of the most prestigious and oldest biblical books." She looks up, appearing to be in thought. "Hmm, now I'm not sure if you can get access up there. Most of those books have been untouched for decades due to their delicacy and value."

Alannah sighs, deflated. "Well, that's sad."

"Was there a specific subject you wanted to research? I could maybe ask someone to search the system to see if a replica has been made."

Perking up a little, Alannah replies, "I'm looking for an entry in the Bible pertaining to the Smashing of the Clay Pots. Are you religious at all?"

"Yes," she replies sternly. "Why do you seek this specific verse?"

"I've been asked to conduct some research."

"Research?"

"Oh, yeah, sorry, I should have said, I'm a nun, you see. Erm, so I've been sent across to New York to get as much information as I can from the American libraries and then feed this back." Alannah feels uneasy. Not only has the quick judgemental reaction from the young girl caught her off guard, but now she finds herself lying to try and justify her request. "I mean, I have studied this a little already during my enrolment, but I haven't really ventured into this in any depth as we don't hold much information about this particular subject in rural Ireland, which is where I am from."

A slight pause ensues, making Alannah feel even more awkward. The young girl continues to say nothing and is staring at Alannah with a somewhat cautious and alarmed expression.

"I'm on a mission, you see. My superiors have sent me across the gigantic pond that separates us so that I could visit the second biggest knowledge holding venue in America to investigate this further and pull out any information possible so that we can educate those back home."

"I see," she replies. "You don't look like a nun. Why don't you wear the same clothes that they wear?"

"Oh, my superiors just decided it might be best for me to dress down during my trip to not stand out and draw any potentially unwanted attention to myself as I'm on my own."

"Oh, okay," the girl replies, appearing to believe what Alannah is saying to be true.

Putting out her hand, Alannah says, "My name's Alannah."

Shaking this, the girl replies, "Julianna."

"Julianna, do you think you could help me at all?"

"I... really shouldn't—"

"Julianna, if you know anything about this, please, I beg you to help me."

Taking a deep breath in, Julianna looks to the ground.

Making her way around the table, Alannah kneels at the side of her. Forcing eye contact with Julianna, she whispers, "Please."

Appearing reluctant, Julianna says, "The verse you speak of is not in the Biblical section."

"Okay, so where might I find this?"

"It is located in the Dark Ages section."

"Brilliant," Alannah replies, relieved that she got the answer she needed.

"Huh, I'm not sure it's brilliant," says Julianna.

"What do you mean?"

Shaking her head with her eyes wide, Julianna replies, "I have been to the Dark Ages before, and it is not a section of the library I profess to like. It is just as it says: dark. And the energy makes the hairs on my body stand to attention."

"Really?"

"Yes."

"I have to go there. Can you show me?"

A moment or so passes.

"I wouldn't ask if I wasn't desperate."

Julianna says nothing as she twiddles her fingers.

"You don't have to stay with me – just point me in the right direction."

Julianna says nothing. She looks around furtively.

"Maybe you can just tell me what floor this is on?" Alannah tries.

Looking Alannah directly in the eye, Julianna says, "I can assure you, it is not on any floor. The Dark Ages section is way out of sight. Only those who know where it is can locate it." Julianna's eyes are starting to look as though they're turning black. "Those who run the library have even stopped telling its own staff members that this area exists. It's too dangerous. If these books fell into the wrong hands, a whole new realm of evil could be awoken."

Aware that evil is already amongst them, Alannah says, "If only you knew."

"Knew what?"

"Nothing. Ignore me." Alannah exhales heavily, regretting the comment. "Please, you must show me. You are my only hope." Trying one last time, Alannah plays the religious card. "Think of it this way – the Lord has guided me to you for a reason. You say this section is secret and not many people are aware of its existence. Look around the room and ask yourself – how many people in this room would have known about the Dark Ages?"

Julianna says nothing and breathes deeply.

"Exactly. None of them. So how and why have I, out of all the people in this library, been immediately guided to you?" A brief pause. "Because the Lord knew it was you who could help me. No one else in this entire building, just you."

"I suppose when you put it like that..."

"I'm certain you can feel the chill in my hands from the outdoors. I have honestly just walked into the library minutes ago and have been guided to you. Look, there's not a spare seat in sight except this one, directly facing you. Clearly, the Lord wants you to help me. Please, Julianna, I need your help."

"What if..."

Desperate, Alannah grabs both of Julianna's hands. Remaining on her knees, she begs, "Please, please show me where it is."

"Okay. I will show you where you can find the verse you seek."

Hugging Julianna, Alannah says, "Thank you. Thank you. Thank you."

"I am certainly familiar and aware of where the book you require is – it's in the Absence of Light section."

Relieved, Alannah replies, "I honestly cannot thank you enough. You are going to make a huge difference."

Putting her jacket back on, Alannah helps Julianna to collect her things. "After you," she says.

They walk down staircase after staircase and a variety of hidden passageways for what feels like miles, eventually reaching a narrow and dark corridor. The grey slate brick is damp, with tiny areas of green moss. Not a single person can be seen. The space around them is so tight that Alannah's slender body can barely fit down it. With her phone in her hand, Julianna puts on her torch. Looking around, Alannah begins to realise why this section of the library is not signposted. The energy is nothing like that of the rest of the library. It's intimidating, relentless and taunting. Hugging herself, Alannah feels the presence of the unwanted kind breathing down her neck. She closes her eyes and bravely looks behind her. There's nothing and no one there. Aware her mind is playing tricks on her, she continues to follow Julianna. As Julianna looks back at her, Alannah notices the dark oak wooden oval door in front of her. They've arrived.

"You ready?" Julianna says.

"Ready as I'll ever be." Retrieving the rosary bead from under her top, Alannah kisses it and makes the sign of the cross. "And may our Lord be with us."

"Let's go, then," Julianna says as she pushes the door open.

The smell of damp and dusty old paper hits Alannah's nose. True to its name, the room that contains the forbidden books is murky, oppressive and has a bad energy. Alannah wastes no time. She wants to leave as quickly as she can.

"Where is the Smashing of the Clay Pots book?"

"This way," Julianna replies.

Alannah covers her mouth and nose with her scarf.

"Kicks you in the nose that smell, doesn't it?"

"Yeah. It's hurting my head a little," is Alannah's muffled response.

They walk through the maze of bookshelves and a never-ending number of seriously old, worn-looking books and finally come to a stop. Standing on the bottom shelf and reaching up high, Julianna retrieves a thick hardback book with a deep red leather jacket.

Passing it to Alannah, she says, "There you go."

Holding it in her hands, Alannah reads the gold lettering, *A Curse to Behold*, engraved deeply into the leather.

"The answers you are seeking lie on those pages."

"How do you know about this book? Wait, have you already read this? If so, just tell me the information."

"This book was one I came across many years ago. I was a dark-minded teenager. I didn't have any friends and so I'd spend a lot of my time in this section of the library. I would find myself sinking into a whirlpool of depression down here. My head was filled with all the dark stories hidden underground. I couldn't pull myself away from the dark mysteries of the world. But this book… When I came across this book and I read about the Smashing of the Clay Pots and the repercussions of those actions taken by mankind, I had to stop reading. Never have I slammed a book closed so quickly in my life.

If the premonitions spoken of in this book are true, then may your Lord have mercy on our souls."

"What? What was it?"

"I told you, I didn't read it all. I don't even want to speak about it. It gave me nightmares for months. You must read it for yourself."

"Seriously?"

"Seriously," Julianna replies, her expression stern. "I don't know why you seek this verse. I would like to believe that it is just curiosity, but my gut is telling me it's something else. And Alannah, you should know that my gut instinct is pretty much on point with this sort of freaky stuff."

"Don't worry. All will be okay."

"Is that your final words on the matter then, sister of God?"

"Yes."

"Well, then I guess I'll have to trust you or start living my life as though every day is gonna be my last."

Placing her hand on Julianna's shoulder, Alannah says, "I will do everything in my power."

The pair smile at each other.

"Thank you for helping me, Julianna."

Glancing at the book held firmly in her hand, Alannah is nervous and yet intrigued as to what secrets these pages might hold.

Reaching inside her backpack, Julianna retrieves a piece of paper and a pen. Clicking the button on the top of her pen, she writes her number. "Here, take this. It's my cell. If you need me for anything, just call. With you being new and alone around here, I'm sure you're gonna need a friend with whatever mission you're about to embark on thanks to those sisters of yours back home. Huh."

"You're too kind, thank you so much." Alannah places the piece of paper safely into the zip pocket on the inside of her handbag. "Suppose I best go check this book out. Again, thank you."

"You're welcome."

Leaving the Absence of Light section, Alannah makes her way to the librarian to check out her book. And now she's even more nervous about what's to come, thanks to Julianna's discouraging words and Matthew's random request.

Chapter Thirteen

"Bravery or Stupidity?"

"Mate, have you phoned Hermon?" Phil asks as he lies on one of the single beds, browsing the room service menu. "I'm starving. You?"

"No, I'm alright," Matthew replies. He sits at the desk and turns on his laptop. "I emailed him when we landed, and last time I checked, I didn't have a reply."

"Aw, mate, he best not bail on us now. I'll be well pissed," Phil says.

"It's what, nine-thirty now. Maybe he likes to go to bed early. I'll email him again. If I don't get a reply, we'll get our heads down and I'll call him in the morning."

Phil's phone begins to ring. "Sorry, one sec, mate." He answers the call. "Hey, yeah we landed. Uh-huh, we just got to the hotel now. Yeah. I'll call you later." He then whispers, "Love you, too."

Blushing slightly, Phil puts the phone on the bedside table and resumes his task of finding what stack of food he's going to order.

"Selena?" Matthew asks.

"Yeah, mate." Phil's cheeks turn a slight shade of pink.

"Cute."

"Yeah. Yeah. Yeah. Don't start."

"I'm not," Matthew protests. "I'm just saying it's cute of her to check in on you, that's all."

"Mate, why the fuck is there no bacon on this menu? I'm itching for a bacon sarnie."

Matthew laughs. "You're such a dick at times. They don't eat pork here, you absolute wally."

"What? You mean they've gone through life without a sausage or a stack of crispy bacon? Wow, who made those rules up? That's well tight." Phil's stomach begins to rumble.

This sets Matthew off laughing again.

"I'd kick off if that was me."

"For fuck's sake, Phil. They don't know any different, so how can they kick off? I swear, sometimes I worry about you." Matthew's laughter eventually subsides and into the odd uncontrollable chuckle.

He's grateful he has Phil by his side. It's these moments that he cherishes. Tiny snapshot moments when they can laugh and forget about the enormous task at hand. Rare, but wonderful moments. Jumping on his bed, Matthew places his hands on his chest and gazes at the ceiling.

"We're gonna find 'em, aren't we?"

"For sure, mate. Don't you start with the doubt. You're the tough one."

"I know. I know. I'm not doubting, I suppose I'm just way more nervous now that I have a granddaughter to fight for and protect. Well, now that *we've* got a granddaughter to fight for. It's just a little mind-blowing. We've got to somehow find, fight and collect them all and make sure that none of them get harmed, and one of them, we know, is practically a newborn baby. If I'm totally honest, I'm starting to feel the weight on my shoulders a little."

"Believe me, you're preaching to the choir. I'm a wreck half the time. If it wasn't for Selena calming my nerves, I'm not sure how far I'd have come. And you, of course. I'd have ended up dead in a ditch without you. That I am certain of. Addiction well and truly got me good."

"I know," Matthew replies as sadness overcomes him.

Phil's words trigger a memory of the unwanted kind.

Swaying with a bottle of vodka in his hand, Matthew sees himself standing by the lift in what was once the busiest section of Honey Productions. The derelict space haunts him. He's drunk, dirty and shouting at nothing and no one. Just as he's about to get in the elevator, he drinks the remainder of the vodka and throws the bottle across the room.

Cringing inside, Matthew squeezes his eyes tightly together to get rid of the painful memory. But another one flashes through.

Positioned on top of a woman he met just a few hours earlier, Matthew is sweating in bed having rough sex with her. It's Marilyn.

A knot forms in Matthew's stomach. This memory disturbs him greatly. It is a struggle for him to come to terms with the fact that he used a woman for sex while he was drunk. It goes against his morals; the guilt Matthew feels because of this drunken mistake is intense.

Looking to Phil, he says, "Believe me, I walked in your shoes, my friend. I know, more than anyone, what a slippery slope addiction can be. It makes you do things you wouldn't even dream of while you're sober. There was no way I was going to let you destroy yourself like I did. And overcoming addiction is all about turning to the next addict and helping them through. Making right from the wrongs we may have done during active addiction."

"Well, I'm grateful that you came out the other side because if I didn't have you, I don't think I'd have made it."

"Do you ever think about the first day they're home?"

There's a brief silence.

"For sure, mate," Phil replies.

"You know what I think about? The moment when it all really sinks in. That true moment when I know it's over and we've got them back. They're all home where they belong."

"Mate, I think about nothing else."

"You know what, I actually don't think I'd go to sleep at all that night. I often visualise myself sat in a chair at the side of Eve's bed, watching her sleeping all night. I just want to take in every movement of her beautiful face for the first time again." Matthew smiles as he pictures the moment in his mind's eye. "Then, as she wakes up, I'm going to be the first person she sees. I'm right there, you know. And she's going to realise that I am going to be there for her always. I want nothing more than for her to know that I've been fighting for her all this time. I want her to see that I never gave up on her. And let me tell you this – she will never be taken from me again. Not a chance."

A great big grin spreads across Phil's face.

"Just knowing that I'm going to be able to look out for her and watch her grow and be a wonderful mother to her daughter just like Lauren was to her. I mean, come on, how precious is that?"

"I know, mate."

"It's the next generation. And I know we have no clue what Honey looks like, but I'm sure she's probably got a mixture of Eve, Lauren, Alice and Dorothy. Our granddaughter is a creation from a long genetic line of beautiful women."

"I hear you. I hear you. I've got a daughter and a granddaughter to meet." Phil puffs. "Aye, our kids are going to be the most protected kids on the planet."

"Oh, you don't have to tell me that," Matthew replies with his brows raised. "You know what I can't wait to do?"

"What?"

"I can't wait for us all to walk along the beachfront together as one great big, blended family. Arm in arm." Matthew gets teary-eyed.

"Aw, mate, we'll get there. All of us. We're going to be walking along the beachfront, watching the sunset in no time. The little ones will be running around causing havoc and we'll be standing by just watching them all."

Matthew clears his throat. "I know. Visions like that keep me going. I don't know what I'd do without my visions. They give me faith that we will be reunited one day."

"Well, let's pray that this Hermon guy has some vital information for us."

Matthew gets up and checks his emails again. Still no response. "You still hungry?"

"No, mate, lost my appetite. I'm all good."

"Well, we best get some rest because we're gonna be on a full alert demon hunt tomorrow."

"Oh, I can hardly contain my excitement," Phil says sarcastically.

Matthew smiles.

Feeling warmth upon his face, Matthew peeks his eyes open ever so slightly. The light from the sun is blaring through the thin material of the curtains. Glancing at the digital clock on the bedside table, he sees the time is flashing 08:40 AM. Reaching for his phone, he immediately clicks onto his emails. There it is – the reply he has been waiting for.

Sent: Hermon.Shimai@historicinvestigations.com
To: MatthewHoney@honeyproductions.com
Subject: Meeting Location.

Dear Matthew,

I am happy you and Phil made it to Israel. Welcome to the land of secrets. Your time here may change you – for better or for worse, we will soon find out. Be warned, Israel is not for the fainthearted. I am not sure if you are aware of the traditional dress code and respectful requirements of travelling around Israel, but if you and Phil can follow these guidelines then our journey together today will be easier. We will be passing by many locations where strong religious backgrounds remain and they have strict rules about dress codes. Therefore, you should avoid wearing shorts or tops with short sleeves or anything that might leave any skin areas exposed. At Jewish places of worship, men should keep their heads covered. As I say, we will be passing through these areas, so if you could be respectful and wear a hat that would be most appreciated.

> I am aware of your location at the Hilton Tel Aviv on the beach front and so I will collect you from your hotel at 10:00AM sharp. Be ready, as we have a lengthy journey ahead of us to get to the tainted Valley of Hinnom.
>
> Best
> Hermon

Looking to Phil, who is also just waking, Matthew says, "Looks like we're on."

"Huh?" Phil says, sleepy-eyed.

"Got an email from Hermon. We best get moving. He'll be here at ten to collect us."

"What? He'll be here in ten?" Phil says as he bolts upright from his pillow.

"No." Matthew chuckles. "He'll be here *at* ten."

"Oh, okay." Phil replies as he throws his head back on the pillow. "Aw, mate, I need food before we go anywhere."

"Well, you go get your arse in the shower, and I'll order room service. Oh, and be sure to cover up. Like, head to toe cover up."

"Head to toe? What like wear one of those veil things?"

Laughing, Matthew replies, "No, you wally! Wear a hat."

"Phew." Phil exhales. "I ain't brought a hat. I don't wear hats – why would I cover this beautiful head of hair up?"

"Mate, don't be a dick. It's a respect thing. I've only got a Yankees baseball cap myself, so I guess we'll have to see if they've got a hat for you in the hotel shop."

"You've gotta be kidding me."

Amused, Matthew replies, "Rules are rules, mate. Sorry."

"Well, this trip just went from shit to even shittier."

Just over an hour later, Matthew and Phil are standing in the lobby of the hotel, wearing all black. Although they have sports branding on their tops, Matthew hopes that this won't be an issue as at least they don't have any skin on show. He's thankful that he packed a black pair of jeans and didn't have to purchase the black trousers that were for sale in the hotel store. Particularly as he's stood laughing at Phil, who had only brought shorts with him.

"You look a right twat," Matthew says as he howls with laughter.

"Aw, right, I'm not 'avin' this. You can go on your own," Phil says, crossing his arms.

Phil is wearing a long-sleeved Adidas black top with white stripes down the arms and a white logo on the chest, accompanied by black dress trousers. Perched upon his head is a black, mafia-style hat.

"Mate, I'm pissed."

Unable to contain himself, Matthew's already whipped his phone from out of his pocket and is taking an endless number of pictures. "These are definitely going in the album."

Phil pulls a face.

"Oh, oh, I've got a good idea – I'm gonna send these to Terry and Alannah." Matthew laughs. Tapping the screen, Matthew says. "And… send."

A *whooshing* sound blares from Matthew's phone, and then it begins ringing. Attempting to compose himself, he answers the call. "Matthew Honey speaking."

"Matthew, it's Hermon, I'm out front. I can't see you."

"Oh, hi Hermon. Sorry, we'll come out now."

"Okay. Thank you."

Matthew puts the phone back in his pocket and turns to Phil, his expression now serious. "Well, let's get this show on the road."

The pair walk through the lobby and head out to the front of the hotel. Looking to his right, Matthew sees a fairly new burgundy Toyota Corolla. Behind the wheel is a slender, tanned looking male with a black hat upon his head and thin metal-framed glasses perched upon the bridge of his nose. Matthew waves and mouths, "Hermon?"

The man behind the wheel nods his head and beckons Matthew over to the car.

Opening the passenger door, Matthew says, "Hermon?"

"Yes. Matthew?" Hermon responds.

Taken aback by his British accent, Matthew replies, "Yes. Nice to meet you." As he seats himself on the passenger's seat, he puts out his hand.

"And you must be Phil?" Hermon says.

"Yeah, mate," Phil replies as he gets in. "Nice to meet you. And can I just clarify that I don't normally dress like this? Just trying to follow your rules."

Nodding his head, Hermon replies, "Yes. Sorry about that, I should have warned you before your arrival."

"It's not your fault." Matthew responds. "We should have done our own research before we came. Don't worry about it. He's going to be my day's entertainment, aren't ya Phil?" Matthew laughs.

"Shut up," Phil replies.

"So, if you don't mind me asking, are you British?"

"Yes, I am. Well, I am first generation Brit in my family line," Hermon explains as he pulls off and edges into the traffic.

"Was it your parents that moved to England then or…?"

With his eyes fixed firmly on the road, Hermon replies, "Sorry, the traffic's not normally this bad. Everyone is getting ready for Hanukkah tomorrow. What was it you just asked?"

"Did your parents move to England with you?"

"No. My genetic line goes right back to Jerusalem – both my father's and my mother's – and it would have stayed that way if it wasn't due to the world wars. That's when the line got broken, really, and our DNA started to spread around."

"Oh wow, that's a real shame."

"Yeah. My great-grandparents on my mother's side retreated and took solace in Poland. They remained there for some years, and they already had my grandpa Jan when they moved across to Poland. Then my grandpa Jan, met my grandma Magda, who also had the same story as my grandpa Jan – she was born in Jerusalem and her family had taken her to Poland as a young girl to retreat. They eventually got married and they had my mother."

"Wow, that's some story."

Hermon smiles.

"How did they end up in England, then, and what about your father? Please, tell me to shut up if it's none of my business. I just find it fascinating how you've ended up back here after all those years of your family running away from the only place they'd called home."

Hermon sighs. "Quite a sad story, really." He turns the car onto the highway. "Sorry about that, just didn't want to miss the turn."

"It's okay," Matthew replies, double checking his seatbelt is firmly locked.

"Yeah, so as I was saying, it's quite a sad story really. My grandpa Jan was a highly intelligent man. When Hitler was appointed Chancellor of Germany back in nineteen thirty-three, my grandpa Jan just had a really unsettling feeling about him."

The mention of Hitler makes Matthew's toes curl.

"He'd heard that this Hitler man was quite angry and was always shouting about becoming a true dictator, reclaiming lost land and waging war upon the world for those who didn't agree with him. I suppose something just never sat right with him."

"Yeah, mate. I think a lot of people would agree with you on that one," Phil chimes in.

"Well, back then, people really didn't know how dangerous he was going to become. In nineteen thirty-four, Hitler proclaimed himself as Führer, Leader of the German Reich, and my grandpa Jan had a vision and a firm belief. He knew this was not going to be good for the people of Europe, particularly for the Jewish community, and so he started looking for a safe place to transfer to."

"Clever man." Matthew nods.

"Yes, for sure. He was a great engineer, you see. Most nights he would tell my grandma Magda that this was not good news for the world and that this Hitler man was going to bring bad amongst the land, especially for the Jewish communities. Naturally, my grandma thought he was going insane."

"I don't think anyone was prepared for what was to come at the hands of that man," Matthew responds.

Hermon falls quiet for a brief moment as he indicates to weave through the upcoming traffic. He settles in the outside lane before continuing. "Sorry about that. Where was I?"

"You said your grandma thought your grandad was insane," Matthew confirms.

"Yes, that's right. So with that, in nineteen thirty-five, when Hitler signed an agreement and had excluded Jews from fighting in the army of Germany, my grandpa Jan made a decision. That night, he left with my grandma and my mother and headed for England on the back of a cargo ship."

"Smart move," Matthew says, raising his eyebrows.

"I know, right. He had begged his parents, my great-grandparents, to follow him, but they refused to go. My grandma almost refused, too, but she knew he was serious, and she didn't want to split the family and allow him to take her daughter, my mother, and she'd have been left behind. So instead of facing that choice, they left everything they had and boarded the ship. It was on the ship that my mother met my father. They were young children. My grandparents had become friends with one of the other families on the ship."

"That's sweet," Phil says with a smile on his face.

"Wow. What a history," Matthew says. "So, what's brought you here specifically?"

"I just got interested in my roots. I think we're always intrigued in some way about where we came from to better understand who we are. I spoke to my grandpa Jan a lot before he passed."

Hanging his head, Matthew is finally feeling the weight on his shoulders from the mention of death. "Oh, I'm sorry for your loss."

"It's okay. He was a great man and did great things while he was alive. He lived a long and successful life. Even got a letter from the Queen of England for passing one hundred years old. His pride and joy."

"I'm gonna get me one of them." Phil grins.

"That's awesome," Matthew says.

"Yeah. That's grandpa Jan, alright. He was a truly awesome man."

"Sorry, you were saying you spoke to your grandpa Jan…"

"Yep. I spoke to him and to my mother at great length, but my mother can't really remember much as she was only very young when they fled Poland. Other than seeing pictures, England is all she knows."

"What part of England were you raised in?"

"Greater Manchester. You know it?"

"Know it, are you kidding me? That's where my hometown is," Phil pipes up from the back of the car.

"No way, where about?"

"South Manchester. Well, Wythenshawe, to be specific. You?"

"I'm from Prestwich."

"No way. That's wicked. I know it well. There's a lot of Orthodox Jews that live there, right?"

"Yes, that is true. However, because of the war, my grandpa Jan westernised my mother so as to not stand out at all. They lived in fear a lot and so the dressing traditions were a thing of the past for us. We are still deeply religious, though."

"What a small world," Phil says.

"Huh, I know, that's crazy," Matthew says. "Sorry for changing the subject here, but how did you get onto the Smashing of the Clay Pots?"

Hermon takes the exit off the highway and parks the car in a layby. He looks at Matthew with an element of fear in his eyes. "I don't even know where to begin with this." Hermon's tone has become serious. Rubbing his face with his hands, he continues, "Much like my grandpa Jan, I've been given a sort of sensory gift, let's say. It's like a psychic visionary ability. I can't speak to the dead or anything like that, but I get intense premonitions of sorts. Like I can see what's to come. Now please, hear me out before you think I'm nuts."

"Believe me, after what we've seen and been through, you're in safe hands here. Neither I nor Phil are gonna call you nuts. Ain't that right, Phil?" Matthew says.

"Oh, for sure, Hermon. No judgement here. One Mancunian to another."

"Thank you, lads. That means a lot." Hermon shifts in his seat to face them both.

"Where to begin, where to begin… Okay, so I was at home one day, maybe three years or so ago now, and I got this sharp shooting pain in my head. It hit me with such force, I fell to the ground. Literally curled up into a ball, screaming out. My mother didn't know what to do so she rang for an ambulance. I thought I was having a stroke or something. Anyway, after numerous tests, they couldn't find the problem, so the professionals wrote it down as a severe migraine. I felt like a hypochondriac, although I knew the pain was real. Anyway, it happened again about a week later. I'd collapsed to the floor much like I did the week before, but this time a snapshot vision of a horrific demonic-looking female entity appeared. Scared the absolute shit out of me."

At the mention of the demonic woman, Matthew and Phil exchange a meaningful glance.

"I didn't know what to make of it," Hermon goes on. "And as time went by, the pain got more intense and lasted longer. The visions also got longer and were more disturbing each time. Popping up no matter where I was or what I was doing. It was a scary time for me. She's not a pretty sight."

"I've seen her, too," Matthew says. "So, I know first-hand how horrifying it must have been."

"Exactly. Evil in its truest form."

"Yeah," Phil contributes.

"The visions just kept coming, and so I started to make notes and journal what I was seeing. I knew this part of me, whatever it was, wasn't going away and so I had to start embracing it. I remember coming round after an episode one day and I started thinking to myself, maybe it's coming to me for a reason, like maybe the reason was that it was going to be the perfect fiction novel or something. No way did I ever think it would lead me where it has."

"Huh," Matthew says. "I would have loved nothing more than for this to have been a crazy fiction novel and not my real life."

"So true, my friend."

"Yeah. Me too," Phil says.

Taking a deep breath in, on his exhale, Hermon continues, "After about a year, I sat down and started piecing all the visions together. When I was a young boy my grandma told me about my grandpa Jan and how he was gifted. That he had visions and that these visions saved the family bloodline. And she carried on about how I wouldn't have been alive without his bravery and gift. So I gathered all my papers and I went and spoke to my grandpa Jan about it."

"Really?" Matthew questions. "And what did he say?"

"He was shocked, initially. He didn't realise that his gift was hereditary. And that's when he told me that he believed I was gifted like him and that the things I was seeing were going to come to fruition. But then he told me that from his own personal experience, I was to keep this to myself. Much like how people reacted to his vision of the war and the holocaust, he didn't want me being treated the same way. He was almost sectioned. At that point I decided I was going to keep it to myself until I had more answers. Hard facts that couldn't be ignored. So, I got online and started researching. It became an obsession."

"Yeah, I've been there, too," Matthew says.

"Oh really?" Hermon says.

"Oh yeah," Matthew replies.

"Wouldn't wish it on my worst enemy," Hermon says, shaking his head. "Anyway, I knew from my visions that she'd been created on unholy land, and I knew it was due to the sacrifice of children, so when I saw the story about the Kings of Judah who sacrificed their children on holy land to fake gods for their own righteousness and selfish desire, I knew that it had to be where this demon had been created. I mean, how could it not be?"

Matthew raises his eyebrows at this. "Is that all you're basing your findings on?"

"A curse had been bestowed upon the land from that point forward deeming it unliveable to mankind. How could I not be drawn to this land?"

"I'm just saying." Matthew puts his hands up. "I mean, was there nothing in the visions that confirmed it was here? You said in your article that you've visited the land and that—"

"Yes, I did say that. I said I have visited this land in my mind's eye, and I know that the answer on how to defeat the Dark Empress lies here and I believe that to be true. I know this is where she was created. I feel her presence even now. I know she was formed on the tainted Valley of Hinnom. And I also know that big things are coming and they're not things of greatness."

Optimistic, Matthew says, "So these visions, how far do they go?"

"You have to believe me. I have seen the end. I have seen what happens to mankind if she isn't stopped, and I pray not only that we're in time, but that I am right and that the answers we seek are, as I believe, on the land."

"Are you suggesting that we cannot defeat her?"

"I'm not suggesting anything, I'm merely saying I have seen how the end of the world happens. And I have also seen the only possible way that this won't be our reality."

"So, you do know how we can defeat this?"

"Like I said, I haven't been to the tainted Valley of Hinnom, but from my visions, I believe I know exactly where the answer awaits."

"Are you sure?"

"Yes." Hermon looks Matthew dead in the eye. "Matthew, I tell no lies. There is only one sure way to defeat this entity and I believe it's you who has to see this through to save us all."

In shock, Matthew says, "Me…? I have to…? Wait, are you sure you've seen that right?"

"Never been surer about anything in my life."

"Well, I guess we best get driving to the tainted Valley of Hinnom, then," Phil says, leaning over the seat and patting Matthew on the shoulder.

Matthew has always wanted to have his day and take out the bitch who stole his daughter from him. But now, just knowing that the fate of the world lies solely with him – well, that's kicking up all sorts of emotions and nerves. Not knowing whether to cry or jump out of the car and get the first flight home, Matthew decides it's best to say nothing for fear of saying the wrong thing. Figuring he's asked enough questions, and fearful of any further answers, Matthew falls silent for the remainder of the journey.

Chapter Fourteen

"What's the Truth and What's the Lie?"

Eve and Lewis are curled up in bed. The room is gloomy, and the black curtains have been drawn around the bed with a gap just large enough so that Eve can see Honey inside her crib and feel assured that she is okay. Eve is patiently waiting for her husband to stop mumbling and fall asleep. Her forehead becomes slightly sweaty as her nerves kick in. Tonight, she took a very risky move. One that could potentially get her killed or, worse than that, put her daughter in harm's way. Yet, even with the high stakes, Eve knew she couldn't miss this opportunity to gain clarity and get answers.

Lewis continues to ramble on about his successful possessions of the night and how he cannot wait for their ownership of the universe to begin, but Eve doesn't engage. Eventually, he tires of the one-way conversation and quiets down.

"Night, baby," Lewis whispers.

"Goodnight, handsome," she replies.

Eve peers up at the clock above the crib. The time is five-thirty in the morning, and her thoughts are racing. Her head is jam packed with unanswered questions and fear. Thomas's words haunt her: "*Your name is Evelyn Jade Honey, and you were born, not created.*"

Born and not created? After all this time, could she really be human? Surely not. There's no way that can be true. Eve gently extracts her hand from Lewis's. She gets up and steps softly to the foot of Honey's crib. With one last glance at Lewis, she reaches inside the crib and lifts the bottom part of the mattress. Placing her hand underneath, she collects a hidden item: a phone that she took from one of the children's bedrooms during a possession earlier that night. She had returned to the orphanage before Lewis and was able to hide it from him.

Eve cannot stop her hands shaking. Petrified that she's going to drop the phone, she swiftly moves to the rocking chair and sits just as the phone slips from her grip... and lands inside her lap. Feeling nauseous, Eve places her head inside both her hands. A pain like no other hits her like a bolt of lightning through her brain.

"Go on, check it," she hears.

And just like that, a tingle travels down her spine and the pain stops.

"Check it."

Opening her eyes, Eve sees there is no one in the room besides her, Lewis and Honey. Putting her head back, she looks up high and takes a deep breath before staring at the phone in her lap again.

"Okay," she whispers.

She clicks the button on the side and the screen lights up. Sliding the button to unlock the phone, she locates the internet app icon. Her thumb hovers over it. Her chest has gone tight.

"What am I doing?" she whispers.

Fear has taken over from curiosity, and she's now unsure whether she has the courage to look for answers. If what Thomas has said is true, then what can she do about it? Absolutely nothing! Eve knows that she would be torn down from the inside out. She couldn't possibly go against Jezebel – could she?

"But what if he's lying?" she breathes.

Just then she hears Thomas's voice again. "There's only one way to find out, kid."

"Where are you?" she says, raising her voice slightly.

This time there's no answer.

She hits the internet icon button and quickly types *Evelyn Jade Honey* before she can change her mind. But something warns her not to click the enter button. Eve closes her eyes and sobs quietly. When she opens them, she jumps as she sees Thomas kneeling on the ground besides her.

"You can do this, Eve," he whispers.

"I… you…" Putting her head back inside her hands, Eve can't bring herself to say the words she wants to speak.

"Just take a look. What's the worst thing that can happen?"

"You could be telling the truth, and my whole existence has been a lie. How about that?"

Lewis begins to stir.

The pair fall silent.

Eve's voice is now so quiet she's practically mouthing. "You shouldn't be here." Pointing up high, she continues, "She already knows something suspicious is happening."

"Are you not curious about who you truly are?" Thomas pauses. "Like why is your daughter called Honey? Did you not think that deep down somewhere you had an internal impulse of some kind to name your daughter that? Now that I have told you your birth name, can you not see how something deep within you clearly chose that name? I can, and it's because it forms part of your human identity. And that identity is still living within you."

Scared out of her mind, Eve decides it's best to say nothing.

"I know you sense that something's wrong. Why else would you have stolen that phone from a child's bed?"

"I'm going to put it back tomorrow. I'm just using it for now. And yes, so what, I might be a little curious about the things you're saying, but only to prove that you're lying and so I can hand over my daughter to the right side without wondering if I am human."

"You don't honestly believe that dribble that's just come out your mouth, do you?"

"You're going to get me and my family killed. So that's honestly the only thing I care about right now."

"Is this what you believe you were destined for? To live in fear. My darling sister, you were created to leave a legacy. You will save the world and mankind."

"Shut up," Eve snaps.

"Please, listen to me. Your daughter, your beautiful Honey, is an extra gift to the world. A beautiful, innocent and joyful gift that is ready to continue your legacy after you've gone. She will achieve great things and change lives."

"After I'm gone?"

"Eve, I have told you all I can for now. If you do as I ask and you see that I am telling the truth, I will trust you with the rest."

"But…" Eve says.

It's too late. Thomas has disappeared.

She shifts in the chair and the phone slips from her grasp. It hits the floor with a huge *bang*.

Lewis bolts up from the bed. "What was that?"

Eve quickly collects the phone and hides it behind her back. "Oh, nothing," she replies. "Erm, I was just checking on Honey. I dropped her toy on the floor."

Glancing at the crib, Lewis sees Honey is still sleeping. "She's fine," Lewis says. "Come back to bed."

Opening the covers, he pats the empty space.

"Sure, just let me put her toy back inside her crib." Eve says as she steps towards the crib. She lifts the mattress and slips the phone underneath.

Lewis kisses Eve on the head when she crawls back into bed. "Why are you sweating?"

"Oh, erm, nothing. I'm just a little hot, that's all. I was thinking about this evening and how intense it was. I got a bit of a kick out of it and started sweating."

"Oh, okay. Night, baby. I love you so much."

"I love you, too," Eve replies.

Eve peers over at the crib. She didn't have a chance to turn the phone off! If the phone rings, she's most certainly going to be in a whole load of trouble. She'll have to wait for Lewis to fall asleep again and then get out of their bed to collect the phone. As she watches the hands on the clock tick by, the rhythm puts her in a trance. Her eyes slowly begin to close. And just like that, she's fast asleep.

Darkness is upon her. She sees nothing but a blanket of black.

"No!" Eve shouts as she throws herself forward.

But Eve is not inside her own room. This room is bright.

Panicking, she calls out, "Honey."

But her daughter is nowhere to be seen. Neither the crib or a picture of Honey is in sight. Looking to her right, she sees Lewis isn't there either. Confused, she notices a bedside table. And on the table is a framed picture of a girl who looks identical to her, with an unknown woman smiling in the background on a bed. Retrieving the frame, Eve inspects it further.

"How is this possible?"

Slowly glancing around the room, Eve feels a strange connection with the space and all the items within it. To her left, she sees a tiny little bear on the pillow next to her. He looks worn and either over loved or uncared for. Turning her head to the wall behind her, Eve gasps. She's staring at a huge heart mosaic of pictures. Each image contains the girl and the woman from the picture in the frame. In some of the images, a man is present, and they all look super happy. A proper family.

Putting the picture frame on the bed, Eve gets up on her knees and touches each of the images, scanning them with great intensity. Her heart begins to race as she notices a specific picture in the centre of the heart. The girl is sat in a chair with a party hat on her head. She appears to be blowing out the candles on a cake. All appears to be normal. Behind the girl's head is a banner. And on the banner, it reads: "Happy Birthday Evelyn Jade".

Eve scrambles to get up, her legs tangling in the bedsheets. Her eyes on the images, she stumbles back, and her butt hits the desk. She turns quickly, her heart racing. On the desk is a thickly bound leatherback diary with an open lock on it. She flicks the front cover open and jumps back slightly, as if something might leap out at her. When nothing does, she pulls out the chair and sits down. Her eyes are drawn to the bold writing on the front page in black marker:

This Diary is Property of Evelyn Jade Honey
Do Not Read or I Will Know.
Stay Out Dad!

Turning the page over, she sees an entry written with blue ink. Some of the ink is smudged. It appears to have been damaged by drips of liquid.

Dear Diary,

Well, I guess it's just you and me from now on. My first year of high school has been awful. Just awful. Not only have I had to try and meet new friends, learn new skills, but my mum died too. Yeah diary, my mum DIED. She's DEAD and she isn't coming back! And now I'm coming to the end of my first year at high school and I've realised one thing: I can't tell anyone my feelings and I can't possibly try and make friends because I get teased. I have tried and tried and tried to get people to understand my pain, but instead they look at me like I'm weird. Someone has started a rumour about me. They say that I pushed my mum into the road, and they all call me the "Mum murderer". They say that I killed my own mum on purpose. I get told at least five times a day that I should just go and kill myself and diary, if I didn't think it would destroy my dad, I would do it in a heartbeat. Why should I live when my own mum doesn't have the privilege? The woman who brought me into this world and gave me nothing but love… because of my stupidity she died. I know you won't have the answers for me, but I thank you for listening.

What does all this mean? Suddenly Eve hears laughter coming from outside the room. Cautiously making her way to the door, she puts her head to the wood. A radio is playing, and a woman and man are singing along. They sound happy. Hearing the clanging of pots and pans, Eve concludes that they must be in the kitchen. She twists the doorknob. Opening the door a fraction, she pokes her head outside. There are multiple closed white wooden doors in a bright and airy hallway. As she steps out of the room, a floorboard creaks. Eve stands still to be sure she wasn't detected. When no one makes an appearance, she bravely continues to walk towards the staircase where she can hear all the commotion taking place.

Dropping to her knees on one of the steps, Eve peers down through the gaps in the banister. She can see the handsome man from the pictures in the kitchen. He smiles and grabs the hands of a girl who is of a similar height to her. The girl is laughing as the man sings and moves her arms.

"Dad, stop it!" the girl says with a giggle.

"What? Too cool to dance with your dad now you're in high school."

And just like that, he twists the girl around. Gulping, Eve sees the girl's face. It's her!

CHAPTER FIFTEEN

"We've Arrived."

"This is as far as I can take the car. We need to walk the rest of the journey to Mount Zion," Hermon says as he pulls up the handbrake. The car is parked at the side of an oversized sandy coloured mountain.

"How far is it?" Matthew asks.

"Not far. It will only take around an hour or so. Be prepared, it gets quite hot. I packed us all some iced water. This should keep us going."

"Are you okay?" Matthew says, turning to look at his friend. "You've been quiet the whole journey."

"Yeah, mate, I'm fine. Just nervous, I think. I mean, if he's right, then she was created here. Like, will she know that we're sniffing around? You know what I mean?"

"That's a very good question," Hermon replies. "But we do not know the answer. We must pray before we step foot on the land. We must pray for protection and camouflage so that we can enter undetected. We will promise, in exchange for safety, that we will be quick and will not disturb any artefacts that we find."

"What, and you think your God is going to protect us from that when he hasn't even protected almost one hundred children from this evil—"

"Phil!" Matthew says.

"What?"

"No, Matthew, it's okay," Hermon says. "I understand. I know that your faith has been hindered by the terrible events of your life. But right now, I really need you to just have faith in me. I'm trying to help." Turning to face Phil, he stares him directly in the eyes. "Can you do that for me, Phil? Just have faith in me. Please."

Rolling his eyes, Phil says, "Sure, mate."

"Thank you," Hermon says with a sincere smile upon his face.

Matthew doesn't know what to expect out of today. His palms are getting sweaty. His nerves are slowly getting the better of him. And he could do without Phil having one of his moments and kicking off.

"Okay, let's get out of the car. I know my legs can do with a stretch after three hours of driving."

As the door slams shut, Phil grabs Matthew by the shoulder.

"Mate, what if this doesn't go to plan? What if he's, like, using us as bait or something?"

"Don't be stupid."

"Come on, it's a bit weird. He's got some magical gift where he can see into the future. And that bullshit story about his grandfather predicting the holocaust. I mean, if that ain't a slap in the face to every person who lost someone in the biggest murder spree ever known to mankind, then I don't know what is. And now what – this guy just knows how to get rid of this entity? Nah, something just isn't sitting right with me, mate."

"Look, Phil, you don't have to come. You don't have to believe this guy at all. That's totally your right. But me, I'm choosing to go with him, because you know what? I've got nothing to lose. I have looked in the face of evil and if evil is going to come at me here, then bring it on, because I'm ready and waiting." Getting out of the car, Matthew pops his head back through the door. "It's up to you what you do from here, Phil. No one's forcing you." Matthew slams the door shut and makes his way across to Hermon.

Hermon holds a huge map in his hands. "So, what's the plan?" Matthew says. "Where do we go from here?"

Pushing his glasses back up the bridge of his nose, Hermon says, "If my calculations are correct, we need to head up this way."

Staring out at the never-ending sea of sandy-coloured rocks and hills, Matthew lets out a huge sigh. Placing his hands on his hips, he sets off, panting. His nerves have subsided. All he can think about now is how blooming hot it is! It's practically the desert, and he's been forced to cover his whole body. And not only this, but he's also wearing all black.

"Aw, mate, it's hot innit?" Phil says as he steps out of the car and slams the door shut behind him.

"Aye, bet you're glad you've got that ridiculous hat on your head now, ain't ya Phil?" Matthew sets off laughing.

"Ah, shut it. You won't be laughing when I use it to fan myself down." Making his way over to the pair, Phil glances at the map. "What's the plan now then, lads?"

"Okay, so we're going to head across to the right and continue down that path for around four miles or so—"

"Four miles!" Phil shouts. "Are you kidding me? I'll die out here in this outfit in four miles."

Matthew laughs.

"I have water for us. It won't take us too long if we start moving now."

"No time like the present," Matthew says as he taps Phil on the back.

"Fuck," Phil whispers under his breath, just loud enough for Matthew to hear.

Hermon conducts his prayer and they all set off on foot. Matthew puts his hand inside his pocket and feels the edges of the crucifix. He holds it in his hand and silently prays to God, requesting guidance, love and support. He feels a sudden tingling sensation up his spine that travels to his heart, creating a surge of warmth. He decides against announcing this, for fear of freaking out Phil and Hermon. Matthew stays quiet and continues walking.

The minutes feel like hours and the hours feel like days. Matthew's feet are beginning to hurt and his ankles feel swollen. Desperate to get to the destination, but urgently needing some rest, Matthew stops and puts his hands on his knees as he bends down to catch his breath.

"Hermon, pal, how long do we have left?" Matthew asks, huffing and puffing away.

"Yeah, come on, mate, I feel like we've been walking round in circles," Phil agrees, fanning himself with his hat.

Hermon points to the right and says, "It's just over that hill there."

Matthew walks quicker than he's walked all day, battling against the stones and rocks. They reach the top. He can see them out to the other side of the hill – the ancient rock-cut tombs that Hermon had been describing during their walk.

"Can you believe it… All this time and we've finally made it." Matthew's emotions are running high.

Tears begin to well in his eyes. This ancient rock-cut tomb might be just some derelict land that holds history and stories, but to Matthew, this place is so much more. These rocky caverns hold his future. His life. His everything. Falling to his knees, Matthew is unable to hold himself together.

"God knows I pray he's right, Phil."

"I know, mate," Phil says as he kneels with his friend and holds him. "I know."

Joining the pair, Hermon says, "Beautiful isn't it, lads?"

"Breathtaking," Matthew responds. He wipes his face, clears his throat and dusts himself off.

"So, the answer is in there?" Phil asks.

"I believe so. But there is only one sure-fire way to find out." Opening his backpack, Hermon retrieves three torches. "Here," he says, passing them a torch each. "I don't believe there will be much in the way of lighting inside so we'll need all the help we can get."

"So, what is it we're looking for?" Matthew asks, his voice still somewhat hoarse.

"From the visions, I've seen that the answers we seek are hidden behind a wall."

"Oh great!" Phil exclaims. "How the blooming heck do we find a hidden *wall* in that thing over there?"

"Don't worry, our ancestors did not make this task impossible for us. They left clear markings upon the chosen wall. They're drawings that resemble those of our Egyptian ancestors."

"Oh, like hieroglyphics?" says Phil.

"Yes. Exactly," Hermon replies.

"See – not just a pretty face," Phil says with a rather proud expression.

"You might have a pretty face, but your fashion sense is terrible." Matthew laughs.

"Oi, leave it out."

"Sorry, Hermon," Matthew says. "What were you saying? These hieroglyphics that we need to look out for – what are they exactly?"

"I will know them when I see them." Hermon says as he begins walking towards the tomb.

"Well, we best follow him," Matthew says.

Stumbling their way down the hill, they eventually reach the tombs. Matthew can't believe how big they are – from afar, they looked small, but they're easily the size of the Colosseum in Rome, and that's just the outside. Matthew's heart begins to race.

Looking to Phil, he says, "What do you think, does this location really hold the truth on how to defeat that evil bitch?"

"Well mate, there's only one way to find out." Putting out his hand, Phil says, "After you."

"Ever the gent." Matthew laughs.

As he enters, Matthew's nose is hit by the pungent stench of decaying corpses. There's no denying something or someone is rotting inside here. With his torch in one hand and the other hand firmly placed over his mouth, Matthew follows Hermon's lead. Flashing the light up above, he jumps as a group of bats swoop down in his direction. A collection of *screeches* from the bats and screams from Matthew and Hermon radiate round the tomb. There's a scuffling noise and Matthew looks down to see Phil on the ground.

"I'm so sorry," Matthew says, helping his friend up.

"I think it's best we keep our lights shining directly ahead of us," Hermon says quietly. We don't want to disturb anything."

Dusting himself off, Phil says, "How long we gonna be in here?"

"I think it's just this way," Hermon says, moving on.

The energy is eerie and yet familiar. As they travel deeper inside, Matthew hears children singing.

"Wait," he says, putting out his hands. "Can you hear that?"

"Hear what?" Phil and Hermon both say.

"You can't hear those children singing?"

"Mate, don't start joking around and shit. This is not the place of the time to be playing pranks."

"I'm being serious. They're singing Ring a' Ring o' roses. That's her fucking song. I'm not lying. That's it."

"We must be getting close," Hermon says. "Let's keep going."

As he takes his next step, Matthew gets an intense tingling sensation down his spine. And just like that, the singing turns into insane childlike laughter. Crying out, Matthew closes his eyes and puts his hands to his ears. Unfortunately for him, the noise isn't coming from an outside source. It's circulating inside his mind. No sooner has he closed his eyes, he sees the children playing with sticks and stones as they sing along to the haunting nursery rhyme. Opening his eyes, Matthew jumps as he sees Phil in front of his face. He can see his mouth moving but he can't hear any words coming out of his mouth. The only thing Matthew can hear is his own breathing, and it's getting heavier.

Matthew backs up against the wall. He feels claustrophobic and there's nowhere to turn. Opening his backpack, Hermon grabs a small vial of liquid. Pulling the cork, he throws the liquid on to Matthew.

Feeling a burning sensation, Matthew cries out. He falls to the ground, his breathing erratic. He can now hear again and the sound of Hermon chanting in what must be Hebrew reaches his ears.

Kneeling next to him, his face sweaty and his hands shaking, Hermon says, "I am so sorry. I should have warned you. Matthew, you are going to be affected here. You are the chosen one on behalf of mankind. The children do not want you to stop the entity from taking vengeance upon the world that neglected them, and so they're going to try and weaken you and tear you down from the inside out."

Clutching at his chest and putting out his hand to Phil, Matthew replies, "Yeah. Thanks for the warning. So I can expect more of that, then?"

Hermon reaches inside his backpack. "Here, take this," he says, passing Matthew some rosary beads.

Matthew places the beads around his neck.

"This way," Hermon says.

As they continue walking, every now and then, the walls shake. Matthew has lost all concept of time. They walk on for what feels like an hour, but is more likely five or ten minutes. Matthew bumps into Hermon as he comes to an abrupt halt.

"I don't believe it."

"What?" Matthew asks.

"There…" Hermon points to his right.

Shining his torch, Matthew sees a ginormous marking of an oversized bird with its wings spread on the wall. Underneath the bird are what appear to be figures of children in the hundreds, maybe even thousands. It's a sea of small childlike figures. Walking up to the wall, Matthew grazes his fingers against the markings. The texture is rough. Each childlike figure he touches gives him a slight tingling sensation and tears well inside his eyes. Trapped souls. Tiny, trapped souls, just waiting to be saved and released into the serenity of the abyss of afterlife.

Placing his head to the wall, Matthew whispers, "I will release you."

A silent tear slides down his face.

Matthew jumps as Hermon shouts, "Guys, this way, here's the rest of them."

Catching up with him, Matthew can see that Hermon's energy is high. He's overly enthusiastic about his findings. Matthew gets a sense that Hermon didn't truly believe what he saw in his visions, and yet now that it's in front of him, he's forgotten the sinister reason why they're actually inside the tombs. Shining his torch around once more, Matthew sees markings. Walking towards them, Matthew homes in on that of a crucifix piercing a heart, and one of a baby.

"Look, here's the rock I saw in my vision," Hermon announces as he sets down his backpack and retrieves his tools. "Lads, can you shine your torches over here for me, please.

"Sure," Matthew says.

"We're almost there. We've almost got the answers," Hermon says excitedly.

"What is it exactly on the other side?" Phil asks.

"From what I've seen, it's a scroll laced with gold."

"Oh shit," Phil says.

As he chisels away, the walls begin to shudder.

"You're going to have to hit it harder than that, mate," Phil says.

"I know, my glasses just keep slipping."

"Give it here," Matthew says, passing Hermon his torch in exchange for the tools.

With a swing of his arm and a bang on the hammer against the metal chisel, the rock instantly *cracks* and shatters to dust.

"Now what?" Matthew asks.

"Reach your hand in," Hermon says.

"Not a fucking chance."

"You have to, Matthew. Clearly these walls are weak to you. It has to be you."

Closing his eyes, Matthew holds his breath as he places his hand inside the gaping black hole.

"What can you feel?"

"Nothing, it's just another rock."

"Push it," Hermon says.

Pushing the rock with all his might, Matthew hears a *click*. And just like that, the hidden door opens. Cringing at the sound of scraping rock, Matthew retrieves his torch from Hermon and shines it into the darkened space. There, in pride of place, surrounded by markings galore, is the golden laced scroll.

"Oh my, I was right," Hermon says, bouncing up and down.

"What now?"

"Matthew, you must go and collect it."

"What, on my own?"

"Yes, I'm afraid that if we all go inside, we might cause a stir. It is safer for us all if you go in alone."

Looking to Phil, Matthew says nothing. But the fear he feels can most certainly be seen in his eyes.

"You've got this, mate," Phil says. "Just think, you're doing it for the kids. It's almost over."

Creeping his way into the space, Matthew shines his torch on the walls. There are markings everywhere. Children with dark eyes, fire, upside-down crosses, and everything of the impure kind has been carved into the space.

"What can you see, Matthew?" Hermon shouts.

"I'll tell you when I get out," Matthew hollers back. "What have you come for?" Matthew asks. Each marking is more disturbing than the last.

Breathing deeply, he focuses on the task in hand. Kissing the rosary beads around his neck, Matthew reaches out and quickly grabs the scroll and then runs towards the doorway. The walls begin to shake, and rocks fall from a great height.

"Run!" Hermon shouts.

Matthew makes it out of the hole by milliseconds, grazing his hand as the door almost closes on him. Catching up to Hermon and Phil, Matthew falls to the ground as the sound of children giggling penetrates his eardrum.

"Argh!" he cries out.

Phil runs back to Matthew and shouts something, but there is no sound again – Matthew can only see his mouth moving. It's as if time has slowed down and all reality has been lost. Now the walls are shaking, and the rocks are falling at a rather dangerous rate. Any minute now they're going to be trapped inside the tomb, with no way out. Grabbing Matthew by his arms, Phil and Hermon carry him. The noise of the children is unbearable.

"Why?" Matthew shouts. "I will release you. I will release you," he cries repeatedly.

They just manage to get out of the tombs before the whole building caves in. Smothered by a cloud of sandy coloured dust from the crumbling rocks, Matthew, Phil and Hermon cough profusely while they lie on the ground. Matthew retches from the dust that's lodged at the back of his throat, then throws up. His ears are ringing, and he feels as though he's going to pass out at any minute.

He peers to his left and sees Phil coughing. Strings of saliva drip from his mouth. Feeling lightheaded, Matthew reaches out his hand. "Phil. Help me," he says right before his eyes close.

And he's out!

Chapter Sixteen

"You Will Obey Me."

Eve is stuck inside the depths of her own mind. She has been flung into the all too familiar forbidden forest, and there's nothing but darkness surrounding her. Wearing a white cotton gown, she sits on the ground. Her hand is filled with leaves and soil. Something slimy wiggles between her fingers, and she flings the contents of her hand away. Shaking from head to toe, she wipes the residue onto her gown.

"Please…" she cries out. "Honey, where are you?"

"Ring a' Ring o' Roses… Remember me now?"

Pain surges through Eve's eyes as they transform. The white disappears, and they become gaping holes in her face.

"Hmm, so compliant." Jezebel appears in the distance, beneath the trees. She drags her feet towards Eve, who is still sitting on the floor crying out in agony.

The tingling sensation takes over her entire body and the transition is finally complete. She's now in her true form. A mirror reflection of her owner!

"Stand," Jezebel demands.

Without hesitation, Eve rises to her feet.

"My chosen one… How loyal you once were."

"Dark—"

"Do not speak until I command you to!"

Eve shakes from head to toe as fear travels around her body. Her head low, she doesn't dare make eye contact with Jezebel.

"That's better." Putting her finger under Eve's chin, she lifts her head. "Have I not given you everything?"

"Yes, Dark Empress."

"Then why do I get the distinct feeling you're attempting to betray me?"

"I… I… don't know, Dark Empress."

Breathing heavily, Eve sees Jezebel's bottomless eyes staring directly into hers. Behind those dark lenses, Eve sees something she's never seen before. It's children. Thousands of tiny children. Positioned in groups, they're dancing around and around in circles, holding each other's hands.

"Do you know why I have summonsed you here?"

"No, Dark Empress."

"Well, I'll tell you." Jezebel lets go of Eve's chin. "I have summonsed you here for you to pick where your loyalties lie. By the time we leave this beautiful sadistic creation of mine, you will either be alive and ready to take charge of our universe as we've always planned and been destined for, or your soul will be crushed, and you will cease to exist."

As the words register inside Eve's mind, she suffers an almighty gut-wrenching pain.

"Do you understand?"

Trying to be strong and not show her internal pain, Eve replies, "Yes, Dark Empress."

"Yes, Dark Empress what?"

"Yes, Dark Empress, I understand."

"It has been brought to my attention once more that you have been communicating with others outside of our realm."

Raising her arms, Jezebel stares intently at Eve. Feeling her feet lift from the ground, Eve panics.

"Please, no," she begs.

As Jezebel clench her fists, Eve's throat becomes tight. Something is suffocating her from the inside. As she's being choked to death, Eve sees Honey's beautiful face. She cannot die this way. She must do and say anything she can to get home and protect her daughter. Choking, gasping and feeling as if at any moment the last molecule of life is going to leave her body, Eve manages to summon just enough strength to beg for her life a final time. "Please…"

Bringing down her arms abruptly, Jezebel shouts, "*Moriere Tradet*!"

Eve drops to the ground, coughing and retching as she desperately tries to regulate her breathing. The veins on her head begin pulsating. Her head is swollen, bright red and heavy. Dirt is sticking to her face.

"Get up, Eve," Thomas's voice whispers in her head. "Do it for your daughter."

Aware that she cannot show any weakness, Eve manages to stumble up to her feet. There is no way she's going to die in the forbidden forest, never to be found again. She will get back to her daughter, and she will protect her. She now stands tall, with her head held high. Her chest still moves at a rapid rate, but this time she is staring Jezebel directly in the eye. Never again will she allow her to try and kill her. Eve clenches her fists.

"Anger. I like it," Jezebel says as she basks in the glory of her torture. "Made your choice, have you?" A deceitful smirk spreads across her face.

Eve throws her shoulders back, grits her teeth and replies, "I serve you and only you, Dark Empress."

Eve can feel the aggression bubbling up inside of her. She wants nothing more than to strike back. She knows she is powerless right now, and she would almost certainly be destroyed in an instant. There's not a doubt in her mind that Jezebel is much stronger than her. Timing is everything. And now that her daughter's safety has a big question mark looming above it, more than ever, Eve's ready to hear what Thomas has to say.

Chapter Seventeen

"Blood Must be Sacrificed."

"Baby, before you get started in here, are you gonna come eat something?" Brennan says as he enters the study. "I've made breakfast… It's your favourite – pancakes with a side of crispy bacon and syrup."

Her sight fixed onto the front cover of *A Curse to Behold*, Alannah doesn't turn her head or acknowledge her husband's entrance into the room. "No thanks. All good. I'm working," she quickly replies.

"Please, it's Christmas Eve. Can't you just break away for like thirty minutes?"

Alannah is eager to start reading the book of secrets and unknown tales, but she knows her husband, and he won't leave her alone until she agrees to eat something.

"Look, I know I'm not going to see you for pretty much the rest of the day, and I'm okay with that. I've got to wrap the rest of your presents that got delivered yesterday…"

The words "your presents" instantly spark Alannah's interest. "Oh, really now," she says as she puts the book on the desk and makes her way to Brennan. Flinging her arms around his neck, she continues, "And what might those be…?"

"Oh, now someone's interested in me, hey?"

Alannah kisses his neck and playfully nibbles his earlobe.

"Someone's perked up. Hmm, now you wanna come have some fun because you heard presents – why didn't I just say that sooner?"

Running her fingers through his hair and kissing his lips gently, Alannah replies, "Honestly, I'd love to, handsome." She kisses him again. "But I've really got to get started with this book. I'm sorry, I just have to do this."

"Right, well I'll leave you to it… but, and this is a big but, that's only if you come have breakfast with me... deal?"

Looking at Brennan, with his oh-so-handsome face, Alannah smiles. "Fine," she says as she surrenders to his cuteness. "I'll come eat with you. *But*, and this is also a big but, you have to keep your promise and leave me alone for the rest of the day. Deal?"

"Scout's honour."

Leaving the study, Alannah seats herself at the dining table. The tastebud tingling, mouth-watering scent of cooked smoky bacon journeys its way up her nostrils, igniting the rumbling in her tummy.

"See, told you, you needed breakfast," Brennan says with his know-it-all expression.

"Okay. Okay. Maybe I am a little hungry." Rolling her eyes, she puts her hands in the air in a sign of surrender. "You were right, as always. I was wrong."

Brennan places the platter of pancakes, bacon and a selection of colourful fruit in the middle of the table and plants a kiss on top of Alannah's forehead.

"Happy Christmas Eve, my baby," he says as he pushes his glasses back up the bridge of his nose. "Now eat up, because you're going to need it, judging by the size of that book you've got in there. Looks like it's got some heft to it, that one."

"Yeah, that it has," she replies. "Hmm, this smells great. Thank you so much handsome. And it looks amazing by the way."

As he retrieves the maple syrup from the cupboard, Brennan says, "You were quiet when you got back from the library last night. Is everything okay?" He sits himself across from Alannah at the table. "Anything I need to know about?"

"Oh, no. Nothing to worry about at all." Alannah can feel her face going slightly red from the lie that has just blurted out of her mouth. "It's just a bit of research Matthew wants to me do. No biggie."

"Oh really. What's the subject?"

"Just a verse from the Bible, that's all."

A confused expression crosses Brennan's features. "Wait, you need to research the Bible? Haven't you already like blasted your way through that when you got initiated into nun-ism?"

Caught off guard by Brennan's choice of words, Alannah almost chokes on the huge piece of pancake she's shoved in her mouth. "Nun-ism… What's that, then?"

"You know what I mean…" Brennan replies, joining in with the laughter. "You know, like being a nun and all that – nun-ism, like Judaism or something."

Alannah breaks out laughing.

"No, like didn't you guys have daily Bible study meetings on that sort of stuff?"

"I love you so much," Alannah says. Her heart warms at Brennan's innocence.

"I love you, too," Brennan says, hanging his head.

"To answer your question, yes, we did conduct Bible studies. We would dissect the Bible as much as we could with the children. And, well – because we were with the children most of the time, it was never studied in any depth. I have, during my own time, studied the Bible myself. However, this specific verse that Matthew has requested, I don't have much knowledge on."

"Okay, well what's it about?"

"I'm not sure really."

Alannah doesn't want to scare Brennan and potentially have him on her case every day, trying to talk her out of her mission to help get the children back, so she decides it's best to play the subject down and not tell him too much about what she's up to.

Brennan frowns. "You're going to a lot of effort for something you're not sure about."

"No… erm, well…" Alannah stutters. "It's not that I'm not sure about it – I know that it's a certain verse, I just don't know an awful lot about that specific verse."

"Ah, okay. Well, what verse is it?"

"Why do you want to know?" Alannah asks suspiciously.

"What…" he says, shrugging his shoulders. "Is it a crime to take an active interest in what my wife is spending all her time working so hard on?"

"Of course, it isn't."

"So, what's it about, then?"

"It's just this verse – the Smashing of the Clay Pots."

"What's so special about that one?"

"I'm not sure. It's just that Matthew said that the guy he is meeting mentioned this verse and he wanted to know if I knew anything about it. So, to cut a long story short, I told him I didn't, and he asked me if I would look into the verse and see what information I could find. I went to the library yesterday and a very helpful young lady called Julianna showed me where I could find the book. And that's it. Now I'm about to lock myself away and research it because last night when I got home and you woke, I wanted to give you my undivided attention because I love you so much and you just looked exhausted."

Alannah shovels an oversized mouthful of pancake and bacon into her mouth. Giving Brennan a cheeky smile, she secretly hopes that she's satisfied his curiosity and that there will be no more questions on the subject.

"Aww, I know, my baby. I really was exhausted. I've not stopped worrying about you for days now. But I just want you to know that I appreciate you putting me first last night. Having you snuggling with me watching movies and giving me your undivided attention was just what the doctor ordered."

Stretching out his hand on the table, Brennan gestures for Alannah to hold his hand. Taking the hint, Alannah smiles as she places her hand inside his and their fingers intertwine.

"So, Julianna…"

"Huh?"

"Julianna. It's nice."

Wondering what on earth he's talking about, a confused expression crosses Alannah's face.

"You've met a new friend. It's nice. So, what part of New York does she live in?"

Alannah swallows and says, "I wouldn't really say a new friend, she just helped me get the book. That's all."

"That's a shame. It might have been good for you to have made a new friend to go off and venture into the city with."

"I'm not really too fussed about all that stuff, you know that" Alannah says as she ploughs the last forkful into her mouth. She gets up and kisses Brennan on the cheek. "Thanks again, handsome."

Closing the study door behind her, Alannah settles down at her desk and picks up the book. On the very first page, she sees an emblem. Grabbing a pen and paper, she traces its outline. She has always been taught to stay away from anything representing evil and not to taunt unknown entities, and she senses that this emblem represents something far from holy. She decides that it is best to pray before she ventures any further into the book. Clasping her hands together, she closes her eyes and bows her head and says the Lord's Prayer.

Alannah's eyes well up with tears. A pain like no other surges through her heart. These precious words have triggered her. The last time she spoke the Lord's Prayer, she was with all her sisters and the children, and they were all very much alive, safe and well. She swallows the huge lump that has developed at the back of her throat.

Squeezing her fingers tighter together, Alannah continues with her prayer: "Father, please, I ask for forgiveness. I know it has been some time since we last spoke. Please know that leaving the convent was not something I thought about lightly. And Father, I do believe that you were looking over me, and I do believe that you saved me so that I can save all the children from the evil that is walking amongst us. The path that I am on is not going to be easy, but with you by my side guiding me along the way and the love of my sisters who are with you now, I know that I can achieve this. I will save the children. And when that day arrives, it is my solemn vow to look after them always. That is my promise. Please, Father, and my sisters, I ask for you guidance, I ask for your love, I ask for you to keep my soul safe whilst I embark on this journey into darkness. Keep the evil that seeks me from finding me. Thank you, Father. Thank you, sisters. With you by my side I can do this. I will get justice for us all. Amen."

Feeling slightly more empowered, Alannah gathers herself and stares down at the emblem once more. It's the outline of an eye. And in the centre of the pupil is a shape. It looks like an upside-down cross. Underneath are the words *Circum Vertere.* A quick search on the internet reveals that they mean "Turn Around".

A shudder runs down her spine. She jumps and looks over her shoulder, scared that she might have awoken or summoned something. Thankfully, there's no one or nothing there. Getting the creeps from the image, Alannah flicks to the next page.

Breathing deeply, Alannah whispers to herself, "Well, here goes nothing..."

She turns the pages and comes to the following passage:

Darkness will strike upon the reader of this book. Entering the realms of the unknown may seem like a brave and noble decision to make, but do not underestimate the powers of darkness and your words thereafter.

We are here to tell hidden secrets of an equitable ending that is to come to mankind.

Mankind created its own fate and mankind is its own biggest downfall.

Mankind only has mankind to blame.

Thank your ancestors for your karma, for they have awakened something unholy and unforgiving.

We request that you retain a clear certainty before turning these pages, for what is seen can never be unseen and what is read can never be forgotten.

Hell exists and you are an occupant.

Undeterred by the warning, Alannah turns to the next page. Here there is another entry, but the words aren't printed. They have been written with blue ink. Beautiful, cursive handwriting, on a golden, worn-looking page. As Alannah scans the contents, she realises the words aren't written in English. It appears to be in the same unknown language that was under the emblem. She types the passage into the internet translate search bar, then copies and pastes the results onto a blank document and prints it.

A Curse to Behold

Darkness has been cast by my cold hands upon those who have wronged the young, the innocent and the vulnerable.

Wronged them by inflicting pain, covering their screams and watching for their own greed.

Your cruelty and your shame have kindled my internal flames and you will not only feel my wrath, you will suffer the consequences of your brutality.

Children, come forth.

You are the righteous ones.

You will live forever within my sight.

You are the children of the night, and you will give our universe eternal fire and you will remain by my side, and I will reign supreme.

Children, you always were and always will be the innocent ones.

Fear me not. Fear me not.

I am your saviour and together we will seek vengeance on their souls.

Welcome to the dark side.

Welcome home.

As she reads the last word, Alannah's heart begins beating uncontrollably. Her temperature rises and she feels faint, her stomach churning. Unsure of what is happening to her body, Alannah's attention is soon focused on the intense amount of saliva that is generating inside her mouth. Freaking out, she feels as if she's about to vomit any second now.

She dashes to the window, opens it, launches her head out into the open air and retches. Thankfully, for those on the streets below her, nothing comes up. Practically hanging out of the window, Alannah takes deep breath after deep breath of the freezing cold air. Slowly, the contracting feeling in her stomach is beginning to wear off.

Tap tap tap.

Alannah jumps at the sound of tapping on the door.

"Baby, are you okay in there?" shouts Brennan through the closed door.

Gathering herself, she replies, "Yeah, I'm fine, just getting some fresh air, that's all."

"I heard a bang and it sounded like you were being sick. Are you sure you're okay?"

"No, honestly. All good. I'm fine. Just choked on some water. It went down the wrong hole."

"Okay. If you're alright, I'll leave you to it. Shout me if you need me."

"Will do."

"Love you."

"Love you, too."

Looking up at the grey overcast sky, Alannah whispers, "Please help me."

Her temperature has cooled thanks to the wintry air and she slams the window shut. She folds the sheet of paper and places it in the back of her notepad, then sits down. Just as her fingertips grace the roughness of the paper, she hears a whisper from a very faint female voice.

"Moycullen."

Startled, Alannah scans the room. There's nothing and no one else inside the room with her. The only sound she can hear is that of her heart beating and Brennan's terrible Christmas carol singing from the room next door.

"Hello…" she whispers nervously.

Silence.

"Please don't be afraid. If you can hear me, erm, if you can just move something, so I know you're here with me."

Again, there's nothing but silence and no movement inside the room.

With her anxiety easing, Alannah bravely says, "If you said Moycullen, can you move something for me?"

A pen rolls off the table and hits the floor.

"Oh, shit," Alannah says. She jumps so far, she falls off her chair.

She quickly picks herself up, her chest thumping, and her hands begin to shake.

"Shit. Shit. Shit." She doesn't know what to ask next. "Erm. Are you from Moycullen?"

Again, there's no movement and silence.

"Moycullen, Moycullen, what could this possibly mean…?" Alannah whispers to herself.

The computer screen lights up. The internet search engine page is open.

"Crap. Okay, it's okay," Alannah reassures herself. "If you want me to search Moycullen, then please, can you give me a sign."

A *bang* comes from the direction of the window.

Alannah leaps across the room as far away from the window as she possibly can, her heart pounding faster than ever. Bending over and placing her hands on her knees, she desperately tries to regulate her heart rate and breathing.

"Right, come on. You got this girl. Pull yourself together. Alannah, remember, this is only the beginning."

She slowly makes her way towards the window. As clear as the daylight, Alannah sees the purest white dove perched on the ledge of her window, gazing through the window at Alannah. As soon as she makes eye contact with the enchanting bird, it spreads its wings and flaps off.

In all the months that she's been in New York, Alannah's *never* seen any doves randomly flying around the streets or on any of the buildings. Certain that this is a message from her Father, and her sisters, she makes her way back to the computer and types in the word Moycullen and hits the search button.

Article after article about the recently built Moycullen Orphanage in Morrisville, Bucks County, fill up the screen. The headlines praise the selfless owner who dedicates his life to looking after neglected and vulnerable children. And this amazing pillar of the community is also the principal of Grange Park Kindergarten and Elementary. His name is – Principal Jesiah.

Alannah is stunned. This is it, the break she's been searching for. She clicks the top link and scrolls past the headline. Underneath is a picture. And in the picture is the person named Principal Jesiah. And right by his side is none other than Eve, who is cradling Honey, Lewis, who has hold of Hope, and Elisabeth. In the background are the rest of Phil's children and every single child from the nunnery. Alannah puts her hand to her mouth. She cannot believe her eyes.

Seeing the children's smiling faces and knowing that they are okay and appear safe overwhelms her with relief. She prints the article and rushes into the living room.

"Hey, hey, hey, you can't come in here. I've not even started wrapping yet!" Brennan says, hurriedly trying to cover a pile of items on the floor.

"Brennan, Brennan, look, I've found them!" Alannah exclaims, waving the piece of paper in his face.

"Wait, what?" Brennan stares at the image on the article. "Good Lord. Oh, my goodness, that's them." A look of shock spreads across his face.

Bouncing up and down, Alannah frantically flips the cushions on the couch as she searches for her phone. "I've got to call Matthew and tell him."

"Good Lord, he's going to be blown away, I'm sure."

"I can't believe it. I can't believe I've found them," Alannah says as she jumps on him.

"Baby, that's just amazing news. I'm so proud of you."

Alannah kisses him, then heads to the kitchen to look for her phone. "The article says they're in an orphanage or something," she calls back to Brennan.

"Not just any orphanage, baby – this is literally a two-hour drive from here."

"You are kidding me?" Alannah says as she walks back into the living room with her phone.

"No, I promise Morrisville isn't far at all. I have friends that live there."

"We have to contact them. Oh, my goodness. We have to go visit them or something..."

"We will, but baby, remember, this is a potential murderer and a kidnapper. We must let the authorities deal with this."

"Brennan, seriously, do you even understand what this means?"

"Yes, of course I do. It's dangerous and it means you could get hurt."

"No, look at the bigger picture, will you. Stop thinking about me. I'm a big girl, I will be fine."

"And what's the bigger picture?"

"I can get the children back and Matthew and Phil can be reunited with their children after all these years."

Bursting at the seams at the realisation that this possibility that seemed so far away is now within touching distance, Alannah abandons her search for her phone. She rushes to Brennan, and he catches her in his arms, swings her around. Sinking into her husband's grip, Alannah kisses him passionately.

"Happy Christmas, baby," Brennan says.

"Happy Christmas, handsome."

"Go on, call Matthew and tell him the amazing news. I'll worry about the dangerous technicalities later."

She wipes her face and begins ringing Matthew. It goes straight to voicemail.

Alannah blurts out, "Matthew, I've found them! Call me, please, you have to call me." She then starts sobbing before she hangs up the phone.

Gratitude is taking over her whole body. Closing her eyes, she whispers, "Thank you so much."

Chapter Eighteen

"Get Ready! Bring Forth the Plan."

After a visit from good old Jack Frost, Morrisville has been coated with a layer of twinkling magic. It's midday on Christmas Eve and there are one or two drivers who have braved the icy conditions and are driving their oversized cars on the unploughed roads. Embracing the quietness of the streets, the children are having a blast. Snowballs are flying from garden to garden and innocent laughter and playful shouts echoing through the streets.

The majority of the residents have taken shelter inside their homes away from the cold. Tomorrow Saint Nick will arrive, and joy will be spread around every home as they open their presents and celebrate the birth of baby Jesus. But that joy will be short-lived, thanks to the plans of the sadistic, powerful Dark Empress.

Standing in pride of place at the back of the Delaware River, the Moycullen Orphanage appears angelic and is glistening in the daylight. You would never guess that evil lives behind those walls. Beautiful twinkling icicles and thick, undisturbed blankets of white snow as far as the eye can see give the orphanage a pristine, Christmassy postcard image.

Inside the orphanage, the energy is far from magical – in fact, it's the complete opposite. The air is dense, and the energy circulating is suppressive and overbearing. In the dining area, the children are under the care of Elisabeth and Lewis. With their heads down, they're learning, reciting and copying entries that have been written and prepared by Jezebel. They are being taught something of the utmost importance: the children are being programmed to speak the universal language that Jezebel has created. Like little sponges, the children's brains are absorbing every bit of information, as Jezebel had predicted.

On the top floor inside her quarters, Jezebel is dragging her feet as she slowly paces up and down the space, rambling to herself. Changing her direction, she makes her way towards the window. She peers through the gap in the middle of her hair at the window and twitches her head. The window flies open, and a gust of icy wind fills the room.

"*Vieni da me mio fedele complice*!" Jezebel bellows.

The clouds turn grey and darkness looms over the streets. Content, Jezebel waits. A *squawk* echoes into the room. The black liquid seeps from Jezebel's smirking mouth. Her precious infamous raven is on her way. Jezebel requires the assistance of her evil accomplice to fulfil her desire and carry out her plan.

Stretching out her arms, Jezebel basks in the glory of her long-awaited destiny, which is soon to manifest into its rightful form. In a matter of hours, her time will arrive! She is ready to launch her attack upon each home across the globe and eliminate, one by one, every individual adult on the despicable planet she has grown to despise with every ounce of her existence. Jezebel's energy levels surge at a rapid rate. She has never felt so powerful. Electricity is pulsating throughout her whole body. Everything she has secretly worked towards will finally come into fruition. After decades, upon decades, mankind will get what they deserve, and the children of the world will unite under her command. An empire of her own design. Ruler of the universe! No one is going to stop her… she is raring to go.

"*Venit desiderabilia mea et pulcherrima.*"

In flies the raven. Her oversized wings are stretched. Swooping down and *squawking* uncontrollably, the raven appears to be revelling in the glory of her owner's commands.

Communicating with her infamous bird, Jezebel shouts, "Our time is now. We must strike."

The raven rests upon the top of Jezebel's bedframe, peers down and lets out a squawk.

"In forty-eight hours, I need you to have planted the final seeds to wake the sleepers."

The raven squawks again and flaps her wings.

"Yes, we have to bring forth the plan. Someone has entered the tombs, and if the scroll has been passed to the only hands who have the power to defeat us, then our plan could be shattered. Sacrifice – that he will not. I am sure. The ties of the bond are much too tight. If it has been placed into his hands, I am certain that our defeat will not be met due to the weakness mankind experiences when they believe they hold love in their pathetic hearts. It is at this point that I will take him down. When he is weak."

Swooping down, the raven flies around the room before eventually landing on Jezebel's shoulder. Tilting her head, the raven's deep blood red eyes connect with Jezebel's and calls out again.

This time Jezebel takes a moment before she answers. "She has been spoken with. You are mistaken. She is not a traitor. My chosen one will never betray me, she is much too wise for such an action. Besides, she has no way of knowing the truth, so there is no risk. She will never know how we could be defeated and even if she did, her loyalties lie with me and only me. She will die before she betrays me. I am her creator, and this is all she knows."

Reaching high, Jezebel strokes the raven's glossy feathers, which are silky to the touch. She then caresses her beak and says, "Do not worry your pretty self about that. It is our time to come together." Kissing her beak, Jezebel continues, "You, my precious, just focus on waking our sleepers, so they attack at the right time!"

As she makes her way across to the open window, Jezebel has not a shadow of a doubt that her plan will follow through, and she will soon rule. Staring out of the window at the sky, she smiles from ear to ear. The universe is already responding to her commands. Power is taking over, and soon she will be unstoppable. As her smile grows, the black substance dangles from her chin, eventually landing on the floor.

"*Nunc tempus est nos!*" she cries as she raises her arms.

Squawking uncontrollably, the raven flaps high into the dark and intimidating sky. As her evil accomplice goes out of sight, Jezebel hears the front door of the orphanage click shut. Peering down, she sees Eve leaving the house with Honey strapped to her front. Eve is battling her way through the snow to the back of the orphanage. Making her way across the room to the window of the other side, which oversees the river, Jezebel tilts her head with confusion. Eve has positioned herself by the river and is seated on a log. Unsure of the reason why Eve would be out in the cold with Honey during the day, Jezebel becomes somewhat suspicious and decides to act fast! Bringing her fingers to her temples, she closes her eyes and telepathically summons Elisabeth to her quarters. Within seconds, there is a knock at the door.

"Enter," Jezebel commands.

The door creaks open, and Elisabeth enters the room. Kneeling immediately, the ever so obedient Elisabeth says, "You called, Dark Empress."

"Yes. Come here."

Standing, Elisabeth nervously walks towards the window.

"You see that…?" Jezebel says as she points in the direction of Eve, who appears to be having a conversation with her daughter.

"Yes, Dark Empress."

"Well, I want you to discreetly see what she is up to – do you understand me?"

"Yes, Dark Empress. Right away."

"Discreetly," Jezebel repeats sternly.

"Of course," Elisabeth says as she bows her head and leaves the room.

Glaring out of the window, Jezebel is adamant that not a single thing can be left to chance. Innocent or not, nothing can go wrong within these next few hours, and so everything must be considered suspicious until proven otherwise. Every millisecond going her way is crucial to her plan coming together and her empire finally being born. Success is right around the corner, and she can taste its glorious sadistic victory.

Chapter Nineteen

"See, I Told You."

Eve sits looking out at the frozen Delaware River, trying to muster up the strength to make her next move, but all she can think about is how cold it is. Her breath forms clouds as it leaves her body, and she shivers and sniffles. On her knee, she cradles Honey, who looks like a baby polar bear in her white fluffy all-in-one. Eve is grateful for her daughter's presence and her warmth. Maybe her daughter will give her the courage she needs to get the answers she's been searching for. After all, these answers no longer impact just her – they're pertinent to her daughter's future and identity too.

"Who's my gorgeous baby?" Eve says, stroking her little rosy cheek. "Who's mummy's gorgeous little girl – hey…? Yes, you are. Yes, you are."

Honey shows a gummy smile and makes a cute gargling noise as she blows mini spit bubbles. Eve's heart warms. She must do this for her and her daughter. The truth must be known. It's now or never.

"Okay, baby girl, are you going to do mummy a huge favour…?"

Honey smiles.

"Aww, my dolly, you're too cute." Briefly looking over her shoulder, Eve continues, "You're going to give mummy some shelter while I check something, aren't you, darling?"

Eve has one last scan of her surroundings. Thankfully, the coast is clear. Slowly unzipping Honey's all-in-one, Eve carefully retrieves the stolen phone. Her hand shaking, she swipes the screen, hits the internet icon and types "Evelyn Jade Honey" in the search bar. And just like that, the worldwide web has done its job. Article after article about Evelyn Jade Honey, a missing girl from Kent. She clicks on one headline, "Evelyn Jade Honey Missing – Have You Seen My Daughter?" As the page loads, she feels sick to her stomach! It's there.

There is categorically no way of ignoring what's in front of her. It's a picture of her! She is the missing girl in the image. It's her face, no one else's. Gobsmacked, Eve scrolls down slightly and sees in bold print the name Matthew Honey. A man who is claiming to be her father. She scrolls a bit further, her heart racing. Right at the bottom of the page, there's a picture of the man. It's the man she's seen in her dreams! Never did she think anything would come of this. She truly believed she was being paranoid and overthinking things. Now she can't come to terms with what she's seeing.

But right now, she doesn't have time to ponder. Scrolling once more, she sees beneath the image a contact number for Matthew. He's requesting anyone with information about Eve's whereabouts to contact him. She almost drops Honey as a pain surges through her gut. Now the realisation hits her like a lightning bolt to the heart. Much like every child in the orphanage, she too has been tricked, possessed and snatched from a potentially loving family. Tears fall from her eyes.

Looking to Honey, who is smiling her gummy smile, Eve whispers, "How can this be true?"

Eve gasps at the despicable things she has done at Jezebel's command. She's encouraged suicide, snatched children and got a thrill from death, all due to the belief that she was created for the whole purpose of reigning across the universe and that Jezebel's way is the only way to exist. And yet it's all been a lie. She too has been programmed to believe that the dark side is the true side. And the worst of it is that she was considering handing her daughter's soul over.

As she tries to digest the contents of the webpage and deal with her inner thoughts, Eve suddenly hears, "I told you."

She jumps slightly. "Thomas?"

"Yeah, it's me. Listen, Eve, don't say anything more and don't turn around. There's a woman hiding behind a tree across the way."

Eve freezes. Now all she can think about is the repercussions if she's been caught by Jezebel. She'll be killed instantly. Playing along, Eve takes Thomas's advice and tries to act as natural as she can.

"Just slowly turn the phone off and discreetly hide it," Thomas continues. "Then speak to Honey and make your way back into the house. Whatever you do right now, do not give cause for anyone to raise any suspicions about you. You're being watched."

Believing every word Thomas speaks, and following orders, Eve turns the phone off and slides it up her sleeve.

"Oh, my little darling, let's do your jacket back up," she says to Honey in an overly loud voice so she can be heard by whoever is stalking her.

Secretly unzipping Honey's all-in-one suit, Eve slips the phone back inside and then zips it up. She then lifts Honey and playfully kisses her cheeks, and blows raspberries on her face.

"Who's mummy's little girl? Who's mummy's little girl?" she says jokingly. "Oh, my little baby, your cheeks are getting cold. Let's get you back inside, princess," Eve says loud enough to be heard once again.

Eve stands and turns and comes face to face with Elisabeth.

"Oh, gosh, Elisabeth, you scared me."

"Why?" she asks blankly.

"What do you mean why? How often do people appear behind you outside from nowhere?"

"Not often."

"Well, there you go, then."

"What are you doing out here in the cold with that baby?"

"Excuse me, 'that baby' is my daughter – and I've brought her down for some fresh air as it was getting clammy inside."

"Hmm, well you haven't been out here too long so she couldn't have needed it that badly."

"Well, I underestimated how cold it is. Since when was it a crime to change your mind?"

"Depends what decision you're referring to."

"Look, Elisabeth, I'm not playing games with you. Honey's cold and I want to get her back in, so please, just get out of my way."

Appearing amused, Elisabeth moves out of the way.

"Thank you," Eve says as she rolls her eyes.

"She's on to you, you know," Elisabeth says as Eve starts to walk away.

Stopping in her tracks, Eve turns back to face Elisabeth. She decides to dig the knife in. "How does it feel to want to be me?"

Elisabeth says nothing.

"You want that rightful place by her side, you want to be the chosen one, don't you?"

Again, Elisabeth stays silent.

"But deep down, you know you'll never, ever be that chosen one. You'll always come second best and that kills you, doesn't it, E-lis-a-beth?" Eve laughs. "You're pathetic. Honey will get by her side before you ever will."

"Shut up," Elisabeth snarls.

"Thought as much. Now do me a favour and just leave me and my daughter alone. She created me, she just possessed you. The Dark Empress's blood runs through mine and Honey's veins and you will never have that. You will always have vile, dirty, human blood in its entirety. Now retire back to your room and get ready to complete your job." Eve turns and continues to walk back towards the orphanage.

Her heart is beating so fast it feels as if it's going to burst out of her chest at any given minute. Her legs suddenly lose their strength, and she stumbles slightly in the snow. Anxiety is taking over all her emotions, and it's making her weak. Picking herself up, Eve doesn't even attempt to wipe the snow off her body. Now that Elisabeth is watching her, Eve knows that her hunt for the truth is fast becoming dangerous. Jezebel must already be questioning her loyalties, and Eve is scared that Elisabeth is going to cast further doubt upon her mind. It will only be a matter of time before she discovers what her so-called chosen one has really been up to. She has to get rid of the evidence, but she can't do anything with Elisabeth watching her every move.

Walking through the front door, she kicks off her boots and hurries up to her room. She places Honey inside her crib, dashes back to the door and locks it. Eve rests her head against the wood and slumps to the ground. She groans in utter shock and dismay.

"She's adorable," Thomas says, leaning on the edge of the crib.

"How can this be true?" Eve sobs.

"I'm so sorry to have to be the one to tell you."

"Tell me. Tell me," Eve says angrily. "Why didn't you come to me sooner?"

"I can't just make myself seen. It takes time. It takes something drastic. The powers that be knew this was going too far. And then when we heard you second guessing your existence as soon as Honey was born and you became aware that she was pure in her entirety, we knew we had leverage to try and come forth with the truth."

"We?"

"Yes, I am not alone. There is an abundance of spirits up there with me living through the command of God. But the *we* I'm particularly referring to is myself and our mother."

"We have a mother on the other side with you?"

"Yes, unfortunately, we do."

"Why didn't she come to my rescue?"

"Too painful for her. She is broken-hearted, Eve. She came to you once during an entrapment, but it was too difficult for her to process and see you again. She wouldn't have been able to complete the mission successfully. It's all too raw for her. Whereas I only know you from afar, and you do not know me at all, so it felt more appropriate that this came from me and not our mother."

"I suppose that makes sense. Nothing else does, though. How can I be human, Thomas?"

"You have been tricked, just like everyone else who lives within this house of evil and all the other homes you're about to take over across the world."

"How can I not remember anything, though? Lewis remembers his mother. He just chooses not to discuss it."

"Lewis's memory is enhanced by yours. Alice was your first trophy, so to speak, you were never going to forget her and so neither will he. You were the first to be taken. You have no recollection because she will never give that memory back to you. The Dark Empress is one of the most sadistic entities out there. And unluckily for you and our family, our fate was sealed the moment father bought mother the silver locket before we were born. Their first-born child was never going to belong to them. And she was always going to make sure they would only have one child."

As the words 'silver locket' radiate through Eve's mind, she gets a swelling pain in her head. Curling up into a ball, Eve moans out loud. Images are flashing in her mind like a movie.

A beautiful, glowing, woman is smiling and giggling as she's swinging her round in the air on a beach. It's a stunning, sunny day and the air is clear.

This woman is familiar. She's seen that smile before. Connecting the dots once more, Eve realises that she's also from the pictures inside the bedroom from her dream.

Positioned around the woman's neck, shimmering away in all its glory in the sunlight, is a necklace with the silver locket dangling from it. As Eve looks back up at the woman from the images, she sees her mouth, "Mummy loves you, Evelyn Jade."

The flashback fades, only to be replaced by another.

It's the man who is claiming to be her father, Matthew Honey. He's standing directly in front of her with a smile on his face. And although he might be smiling, Eve can see the sadness in his eyes as he's cupping the locket which is now hanging around her neck. As he drops the delicate-looking silver heart, he quickly grabs her and holds her tight. He sobs in her ear, and Eve hears him whisper, "This belongs to you now."

Snapping out of her flashbacks, Eve begins to shiver from head to toe. Holding out her shaking hands and staring at them, she's trying to work out what and who she is…

"Eve, I'm sorry you had to find out like this, but father will soon be on his way for you and Honey, and if you don't snap out of her control, he is going to die, and she's going to take over, and that is not a good thing for any of you. Just think of all the innocent children in the world. Think of Honey. Do you really want this evil entity to possess this beautiful baby girl you love so dearly and have her absorb her innocence?"

"Of course, I don't," Eve snaps. "Just give me a minute to process what you've just said."

"Eve…"

Tucking her head into her lap, she says, "Please just stop speaking."

"Eve, we don't have time. You must know now, and you must take action now! You must be told this information, or it could become too late. She has changed her plan and brought this forward. We don't have time. The fate of the world lies with you and your father, Eve."

"Do you even hear yourself when you speak? Can you not process how huge this is? Really? You just expect me to jump up, clap my hands together and say, 'Oh jolly good, let's get started then?'"

"No, not at all. I know how huge this is, but I have seen the world both ways, and I am certain the way where you find out and stop evil from taking over, is an outcome that you would prefer."

"So just tell me, then?"

"I'm trying to tell you." Thomas steps away from the crib and makes his way to Eve. Kneeling by her side he continues. "She is too powerful for our father to fight alone. She will kill him. We need you to help defeat her. We need you to work this from the inside for the mission to be successful."

"Not a chance, she'll kill me in a heartbeat."

"Eve, you can do this. We know you can. We have seen you already. You are brave. The combination of you and father can end this but first a sacrifice has to be made. Eve, please, you have to do this, it's the right thing to do."

"And what if I say no? Huh, what happens then?"

"Then the world as we know it ceases to exist and father will join me and mother on the other side. He will be killed, as will Lewis's father…

"Well, that's where you're wrong because Lewis's father's already dead."

"No, he isn't, sister dearest."

"Don't call me that," Eve says with a very stern expression. All this information is getting far too overwhelming, and she is losing her patience.

"Look, I'm sorry, I know this is a lot to take in, but we just really don't have much time left." Looking Eve in the eye, he says, "Please, you must trust me. Lewis's father, Phil, might be considered a disgrace, but he's very much alive. He faked his own death. He was watching Alice and the children the whole time. He was even watching you and Jesse when you guys arrived. He was watching the house day and night, he just didn't know how to come home. And as soon as he saw all the commotion at the house the night you persuaded Alice to hang herself, he came out of hiding."

"You're lying."

"What will I get from lying, really?"

Eve doesn't have an answer to that question.

"Phil, Lewis's father, has been hunting this entity with our father for almost two years now. He was only a few steps behind you all at the orphanage. And this time you've been found again! Our father and Phil will be arriving soon, and they won't be alone. Your friend, Sister Alannah, is alive and lives not far from you."

"Sister Alannah?"

"Oh yes, she's very much alive. Didn't notice that one, did you, with all your mass destruction of death and kidnapping. She will soon be here, too."

"How did she—"

"Look, Eve," Thomas interrupts. "That isn't what's important right now. What is important is that the Dark Empress knows they're coming. And she hasn't told you for a reason. She has moved her plans forward and time is of the essence. She is going to strike in less than forty-eight hours. It all lies on you and father to take her down."

"Wait… I… that's just way too…"

"Eve, don't try and make sense of it."

"I don't know if I can—"

Eve jumps as someone attempts to pull the door handle to open the door. Then there's a *knock* and Lewis's voice bellows through the door, "Eve, are you in there?"

"Just think about it. And quickly," Thomas whispers as he disappears.

"Eve, are you in there?"

"Erm, yeah, sorry," Eve says as she lifts her body from off the ground and composes herself to answer the door.

As Eve unlocks it, she has a fake smile plastered across her face.

"Why's the door locked?" Lewis asks as he walks into the room.

"Oh, nothing, I was just comforting Honey and didn't want to be disturbed."

Looking at Eve, Lewis has an expression of confusion. "Are you okay?"

Coughing to clear her throat, Eve swallows to hold back the tears. "Yeah, I'm all good. Why, what's wrong?"

"You just look like you're about to cry at any minute. Are you sure everything's okay?"

The words are on the tip of her tongue, but she can't spit them out. She wants to scream from the rooftop and tell Lewis that his father is alive! And not only that, but that she has a father too. She's desperate to tell her husband that she is human and that they have a real shot at being a happy family together in a normal world. Her eyes are welling up with tears. And, that's not even the best bit – their daughter's soul will be saved, and they won't be forced to hand her over to evil. Unable to speak the words, Eve's torn inside. She has no clue how Lewis will react to the sacrifice they have to make in order to be free. Going against their loyalty to the Dark Empress seems so far-fetched. But, if that's the sacrifice that has to be made in order to live a life of happiness with her little family, Eve knows what must be done. She must be defeated.

"Hello…"

Snapping out of her whirling thoughts, Eve zones back in and sees Lewis stood in front of her, waving his hands in her face.

"Earth to Eve."

"Sorry. Yes," she says in a fluster. "Yes. Erm, I just need to lie down." Eve makes her way to the bed.

A concerned looking Lewis joins her. "Come here. What's wrong?"

Feeling brave, she spits out, "What if all this is a lie?"

Sighing, Lewis responds in a less than accommodating tone, "What now?"

Quickly realising that the support of her husband is something she is not going to receive with this subject, Eve decides to shut her mouth. "Oh, nothing. Sorry, I'm just tired. Didn't sleep much last night."

"Well, why don't you nap now? I'll watch over Honey," Lewis says as he kisses her on her head and squeezes her tight.

Judging from his knee-jerk reaction, Eve has decided she cannot tell Lewis anything. She must do this alone. He would freak out if he knew what she was up to, and she's certain that Lewis would spill all if he was placed under pressure by Jezebel. To finally live the happy ending she so desperately craves, Eve realises that she must be strong for her family. She will just have to complete this mission alone.

Chapter Twenty

"They've Been Found."

"Matthew, Matthew, can you hear me? It's Phil."

Phil's distant voice echoes inside Matthew's mind. Feeling as if he's floating in outer space, he struggles to rouse himself. Alongside Phil's voice, he can hear the beeping of machinery and various other voices mumbling in the background.

"Phil," he moans.

"He's waking up! He's waking up!" Phil shouts.

"Hello, Matthew, can you hear me?" says another voice with a strong accent.

Matthew grunts.

"Okay, Matthew, I'm Dr Mizrahi. You've been involved in an accident and you're in the hospital."

Matthew desperately tries to open his eyes, but fails. He can't summon the strength to speak, so he slowly moves his head from side to side in disbelief at the words he's just heard. Surely, he's dreaming.

"Matthew, I need you to try and wake up for me."

Resisting against the heaviness of his eyelids, Matthew slowly opens his eyes. His sight is hazy, but he can see an extremely worried looking Phil standing right by his side. He manages to force a slight smile. At the bottom of the bed is a tall muscular man in a white jacket, whom he assumes is Dr Mizrahi. Matthew is covered in wires attached to various machines. He is overwhelmed by the number of bodies inside the room. There are nurses all over the place who appear to be working extremely hard.

A petite blonde nurse with a clipboard appears and says, "His observations are stabilising, doctor."

"Fantastic. Matthew, you had us scared for a moment then. We thought we were going to lose you."

"Can't get rid of you that easy, can we mate?" Phil jokes.

Matthew laughs gently, then coughs as pain bolts through his chest.

"Okay, just take it easy. You've got a slight fracture to your left ribcage, and you've inhaled a large amount of dust particles, which have lodged inside your lungs. Whilst you were under sedation, we have completed what we call a whole lung lavage. This is a procedure where we use a saline solution to wash out your lungs. We have attempted to remove as many of the particles as possible, and we've also given you some pain relief intravenously to ease the discomfort."

As he's taking in Dr Mizrahi's words, Matthew sees Hermon walking through the door with two polystyrene coffee cups in his hand.

"Hermon, he's awake!" Phil shouts enthusiastically.

"Oh my goodness, Matthew, you're awake," says Hermon.

"Okay, Matthew, we're going to leave you alone for a little while now that you're stable. I'll be back shortly to check in on you." Dr Mizrahi leaves the room, and the nurses follow, closing the door behind them.

"The scroll," Matthew says hoarsely.

"We've got it, mate, don't worry. It's safe. Here, show him, Hermon."

"Yes, of course," Hermon replies as he places the coffee cups down and retrieves his backpack. Taking the scroll out of his bag, Hermon flashes it to Matthew.

"Beautiful, isn't it?"

"Yeah." Matthew pauses. "It tells us how to defeat her?"

"Yes, I believe so. I haven't worked it out just yet but from the gist of what I've seen… Here, look," Hermon says as he points to the emblem engraved at the top. "This appears to be an important part of the puzzle."

"How?" Matthew asks.

"Underneath it says *Circum Vertere*, which means 'Turn Around'," Hermon explains. "At first, I didn't quite understand why this would be written there, but when I turned the scroll upside down, it's clear. Your perception of the emblem changes. If you look now, you'll see an eye shape, with a heart in the middle and a cross in the middle of that. I believe this is the key to defeating the Dark Empress. Gents, I think we need some sort of crucifix, and her heart has to be stabbed with it."

"What?" Phil shouts.

"I mean, I have to take another look at it, but at first glance, this is my understanding of such a symbol," Hermon says.

"Well, you better get reading." Looking to Matthew, Phil says, "Mate, I ain't stabbing anyone's heart. I'll throw up, for sure."

Matthew rolls his eyes and a slight chuckle escapes. "Pussy."

"Aye, leave it out. I've got a weak stomach."

"Phil, it's okay. I'm joking. You're in the clear, I think I'm meant to do it." He raises his head and glances around the room. "Where are my trousers?"

"Oh, they're here, mate." Phil retrieves them from the chair and places them on Matthew's lap.

Matthew struggles to get to his pocket without pulling the wires out of his hand.

"Do you need a hand?"

"No, I've got it, thanks." Matthew holds the crucifix in his hand. "Will this one do?" he says to Hermon.

Hermon jumps up from his seat. "Where did you get that from?"

"A very dear Reverend gave it to me in my time of need a couple of years ago. He told me to hold onto it and that I would need it one day." The memories come flooding back. He takes a deep breath and continues. "It's funny you should suggest that as the way to defeat her as I vividly recall him mumbling to me about stabbing a heart or something with it."

"I don't believe it," Hermon says. "Look, the patterns on the emblem match the engravings on the crucifix. This is it. Oh my goodness, I can't believe it. I can't believe you've had that in your pocket this whole time."

"Holy crap," Phil says, his eyes wide.

"You and me both, lads." Matthew coughs again. "Oh, consider it done. You put her in front of me and I'll quite happily stab the ugly bitch in the heart."

"Braver than me, mate."

"So, is that it, then? I just have to stab her heart? I don't have to chant any voodoo lifting curse?" Matthew says.

Hermon looks down at the scroll. "I'm not sure, to be honest. I'll have to read the rest to find that out."

"I can't believe it. This whole time you've been walking around with that in your pocket," Phil says.

"I know," Matthew replies.

Phil huffs. "That's just crazy."

As he lifts himself up, Matthew says, "Does anyone know where my phone is?"

Phil passes it to him, and Matthew switches it on. Almost instantly he hears multiple bleeps. He scrolls through the notifications and sees a voicemail from Alannah. Pressing play, he puts the phone to his ear.

"Matthew, I've found them! Call me, please, you have to call me."

In disbelief at what he has just heard, Matthew replays the message. He drops the phone, and the vital signs machine starts bleeping uncontrollably. His heart rate has rocketed. Grabbing onto his chest, Matthew cries out.

Flinging the door open, Phil shouts down the corridor, "We need a doctor! Quickly!"

Dr Mizrahi rushes into the room, "Okay, Matthew, just breathe for me, please. It's okay. It's going to be okay. Just lie down for me and take deep breaths."

Struggling to control himself, Matthew begins crying.

"What happened?" Dr Mizrahi shouts.

"Erm, I… I don't know. He had his phone and then he just went like this," Phil stutters.

"I think he's having an anxiety attack. Nurse, get me the paper bag now."

The nurse grabs a brown paper bag and passes it straight to Dr Mizrahi.

Snatching the bag from out of her hand, Dr Mizrahi places it around Matthew's mouth and says, "Deep breath, Matthew, deep breath for me, please. Let's try and regulate that breathing. In and out." Dr Mizrahi simulates the breathing technique. "In." He inhales deeply. "And out." He exhales deeply.

Matthew repeats this, then coughs hard. His chest feels raw, and he's overcome by a sense of light-headedness. After what feels like an eternity, Matthew's chest pain eases and the machine returns to a normal, stable bleeping sound. Moving the bag away from his mouth, Matthew breaks down. Tears stream down his face as the internal emotional turmoil he feels releases itself in a painstakingly loud bellowing.

"Matthew, mate, what's wrong?"

Trying to pull himself together, Matthew looks to his friend and says, "They've…" He breaks down again and is unable to speak.

"They've what?" Phil's appears frantic. "Mate, seriously, what's happening?"

Putting his head in his hands, Matthew takes a final deep breath and pulls himself together. "Crap. Okay. I'm okay. I'm okay," Matthew says, as he wipes his face. "Doc, you can go, I'm alright."

"Matthew, you've just had a panic attack. I can't leave you just yet, I need you to please just keep breathing deeply for me."

"Doc..." he says in between sobs. "I will, I promise. I just need a moment with my friends alone."

Appearing to take the hint, Dr Mizrahi replies, "As you wish, but I will just be outside if you need me."

"Sure, thanks."

As Dr Mizrahi leaves the room, silence takes over. Picking up his phone, Matthew passes it to Phil.

"Listen to that."

Appearing confused, Phil puts the phone to his ear. His eyes go even wider, and he gasps. "No, no, what? She can't have. How?" Throwing the phone on the bed, Phil drops to his knees as he too breaks down.

Sitting in the corner of the room, Hermon says, "What is it?"

Clearing his face, Matthew says, "They've been found." His emotions take over and he breaks down crying again. "I can't believe it."

"Good Lord," Hermon replies.

"How? Mate, you have to call her," Phil says through his tears.

Wiping his blotchy face for a final time, Matthew says, "What do you think I'm doing?"

Finding Alannah's number as quickly as he can with his shaking hands, Matthew hits the call button, places it on speakerphone and anxiously waits for her to answer.

"Matthew!" Alannah shouts down the phone. "Did you get my message? I've found them."

Crying, Matthew's struggling to speak.

"Matthew?" Alannah asks.

"Yeah, I'm here," he says, clearing his throat.

Hermon passes Matthew a glass of water and he takes a sip. He wipes his mouth and continues, "How? I mean… where?" He smacks himself in the head as he tries to get the right words out. "Alannah, where are they?"

"Matthew, you won't believe it, they're in an orphanage in Morrisville, which is two hours away from me."

"What?" Matthew is stunned. "How is that possible…?"

"I don't know. I was doing some research on The Smashing of the Clay Pots, and I received some guidance. I mean, I won't go into that right now, but anyway, I searched just the word Moycullen on the internet and there it was. The sick, sick individual has kept the name Moycullen. I assume it's as a trophy. They've only gone and built a whole brand-new orphanage, obviously to accommodate all the children from the nunnery, and have named it Moycullen Orphanage. There was a news article published on it because when it was built, the man who is running it was also assigned as the new principal of the local elementary school. They've labelled him the most selfless man in America. Matthew, the school has over five hundred children in it of all ages."

"Oh, no, no, no, that isn't good. Shit, shit, shit." Matthew starts punching the bed.

"How soon can you and Phil get here?"

"I'm in hospital. We had a bit of an accident."

"Oh no, are you okay?"

"Yeah. Nothing I can't handle. I'm going to discharge myself and get on the first plane to New York."

"Wait, it's Christmas Eve," Phil pipes up.

"We don't have a choice!" Matthew snaps. "They'll have a flight and we'll be on it. I don't care if we have to stop off four times. We will get there."

"Brennan, my husband, actually has friends who live in the same village, Lisa and William."

"Alannah, do they have children?" Matthew asks.

"Yes, they have twin boys around eight or something."

"And do they go to the elementary school?"

"Oh my goodness, Matthew, I'm certain they probably do!"

"Those children could very well be a target. Right…" Matthew rips the wires out of his hands and off his chest. The machines are bleeping like crazy. "I'm getting out of here. Alannah, contact your friends and ask them as many questions as you possibly can. We'll be on the first flight out there."

"Wait, Matthew, do you even know how to defeat her? I haven't managed to read the book."

"Yes, it's okay. We have an idea of how it's done and… Well, I'm going to run with it and let's see what happens."

"Please keep me posted on your travelling."

"I'll call you when we're at the airport."

"Okay. Stay safe."

"We will. Speak soon," Matthew says as he ends the call. "Right, pass me my—"

Dr Mizrahi bursts through the door. "Wait, Matthew, what are you doing?"

"I'm leaving."

"You can't, you're too weak."

"Well, I'm a grown man. I have to go and I'm discharging myself."

"Matthew, I cannot let you do that. It is my professional opinion that you should be resting and monitored for at least twenty-four hours. You still have a concussion, and your lungs are not operating at their full capacity."

"Doc, I don't have twenty-four hours." Climbing out of the bed, Matthew goes slightly lightheaded and stumbles.

"Please, get back into the bed and let us fix your wires."

"No! I'm leaving – end of." Getting steady on his feet, Matthew says, "Now give me whatever form I have to sign to waiver all rights and let me get out of here now." Looking to Phil, he says, "Pass me my top."

"You're making a big mistake," Dr Mizrahi says.

"Just stop that bleeping and turn those machines off before I smash them up and get me the forms."

Appearing to accept defeat, Dr Mizrahi switches off the machines and walks out of the room.

"Mate, I get that you're stressed, but you didn't need to speak to him like that. He was only trying to help."

Matthew feels bad, but he can't bow to commands… The clock is ticking, and he's got to get out of there now if he wants to stand any chance of getting his daughter back and not be left behind again. Sitting on the edge of the bed for support as he puts on his trousers, Matthew says, "I know what you're saying, but he wasn't going to let me out if I wasn't so forceful and we have to go. Alannah's husband has friends who live in the same village and his children attend the school where the sick bitch is posing as a principal. We must act fast. No more children can be taken. We will not be ten steps behind again. We are leaving now. I don't care about my health."

"Okay, I'm on your side, remember. Here, let me help you," Phil says as he puts Matthew's socks on for him.

"Thanks."

"You're welcome, mate. It's going to be okay, we're going to get them back." Phil smiles. "Mate, I'm going to meet my daughter for the first time and we're gonna meet our granddaughter. That's exciting."

Beaming from ear to ear, Matthew says, "That's awesome."

Sniffling as he's ties Matthew's shoelaces, Phil says, "I can't wait to hold them all again."

"I know, it's going to be magical." Matthew hops to his feet. "We've got a lot of work to do before that happens."

Composing himself, Phil says, "For sure, mate."

"Right, then, let's get out of here." Matthew looks to Hermon, who seems somewhat astonished in the corner of the room. "Can you drive us back to the hotel, so we can collect our things?"

"Erm, yeah, yeah, erm, for sure," Hermon stutters.

"Why don't we just go straight to the airport? Fuck our stuff, I've got nothing important there anyway, it's just clothes," Phil suggests.

Matthew is about to agree when he remembers he's left the locket in his backpack. Having carried it around with him for almost three years since it fell from round Eve's neck the moment she was taken, Matthew wants to shove it down Jezebel's throat as she's dying at his hands. He wants to rid the world of this tainted item.

"I've left something important there. It's irreplaceable and I can't leave it behind," he says.

"Mate, fuck it. I'm sure the hotel will post it back if we ask them nicely, or they might just hold it in one of those lost and found storage places they have."

Not wanting to tell Phil the true reason as he might try and talk him out of it, Matthew decides it's best to leave out specifics.

"We can pick it up later."

Thinking fast, Matthew says, "Our passports are there."

"Oh, yeah. Shit."

Feeling relieved, Matthew looks to Hermon. "So, are you coming with us?"

"Who, me?" Hermon responds, pointing at himself.

"Yeah, you… We're going to need all the hands we can get. And you're the only one who can read that scroll thing."

Remaining silent for a brief second, Hermon replies, "Okay, I'm in."

"Shit, Matthew, we're going to have to call Terry."

"Crap, right, I'll call him on the way to the hotel."

"Do you think he's going to be able to come?"

"Doubt it. It's Christmas tomorrow, and to be honest, I don't want him to leave his family."

"Yeah, true mate."

"Right, fuck it, that doc is taking too long, let's get out of here."

Poking his head out of the door, Matthew checks that the coast is clear. He waves his arm and the threesome run out of the hospital as quickly as they can.

CHAPTER TWENTY-ONE

"Strange Goings-on."

"Brennan! Brennan!" Alannah shouts at the top of her lungs.

"What's wrong?" replies Brennan, looking flustered as he rushes into the bedroom.

"Call your friends," Alannah says, throwing the phone at him. "Call them now, quickly."

"Wait, woah, woah, woah, breathe."

"There's no time, you have to call them now." Rife with fear, Alannah starts crying. "Please just call them."

"Hey, hey, hey, it's okay, it's all going to be okay," Brennan says as he makes his way across the room and holds Alannah in his arms. "Shh, baby, just start from the beginning for me."

"Your friends in Morrisville…" Alannah sobs.

"Yeah…"

"They have children?"

"Yeah, twin boys, Ashley and Kane. Why?"

"Oh crap, this is bad. This is *real* bad." Pushing herself out of Brennan's grip, Alannah sets off pacing the room. "You have to ring them and see how they are. You have to ring them now, Brennan. They have to get out of Morrisville."

"And you need to calm down, baby, you're going to give yourself a panic attack."

"Brennan, please!"

"Look, I'm not calling them until you calm down. I'm not having you hysterical in the background and I'm certainly not telling them they need to leave their own home the night before Christmas."

"Calm down! Calm down…" Alannah says. Her hands are on her hips as she circles the room.

"Yes, you're acting crazy right now."

"Brennan, their children are in danger. I'm not losing any more children on my watch. No way. Not a chance."

"Right, and I totally agree with you, but please just try and calm down because I am not having you scaring them and their boys with your ranting. You have to remember we are the only ones who are involved in this world of evil. Outsiders are going to think we're clinically insane." Walking to Alannah and stopping her in her tracks, Brennan holds her by her shoulders. "Now if you come and lie down with me on the bed, I will call them, but you have to be calm, cool, collected and not have any form of outburst, okay?"

"Okay."

As frightened as she is, she knows that Brennan is right. She cannot project her fear onto others, no matter how dire the situation is. It is imperative that this entity does not get tipped off that they know where she is. The element of surprise is what could potentially win this war for them. They need to get some information to feed back to help Matthew. Lying on the bed, Alannah closes her eyes and breathes deeply. Controlling her anxiety, she opens her eyes and looks at Brennan, who is lying next to her.

"I'm ready. I promise I'll be cool and won't say a word."

"Well, they might want to say hello to you, and that's alright, just don't start shouting about demons, please. I beg you."

"I promise I will keep my mouth shut."

Retrieving his phone from his trouser pocket, Brennan finds William's number and hits call. As the phone begins ringing, Brennan puts it on loudspeaker.

"Brennan, happy Christmas, man. So good to hear from you."

"Hey Billy, Happy Christmas to you, Lisa and the boys."

"Aw, yeah, thanks man. Oh shit, I heard you got married. Congratulations. That's awesome."

"Aw, yeah, thanks man. She's a real diamond. Sorry, we didn't invite you and Lisa, it was one of those run off and get married quick kind of scenarios. No one was invited to be honest with you."

"Don't worry about it. I'm just happy you're happy. Oh, I heard she's got a cool Irish accent." William chuckles.

"Yeah, she has, I've got used to it now."

"So... When am I going to get to meet this awesome Irish wife of yours?"

"She's next to me now. You wanna say hello?"

"Oh yeah, for sure."

As Brennan passes the phone to Alannah, he mouths, "Be cool.".

"Hey, Billy, so good to speak with you."

"Hey! How are ya? I hope that buddy of mine is treating you well."

"Of course. A real gentleman all the time."

"Gentleman." William laughs. "We must be talking about different people."

"Okay, okay," Brennan says, taking the phone back from Alannah. "I think that's enough from you."

"Come on, I was just getting to the good stuff."

"Yeah, yeah, yeah, we know what that means."

"It's good to hear from you."

"Yeah, you too. So Billy, how are Lisa and the boys doing?"

"They're all good. We're just getting ready for the craziness of Christmas day. Lisa's obviously super freaked out because she thinks she's forgotten a million things, but she always pulls it off. You know what she's like, a perfectionist."

"Yeah, that's our Lisa. So the boys, they looking forward to Father Christmas rocking up tonight?"

"You'd think, wouldn't you... They've been quiet for ages. And they're getting right attitudes on them. They'll be lucky if Father Christmas brings them a lump of coal and an orange at this rate."

Alannah grabs Brennan's arm as she puts her ear closer to the speaker.

"No way. Why's that? What's been happening?" Brennan asks.

"Lisa will kill me for even telling you because she can't bear people thinking our perfect little family isn't so perfect. But the boys have been seriously hitting out. They've turned into evil little shits, and I know that's not cool to say about your own children, but man, I'm praying this is just some sort of phase."

"I'm so sorry. That's terrible."

"Yeah, the other day Kane bit me and Ashley went for his mom. They're getting like violent and shit. I don't wanna raise my hand to them, but it's getting hard to hold back, ya know?"

"I can imagine."

"Well, I suggested to Lisa that we should be thinking about getting them some sort of help like a therapist, to see what's going on, but she's too proud to even think about it. Just keeps saying they'll be alright. It's changed her, man, she's a nervous wreck all the time. Doesn't like asking them to do anything for fear of them hitting out."

Alannah looks at Brennan. She knows this is not a good sign. "Have you noticed anything happening at night with them?" she asks.

"Hmm, I mean a few weeks ago they were complaining of nightmares and headaches in the morning, but that's stopped. I must admit, me and Lisa were having nightmares as well, now they come and go."

Nudging Brennan, Alannah whispers, "Ask him if we can visit them."

"Sorry to hear that, man." Brennan says. "That's terrible. Look, erm, I know it's short notice, but we've got a gift for the boys here and a little something for you and Lisa, do you think we could call round with it tomorrow?"

Hitting Brennan on the arm, Alannah says, "Tomorrow?"

"Sorry, just a second, Billy."

"Yeah, sure. Take your time."

Placing the call on mute, Brennan looks to Alannah and says, "What happened to keeping it cool?"

"I'm sorry, but we need to go there now."

"We can't go now, they're going to be busy wrapping presents for the boys. It would be too weird if I just rocked up now."

Reluctantly surrendering, Alannah says, "Fine."

Unmuting the call, Brennan continues, "What you think, buddy, fancy playing beer pong with me?"

William chuckles, "Good lord, beer pong, I haven't played that since college. I'm not sure about the beer pong, but of course you can come round. Your family, Lisa and the boys will be stoked to see you. It's been too long."

"I know. It's certainly been a long time. You guys still living in Morrisville?"

"Yeah. We're still living in the dream home we built all those years ago."

"That's awesome. So, we'll come before you've eaten dinner, is that okay?"

"Sure thing, just get here whenever you can."

"See you tomorrow." Brennan says.

"See you tomorrow."

The call ends. Looking at Brennan, Alannah says, "I pray we're not too late."

Chapter Twenty-Two

"Less Than Forty-Eight Hours and Counting..."

The children are all gathered in the main hall of the orphanage, their heads held low. Eve, Lewis and Elisabeth stand in front of the Victorian styled fireplace. Everyone in the room has transformed into their true sadistic form. They patiently and silently wait for the arrival of the Dark Empress. The green flames from the candlelight and the fire cast a wicked glow upon the room.

The summons from Jezebel were unexpected, and every muscle in Eve's body is frozen stiff. The energy circulating is equally tense. Bracing herself for the arrival of Jezebel, Eve discreetly grabs hold of Lewis's finger. As she breathes in deep, she hears *thud, thud, thud.* It's Jezebel, dragging her feet down the steps, getting closer and closer. Eve's nerves are shot, her thoughts running wild. She's fearful that this gathering has been ordered because of her ongoing betrayal to her superior, which she believed was secret. She's desperately trying to keep her cool, but she is well aware of Jezebel's capabilities. She can easily read terror in someone's eyes, and this is what will potentially give her away.

Closing her eyes, she focuses on the one thing she is thankful for. Her daughter being safe. Tucked away inside her crib, Honey is under the watchful eye and care of Thomas. Eve has set an emergency backup plan. Should this turn out to be an ambush directed towards her, Eve has given Thomas strict instructions to remove Honey by any means possible from the orphanage. The protection of her daughter is imperative. She doesn't fear death for herself, but Eve couldn't imagine Honey's soul being wide open and captured by evil. The moment she has been dreading is almost upon her. There is another thud and Eve flinches.

"What's wrong with you?" Lewis whispers.

"Nothing."

"Then why do you keep jumping?"

"It's nothing."

Elisabeth turns to the pair and shushes them. Almost coated in her spit, Eve snarls back at her, ready to shut the snivelling little toad up once and for all. Venom is circulating around Eve's body, and all of it is directed towards Elisabeth. Believing that Elisabeth may have ratted her out to Jezebel and put her family in jeopardy, Eve has made a clear-cut decision. She's going to personally slit Elisabeth's throat should this be the truth, even if it results in her own immediate demise.

Her thoughts all over the place and her emotions high, Eve is battling with the overwhelming information that has recently been thrust upon her. If this isn't an ambush, then she has no clue how she is going to continue to live a lie. Now that she knows that she too has been ripped away from a loving family, the internal pain from this newfound knowledge is eating her up inside.

Right now, however, Eve knows she has no choice. She must stay strong and continue to play the game, or face a sudden and horrific death. There is one final thud on the staircase, then Jezebel appears, scraping her nails against the wood and dragging her feet towards the front of the room. The children separate and create a pathway leading directly to Eve. Seeing her just a few steps away, Eve's more nervous than she has ever been. She puts on a brave face, refusing to let this surface. As Jezebel glares at her through the gap in her perfectly parted hair, she smirks sadistically. Eve smirks back.

She's now standing only a few inches from her face, and Eve can smell the rotting stench of death on her breath. She attempts to suppress the lump forming at the back of her throat so she doesn't vomit. This is it, her time has come. Clenching her fists, Eve braces herself to lunge in the direction of Elisabeth.

"Are you ready?" Jezebel says to Eve.

Confused, Eve asks, "Ready, Dark Empress?"

Jezebel reaches out and places her cold finger under her chin and brings their eyesight to a deadlock. As they stare intently into one another's deceitful eyes, for the second time, Eve sees what appears to be the spirits of children. Aware that Jezebel is weighing her up, Eve's stubbornness kicks in. She doesn't blink.

"To rule," Jezebel eventually says.

Eve's legs shudder as the relief hits her. Quick to rectify her body's reaction, Eve throws her shoulders back and raises her head high. As the anxiety leaves her body, her stomach turns and she feels nauseous. Clearly, Jezebel has no clue of her disloyalty and rebellious intentions. For once, Elisabeth must have kept her mouth shut.

"Yes, Dark Empress. I serve you."

"Huh." Jezebel huffs as she steps in front of Lewis.

"Are you ready to rule?" she asks Lewis.

Without hesitation, Lewis replies, "Yes, Dark Empress. I serve you."

Stepping in front of Elisabeth, Jezebel repeats the question.

Bowing, Elisabeth replies, "Yes, Dark Empress. I serve only you."

Eve rolls her eyes at Elisabeth's apparent dig by adding the word "only" into her reply. She is going to take great pleasure in wiping that smug grin off her face.

Turning to face the children, Jezebel raises her arms and calls out, "Children, are you ready to rule?"

In unison the children reply, "Yes, Dark Empress. I serve you."

Throwing her head back, Jezebel then lowers her arms and scans the room.

"So loyal," she says. Making her way into the centre of the children, she continues, "Our time has arrived. Our time to rule has been brought forward. In less than forty-eight hours, we will strike."

The children bounce with excitement.

Smiling, Jezebel continues, "This moment right here is everything we have been working towards. And so, I will ask you all again, my loyal ones, are you ready to rule?" Jezebel shouts.

In perfect synchronisation, everyone inside the room replies, "Yes, Dark Empress. I serve you."

Clearly basking in the glory of the obedience of those around her, Jezebel reaches her hands to the ceiling and screams out. The cruel vibrations hit Eve's eardrums, and she feels the floor begin to shake underneath her. The surrounding walls shudder, and the flames on the candles and fire ignite like a blow torch.

A sharp pain travels down Eve's spine. She loses her footing and fights against the pain to prevent herself from dropping to the ground. Suddenly, the shaking stops and the flames return to normal. Breathing deeply, Eve places her hand on her stomach.

"Their time is almost up!" Jezebel laughs.

Feeling sick, Eve wonders how she is going to complete the mission Thomas has been sent to deliver to her.

She looks up just as Jezebel makes her way over to Rita. Placing her hand under the chin of the small child in front of her, Jezebel says, "Rita, my how you have come such a long way."

Bowing her head, Rita stays silent.

Facing the crowd, Jezebel continues, "Tonight we will implement our final possession on our chosen souls. Be on guard and be sure to capture the final element of their existence. Leave not a molecule behind." Dragging her feet back towards the front of the room, she continues, "Implant fear into those despicable parents. Have them urinate inside their own beds. Make me proud." As soon as the words leave her mouth, Jezebel smiles and the thick black substance rolls down her chin.

The children bounce up and down and cackle.

"Dark Empress," Elisabeth mumbles under her breath.

With a sharp twitch of her head, Jezebel looks at Elisabeth with daggers in her eyes. *Thud, thud, thud.* She drags her heavy legs towards Elisabeth. Jezebel stares at her with a less than impressed expression on her face. "Interrupting me… Someone is feeling brave."

Eve's heart and thoughts set off racing. This is it – this is the moment she has been dreading. Elisabeth is clearly about to rat her out in front of everyone.

"Well, spit it out," Jezebel commands.

"Sorry to interrupt, Dark Empress, I just merely thought that this might be an opportunity to discuss what is expected of us during our take over."

"Hmm, so eager, Elisabeth. I embrace your loyalty and your enthusiasm. However, it would be wise of you not to interrupt me."

Putting her head down, Elisabeth replies, "I am sorry, Dark Empress. Please forgive my defiance."

"Forgiven," Jezebel responds sternly as she turns back to face the children.

Eve is pleased that Elisabeth has been put in her place. She must not have any information that could expose her betrayal, otherwise, she would have thrown Eve under the bus by now.

"In less than forty-eight hours," Jezebel resumes, "you will enter your chosen homes and you will waste no time. First things first: form an alliance with the toxic mist which I have created. Work side by side. You will then take full reign over the adults inside the home. As they lie incapacitated by your commands, you will then wake your sleepers, and with their assistance, you will strike against the adults! Crush them, torture them, dispose of their life by any means possible. You just remember that whatever you do, you put their light out. Do I make myself clear?"

Eve joins in with the response: "Yes, Dark Empress."

"It is imperative that this goes to plan. Remember, you must implement your possession as deeply as you can. Violate them internally. Creep into every molecule of their existence. Take over and do not surrender, even if their soul pleads with you."

"Yes, Dark Empress," they all shout.

Smiling, Jezebel makes her way towards the window. She waves her arms high and the curtains open, revealing a star-filled deep blue sky.

"*Nunc tempus est nos. Ego sum princeps universum. Imperio. Liberos meos. Mea est.*" Turning, Jezebel commands, "Say it with me."

Eve joins Lewis, Elisabeth and the children in shouting, "*Nunc tempus est nos. Ego sum princeps universum. Imperio. Liberos meos. Meaest.*"

Jezebel laughs her sadistic laugh.

Chapter Twenty-Three

"We're Finally on Our Way."

Matthew fidgets in his seat as they wait for their flight to New York to depart. As far as he's concerned, the flight can't be over fast enough.

"Mate," Phil says, nudging him.

"What?" he says back.

"Do you think Hermon's gonna be alright back there? I mean, he's practically at the back of the bus."

"He's a big boy, I'm sure he'll be alright."

"I just feel bad, you know."

"What else were we supposed to do? These were the only seats left, and we were lucky to all get on the same flight at such short notice."

"True. It's just a long time to be sat in such a small seat at the back."

Unclipping his seatbelt, Matthew stands in the aisle. Peering down at Phil, he says, "I'm sure if he had a problem with it, he wouldn't have come with us. It's not like we forced him."

"Well, we did kinda back him into a corner 'cause we said we needed him to read the scroll thing. He might have felt pressured into coming." Shrugging his shoulders, Phil continues, "I mean, it's not like he has any missing children. He's doing this out of the goodness of his heart, and we're sat up front practically in first class, and he's right at the back. Just think it's a bit unfair."

"Go swap seats with him, then," Matthew suggests.

"I would, but I don't think they let you do that 'cause it's got your name on?"

"Look, if it makes you feel better, we'll go check on him when we take off and keep him company for a while. What you think?"

"Okay, deal."

"Right, now that's sorted, I need to take myself to the toilet before we take off, or I'm going to piss my pants mid-air."

Feeling like his bladder is about to burst, Matthew heads down the small aisle to the toilet. As he washes his hands, he catches sight of himself in the mirror. His face looks just as haggard as he feels. Dark rims surround his eyes, and there are deep cuts and purple bruises all over.

"We're going to get her back," he says to his reflection.

Just as a smile forms, Matthew feels his phone vibrating. It's a blocked number.

"Hello, Matthew Honey speaking."

Silence greets him.

He removes the phone from his ear to check that he has reception. Noticing he has full bars, he returns it to his ear and again says, "Hello, Matthew Honey speaking."

This time, a faint breathing comes through.

"Hello," Matthew says. "Sorry, can you hear me?"

A female British accent echoes through his ear, "Hello."

Matthew's heart skips a beat. Surely it can't be…

"Father…"

A gut-wrenching pain surges in Matthew's stomach, and the colour drains from his cheeks. Shaking from the shock, Matthew drops the phone into the sink. He is unable to move. A lonely tear trickles down his cheek.

The door rattles and someone outside shouts, "Oh, sorry, didn't see it was occupied." Matthew snaps out of his trance.

"Please, Lord. Please let her still be there," he begs as he grasps the phone and raises it to his ear.

"Eve! Eve, darling, is that you?"

"Yes," she whispers.

"Oh my goodness, Evelyn Jade." Unable to hold it in any longer, Matthew breaks down crying. "Please, how are you?"

"So it's true," she replies.

"What's true, darling?"

But this time Matthew gets no response.

"Darling, please, are you okay?"

Again, silence.

Bawling and desperate to keep her on the phone, Matthew shouts through his tears, "Please, Eve, darling, if you can hear me, I know where you are and I'm coming to get you."

Nothing.

"Princess, daddy is coming to get you. Just keep yourself safe, I'm on a flight now heading to New York. I'm—"

The phone goes dead.

"Eve. Eve. Darling."

Looking at the screen of the phone, Matthew sees the call has ended.

"No, no, no, no," he shouts. He lets out an almighty wail.

He turns to the door and frantically attempts to unlock it. The fiddly lock slides through his sweaty fingers, and he punches the door in frustration. He's breathing at an uncontrollable rate, and his chest pains have suddenly resurfaced. He slumps to the ground, tears streaming down his face.

"Please, phone back. Please… Jesus, I beg you, please bring her back."

Another knock on the toilet door startles him. Wiping his face to try and mask his meltdown, he calls out, "Yeah, be just a minute."

"Hello," says a female voice.

"Yeah. I said I'll be out in a minute," Matthew yells back.

"We're about to do the safety demonstration, so if you could make your way back to your seat, sir, that would be great."

"Okay. I'll be out in a minute, I said," Matthew snaps.

As he lifts himself off the ground using the support of the sink, Matthew's stomach churns.

"Oh no," he says before turning back around and violently throwing up into the toilet.

"Sir, are you okay in there?"

"I'm…" Matthew swallows and wipes the excess vomit from around his mouth. "I'm fine. I'll be out in a minute."

Dragging his weak body up off the ground, he cleans himself and the cubicle up as best he can, then opens the door. He is greeted by a stern-looking brunette flight attendant with a plump face. Matthew smiles awkwardly before putting his head down and rushing back to his seat.

"Mate, you alright?" Phil says as Matthew sits back down. "You've gone pasty looking."

Matthew tries to find the words without exploding into a hysterical mess, then decides it's best to say nothing.

"I knew it. I knew we shouldn't have discharged you from the hospital," Phil says.

Matthew turns to Phil and says hoarsely, "Please, stop." Coughing, he continues, "You don't understand." He coughs again. "She just phoned me."

"What?" Phil asks. "Who has just phoned you?"

Matthew breathes in deeply, exhales and wipes his face. "Eve."

Phil grabs him by his shoulders and pulls him into his chest. Matthew reciprocates, wrapping his arms around his friend and holding him tight. Crying into his chest, Matthew feels a huge release.

"I can't believe it," Phil says. "Are you sure it was her?"

"Yeah, it was her voice." Sniffling, Mathew continues, "I instantly recognised it."

"Oh, shit. I can't believe it. What did she say?"

Matthew's head pounds fiercely. "She… erm… she just said 'Hello' and then 'Father' and something about it being true."

Beaming from ear to ear, Phil mops the tears from his face with his sleeves. "Aw, mate, this is great news." He pats Matthew on the back. "What did you say to her?"

"I… Well, I didn't know what to say to her. I dropped the phone at first in disbelief. I just knew it was her the minute I heard her say

'Hello'. And then, when she said 'Father', I just blurted out that I was on my way to get her, and I knew where she was."

"Holy shit. Mate, that's huge. Then what happened?"

"The phone went dead."

"Oh wait, mate, you don't think that scared her off, do you?"

"Dear God, I hope not."

"No, I'm sure the signal just went out or something."

"Can't take it back now, can I… I just wanted her to know that I've not stopped looking for her. You know…"

"Believe me, you don't have to explain yourself, I would have done the same thing. I'm sure it's going to be alright. Wow, holy shit. You just spoke to your daughter after all this time."

The pushy brunette flight attendant appears and says, "Please, sirs, can you fasten your seatbelts for take-off."

Matthew settles into his seat and looks out the window as the plane begins to taxi down the runway. He has just heard his daughter's sweet, innocent voice. After all this time, she still sounds just as he'd remembered.

Smiling, he sits back with his shoulders high. He knew it. When everyone around him doubted him and told him to stop looking because they thought his daughter was dead in a ditch somewhere, Matthew never gave up hope. He knew she'd be alive, and he knew he'd get her back one day. A huge sense of gratitude takes over his body. Unconditional love and persistence have finally started to pay off in the most magical way possible. Now more than ever he believes that he will be reunited with his precious Evelyn Jade. After all, true love conquers all.

With his palms pressed together, Matthew looks up high and whispers, "Thank you, God."

Chapter Twenty-Four

"Terror."

Lisa wrestles fitfully with her bed sheets. Restrained by the deceitful mist, she has been cunningly summoned to the darkest depths of her mind by Jezebel. Hearing Lisa moaning in her sleep, Jezebel steps out from the shadow of the darkest corner of the room. Basking in the glory of Lisa's agony, Jezebel embraces her current invisibility.

She taunts what tiny elements of Lisa's soul are left in a variety of gratifying ways, having already captured and detained her husband William lying next to her. Content with Lisa's progression, Jezebel drags her feet across the room, leaving trails of the thick black substance behind her. She reaches Lisa's side of the bed and peers down through the gap in her hair at her latest victim's contorted face.

Feeling highly empowered by the delightful scene of pain and suffering, Jezebel leans down and whispers, "*Temimi.*"

Absorbing the command, Lisa's body begins to convulse, and her complexion turns grey.

Placing her hand over Lisa's face, Jezebel chants, "*Non tamen complevit vobiscum.*"

Lisa's body stops and becomes frozen stiff. Satisfied with Lisa's ability to accept her orders and the progression of her entrapment, Jezebel turns and makes her way to the door. Smirking, she says, "I will be back for you both."

Jezebel drags her feet as she exits the room and moves out onto the landing. Thick layers of the mist intertwine with all the fixtures and fittings in the house. Pictures of family memories fall to the floor, shattering to pieces. Jezebel gets a kick from the destruction she's causing. Families disgust her to her very core.

Jezebel arrives at Ashley and Kane's bedroom. There they are! Her two latest prodigies. These boys will take vital positions within her empire once her takeover is complete. They'll be standing directly by her side, within the top layer of trusted individuals. Ashley and Kane will remain under the sole supervision of the Dark Empress. A privileged position for two very obedient and incredibly lucky boys.

Dragging her way to the bottom of the boy's beds, Jezebel takes in the magnificence. The mist has travelled through every pore on their body, taking over their existence. Mirroring that of the Dark Empress, their skin is deep grey and a black substance oozes out of the cracks. True visions of demonic opulence. Jezebel raises her arms, and Ashley and Kane put up zero resistance as they levitate from their beds.

"Ring a' Ring o' Roses. Welcome to the dark side." She aggressively throws her hands down, and the boys plummet back onto their beds.

"Wake and taunt them now," she commands.

Ashley's eyes shoot open. They are like gaping black holes upon his face. He no longer looks anything like the sweet boy in the family photos. Milliseconds later, Kane repeats his twin brother's movements. An identical reflection of their new owner, Ashley and Kane fling their legs off the bed in a sharp motion. Their bodies follow next, and finally their heads. Jezebel monitors every minuscule movement they make. She wants to test their level of loyalty and worthiness to join her elite inner circle.

The boys turn in perfect synchronisation and begin dragging their feet towards the bedroom door. Jezebel watches them like a hawk homing in on its prey. Intertwining with their bodies, the deceitful mist is making the vision even more disturbing. Levitating off the ground, Jezebel hovers over the boys. Ashley leads his brother out onto the landing and into their parents' bedroom. Stepping to his mother's side of the bed, Ashley gestures for Kane to take the side of their father.

"Copy me," Ashley says to Kane in a dulcet tone.

Ashley removes the bedsheet. Hunching over his mother's body, he watches as she struggles to breathe. He inhales the mist through his nostrils, his eyes glowing. Absorbing the scene before her, Jezebel rejoices as this is a clear indication that Ashley's sadistic levels are high. She can see he is enjoying Lisa's discomfort.

Ashley turns and makes eye contact with Jezebel, and she twitches her head and whispers, "Do it now."

Nodding and turning back to face his mother, in a rather angelic tone, Ashley says, "Mummy, wake up."

Mirroring his brother, Kane repeats this to their father. And just like that… Lisa and William's eyes shoot open to a horrifying unexpected image before them.

The pair attempt to scream and Jezebel laughs.

Ashley and Kane bare their grey, sharp teeth to their parents and snarling in their faces. The thick black substance drips from their mouths onto Lisa and William's faces as they get closer. As the pair struggle, Jezebel gradually lowers her body to the ground. Landing with a heavy thud, she whistles to summon the boys to see if they'll follow her command and retreat. But before Ashley follows orders, he reaches out and slashes his mother's face.

"*Veni*!" she shouts.

Kane follows orders and stands beside her, and she pats him on the head. Seething and growling at his mother, Ashley eventually retreats and stands by Jezebel with his head low. Certain she has chosen the right boys to join her inner circle, Jezebel stands arrogantly. She surveys the sheer devastation and terrified looks upon Lisa and William's faces. The orgasmic surge of satisfaction travelling around her body is so gratifying that she raises her arms and calls out loud. Copying their new owner, Ashley and Kane both howl out loud, too.

At the top of her lungs, Jezebel bellows, "*Causam*!"

Jezebel, Ashley and Kane race towards the bed. As they all collide, there are shrieks and an almighty bang.

Darkness and silence cascade over the room.

CHAPTER TWENTY-FIVE

"It's Happening."

"Brennan, you need to put your foot down or we're never going to make it. They land in like ten minutes," Alannah says impatiently. She's sitting on the edge of her seat on the passenger's side.

"Baby, I'm doing the speed limit."

"How far are we now?"

"About forty minutes or so give or take, depending on the traffic."

"Forty minutes?!"

"Baby, listen, I know you're anxious, but it's Christmas morning, we've got more traffic than usual on the roads because of the holidays."

Alannah clenches her fists with anxiety. "Yeah, but look, it's not that busy now, you could at least weave in and out for a little while, so it doesn't take so long."

"Alannah, sweetie, you have to stop. I'm not getting a ticket and a court summons because you're scared of being a few minutes late. They take speeding and lane-hopping serious here in the United States." Placing his hand on his wife's leg, he smiles. "Look, I promise, we'll get there in time. They've got to get through customs when they land. That isn't a quick process as we already know."

She hadn't thought about that. Her mind has been all over the place in the past twenty plus hours. Alannah surrenders slightly.

"And if we're a little late, I'm sure he'll call, and then we'll just ask him if he can wait. Seriously, it's really not that big of a deal."

"Yeah, you're right." Patting his hand, she continues, "I'm just so nervous, you know. Their poor children have been kidnapped, and I was around them and did nothing to put a stop to it."

"Yeah, but how could you put a stop to something you weren't aware of?"

"No, I knew something was off. I just knew it, but I did nothing to investigate it because I didn't want to be locked away like Sister Elisabeth. So like a coward, I kept my mouth shut and then just abandoned them all. If only I'd have said something…"

"Then what? You'd probably be dead. Whatever this demon is, it seems powerful, cunning and relentless. You wouldn't have stood a chance on your own."

"True," Alannah says. She breathes deeply.

"Look, I get why you might be thinking like that, baby, I really do, but it's like you said, you know the Lord had bigger plans for you. Can you imagine if you hadn't run off? Can you imagine if you weren't here with me right now? No one would have a clue where any of the children are because not only did you find them, but the Lord positioned you in the same country as them and as close as he possibly could. You have a huge role to play in this, Alannah, and you had to leave Moycullen and come to New York with me, or the fate of those innocent children might have been very different."

Aware that her husband is right, Alannah smiles.

"So what happens once we've picked them up?" Brennan asks.

"I'm not sure."

"Well, do you think it's wise that we visit the orphanage or should we stay away?"

"I really don't know. I mean, I don't think it's a good idea to just try and burst in there. We could be met by all sorts of danger."

"No, I think now's the time to play it smart."

"I agree."

"Well, we're obviously going to visit William, Lisa and the boys, so maybe we should book them into a B&B nearby… That way we can drop them there, so they can freshen up."

"Yeah, that's a good idea," Alannah says as she gets out her phone. "What's their ZIP code?"

"Erm, one, nine, zero, six, seven."

She taps it into her map app.

"Oh, there's loads."

Scrolling down the screen, Alannah finds a four-star place, clicks through to the website and reserves a family room.

Alannah looks to Brennan. "Brilliant, so we've got them somewhere to stay, and we can just drop them off there, go visit your friends, and then reconvene and work the rest out after."

"Sounds like a plan."

"Now if you could just put your foot down, I'd be even happier."

Brennan rolls his eyes and shakes his head at her.

Chuckling to herself, Alannah rests her elbow on the ledge of the door and peers out the window. Cars are passing them by, and everyone inside their vehicles appear to be filled with Christmas spirit. They're all smiling and chatting. Some have taken it to the extreme and are wearing Christmas outfits and accessories.

Peering up at the sky, Alannah admires its winter beauty. But something doesn't look quite right. At first glance, nothing would seem out of the ordinary with the grey sky and fluffy blankets of white clouds. However, Alannah's keen eye has spotted a highly unusual transformation.

Inside the clouds, tiny black lines are slowly joining together and creating what looks like mini tornadoes. It's almost as if the clouds have an infestation, and it's eating away at their beauty. Leaning closer to the window, Alannah squints. She gasps – her eyes are telling no lies!

Smacking Brennan, she points in the direction of the sky and shouts, "Brennan, look, look!"

Brennan jumps and shouts, "Alannah!"

"The sky, the sky, look at it."

Brennan stares at the sky. "What about it? I don't see anything."

"The clouds, look. They're changing." Bouncing around in her seat, Alannah begins shouting, "Oh Lord, please, no, no, no, this cannot be good. Lord please, no, no, no, no, I'm not ready for this. No, no, no, no."

"Baby, in case you hadn't noticed, I'm driving, and I really need you to calm down right now, or we're going to crash."

Pushing the button and lowering the window, Alannah unclips her seatbelt and leans her whole body out of the car to get a better look.

"Alannah! Alannah! Get your ass back in the car now!"

Her heart pounding, Alannah ignores her husband's request as she fixates on the clouds.

"The end is coming," she whispers, her eyes welling up with tears.

Feeling a tug on her blouse, Alannah pulls herself back into the car.

"What are you playing at? You're going to get yourself killed," Brennan barks.

Alannah says nothing. She breaks down, sobbing into her hands.

"I'm sorry," she sniffles. "It's just…" She sniffles again. "I can see it, Brennan. I can see the change coming. If we don't get them back soon, we're going to miss our opportunity again, and then only the Lord will know where they'll be and maybe he won't make it so simple to find them next time or maybe we'll all die for our failings."

"Baby, stop worrying, we'll sort this. We're not alone."

Looking back up at the clouds, she gets a huge knot in her stomach. This is not good and she knows it.

She places her hands together. "Dear Lord, it is your sister Alannah, and I am reaching out to you right now for your urgent help, for we are in danger. I pray for the vulnerable, I pray for the weak and I pray for us all. May Matthew and his friends land safely today and may we return every child back to their rightful family and carer as safely as we can. I thank you, Lord, for your love and protection. Amen."

"That was beautiful, baby," Brennan says.

Breathing deeply, Alannah sits in silence.

Chapter Twenty-Six

"Twelve Hours and Counting…"

Jezebel paces the floor of her room. She stops at the window and stares through the gap in her hair at the ever-changing sky. As she smirks, there is a knock at the door.

"*Intrabit*!" she commands.

The door creaks open and Elisabeth steps inside the room. "You wanted me, Dark Empress?"

"Yes. Where is Eve?"

"I'm here, Dark Empress," Eve says as she shoves the door completely open and storms past Elisabeth, rolling her eyes.

Jezebel smiles as Eve heads directly towards her and bows before her feet. She reaches out and strokes her chosen one's head. Pleased at the obedience and respect Eve has shown, Jezebel glares up at Elisabeth in a less than impressed way.

"Well," she says to Elisabeth.

"Sorry, Dark Empress," Elisabeth replies as she closes the door behind her and scurries into the room. "Right away, Dark Empress."

Considering Eve and Elisabeth the only trusted members of her inner circle, Jezebel has requested their attendance for a specific reason. Walking past Eve and Elisabeth, who remain kneeling on the floor by the window, Jezebel arrives at her desk. As she seats herself, she shouts, "*Veni*."

Eve and Elisabeth get up, march across the room and kneel on the ground before her. This time, in perfect synchronisation, they position their hands on their knees facing upwards and bow their heads, a sight that gives Jezebel an almost orgasmic, body-tingling reaction.

"Oh, how loyal you both are." She grins.

The pair stay silent.

"I have summoned you here to discuss the official plan for this evening's takeover."

A brief silence. Jezebel has never disclosed this information for fear of vulnerability, and she is still somewhat reluctant to share it with Eve and Elisabeth. Nevertheless, she requires assistance and protection from someone, and these two are her best bet. She concludes that she really has no other choice. She doesn't want to run the risk of being exposed and her empire being torn down. She is far too close to let this be her outcome.

Content with her chosen accomplices, Jezebel overcomes her doubts. "The plan. I am telling you this in the greatest confidence. You do not repeat this to another. Do I make myself clear?"

Replying in unison, Eve and Elisabeth say, "Yes, Dark Empress."

"Absolutely, nothing can go wrong."

"We understand, Dark Empress."

"Tonight, when the clock strikes ten, I will release my raven. She will fly across the globe spreading the mist upon the streets. Embedded within the mist is the final element of my DNA, ready to be implanted to complete my possession over the young. It is imperative that her flight time is lightning speed or my poison will weaken. We have this logged and it is going to take her two hours to tour the globe and have this in place ready for our attack. Using this calculation, as soon as the clock strikes midnight, I will step forward and release my sacred chant across the globe. At this point, the mist will enter every home, building, boat, plane – everywhere possible that a sneaky human could be. Once it locates my victims, every child in every country will awaken and unite under my ruling. And every adult will be restrained so they are powerless. Once the children have transitioned, they will follow my every command, eliminating their parents and any adult they encounter with their bare hands." Looking to Eve and Elisabeth, whose heads are still bowed, Jezebel asks. "Is this stimulating enough for your inner evil?"

"Yes, Dark Empress," the pair reply.

"Impressive." She grins. "Well, as the children are wreaking havoc across land, sea and air, I will rise above to take up my most important stance. Beneath my beautiful black hole. My vortex. Using a combination of this and the mist, as the two unite, it will create the most valuable part of the takeover." Seeing Elisabeth's head lower, Jezebel bangs her fist on the table and barks, "Are you listening?"

Jumping, Eve and Elisabeth reply, "Yes, Dark Empress."

Jezebel smirks, the black substance hanging from her mouth. "I was checking you were following. Nothing can go wrong. Not even the slightest thing. The vortex I will be building is the most important element. It is my sole responsibility to ensure it has enough power to sustain itself. Collecting all the sacrificed souls, the vortex will then pass them through a portal in exchange for the birth of my empire. As soon as the portal has been established within, I will return to oversee the slaying of mankind." Leaning forward, Jezebel places her hands on the desk and arches her back. "You must be aware that if I return any sooner, all will be lost. It is imperative that I complete this part of the process uninterrupted, do I make myself clear?"

"Yes, Dark Empress."

"Good." Sitting back, she continues, "Once the last soul has been received, the vortex will close the portal, and humanity as it is known will cease to exist, and I will finally have my rightful place, ruler of the whole universe."

Envisioning her triumph, Jezebel stands, the empowerment of the moment tingling through her. Lighting up like flames, her eyes beam bright red. Stepping away from her desk, she drags her feet towards Eve and Elisabeth. Standing behind them, she strokes their silky hair.

"So, are you still wondering why I have summoned you here?"

"Yes, Dark Empress," Eve replies.

Elisabeth stays quiet this time.

"For decade upon decade, I have watched these despicable people living within my universe as though they are welcome. I was created because of their cruelty to vulnerable children. They don't care about children. They don't deserve the loyalty children offer to them. I deserve it, and I am going to take it from them. A long time ago I made a deal. A deal that required patience. To produce a universe of my own ruling, the elimination and sacrifice of every adult on this planet is needed. When I fulfil this, every child will serve under my command. Youth will remain with them always, they will never age. Procreation will no longer be conducted using their vile methods." Jezebel spits on the floor. "Disgusting little insects they are. No, no more of that obscene behaviour. Procreation will now be initiated via my precious *carnitine molendini*, which will penetrate straight through the stratosphere at the same moment the last soul has been surrendered and the vortex is closed."

Jezebel opens the top drawer of her desk and retrieves an item. She grips it tight.

She returns to the window and stares at the sky. "It is vital that you protect me at all costs during the takeover. Do I make myself clear?"

"Yes, Dark Empress."

Aware that one person alone potentially has the means and knowledge of how to destroy her and her destiny, Jezebel is going to stop at nothing to ensure she is given maximum shelter.

"You should know, and this is for you both to know and no one else, that during my takeover there will be one point where I cannot be disturbed. No one is to interrupt or approach me as I am summoning the vortex. If this happens and my attention is lost, it will collapse and this could have a detrimental effect. We have one shot at this." Looking at her closed hand, Jezebel continues, "Should anyone attempt to be foolish and try to assassinate me, you are under strict orders to destroy them without any hesitation, even if this is a child. Do you understand?"

"Yes, Dark Empress," Elisabeth says.

This time Eve stays quiet.

Jezebel turns to them. "Eve?"

"Sorry, yes, Dark Empress."

"Terrific," she replies. "Now come here to me."

Eve and Elisabeth obey.

Pointing her finger in the direction of the sky, Jezebel says, "Look. You see those black formations in the clouds?"

The pair look up and say, "Yes, Dark Empress."

"The transition is already happening. Across the globe, those tiny vortexes are forming. Once I rise, they will unite."

Opening her hand, Jezebel reveals the invaluable item she's been holding. It's her heart-shaped locket. Her hunter. Placing it around her neck, Jezebel says, "This stays with me. It is to be guarded with your life. If for any reason this locket gets detached from my body, you must retrieve it and protect it with every ounce of your existence. I don't care if you have to die to protect it. Do I make myself clear?"

"Yes, Dark Empress."

"Excellent." She grins.

Believing she has got her point across without making herself sound too vulnerable, Jezebel stands between Eve and Elisabeth and strokes their hair, embracing the vision of her plan coming together as the darkness takes over the clouds. Jezebel is ready for the residents of the world to know of her arrival.

Chapter Twenty-Seven

"We Meet at Last."

Marching through the airport with his backpack strapped to his body, Matthew is sweltering. He's a man on a mission. Anyone who gets in his way will be bulldozed without a second thought. Time is of the essence, and he is desperate to get to his daughter. Crowds of people are blocking him, standing by the baggage claim conveyor belts, waiting for their cases. Battling his way through, Matthew's thankful that he, Phil and Hermon have all got a backpack each and nothing more.

"Come on, you two, catch up!" Matthew shouts, waving his arm.

"Sorry for not being as physically fit as you," Phil replies, puffing and panting.

"I think I'm going to have a heart attack," Hermon says.

At last, Matthew can see the light at the end of the crowd. He stumbles out of the mass of hot sweaty bodies and rushes to the final security check.

"Enjoy your trip, sir," says the sharply dressed security officer, passing Matthew back his passport.

He rushes onto the elevator and holds the door as he watches Phil and Hermon catch up. As the doors close, Matthew rests his head against the cold metal. He cannot stop obsessing about the call. He didn't sleep a wink during the whole flight and spent it perusing Hermon's translation of the scroll. But he did figure out one thing. The emblem: the heart and the crucifix merging must be exactly how the Dark Empress is defeated. And another he realised, a vitally important piece of the puzzle. The creator of the first chosen child, which in this case is Matthew, is the only individual the Dark Empress is powerless over. She cannot possess nor execute him. And, not only this, but Reverend Andrew was right: Matthew is the only one who has the power to destroy her. He is the only person who can stab her heart with the crucifix.

And if he should fail? The Dark Empress would gain full reign over his soul with immediate effect. Not only this, but she would also be able to execute him in any way she desires. Matthew cringes at the thought. The stakes have been raised, and he's more determined than ever to take her out!

As they step out of the elevator, Matthew's phone begins to vibrate. He retrieves it as quickly as he can and answers the call. "Oh, hey Alannah. We're just coming out the exit now."

"Perfect, we're parked out front. We can't stop long. Brennan said the security here are a pain in the ass for moving you along."

"Yeah, sure, sorry it took a while getting through security and battling through baggage claim. Okay, so I'm just walking out the doors now." Looking around, Matthew sees cars and people everywhere. "Alannah, can you see me? I'm the scruffy-looking guy in all black, with a backpack glued to him, currently waving his arm like a madman."

"Yeah, I see you," Alannah replies, before wolf whistling.

He looks in the direction of the sound and sees a woman waving.

"Found you. I'm on my way," Matthew says to Alannah, before hanging up the phone and turning to Phil and Hermon. "She's over here, lads."

Matthew smiles at the relief he feels to finally meet the woman who has been in his daughter's presence along with his granddaughter. As soon as she reaches him, Matthew wraps his arms around her tightly and twirls her around.

"I can't believe we finally get to meet," Alannah says.

"I know. I know. This is Phil."

"Hi, Phil," Alannah says as she puts out her hand.

"Too formal. Come here, you," Phil replies as he wraps his arms around her. "Thank you for this."

"You don't need to thank me."

"And this is Hermon."

"Hey, Hermon. Nice to meet you," Alannah responds as she again puts out her hand.

"Don't want to be the only arsehole here," Hermon says with a smile on his face, before giving Alannah an awkward hug.

As she chuckles, Alannah points to the car and says, "Oh, gents, this is my husband, Brennan."

"Hey guys. Nice to finally meet you," Brennan shouts out the window. "Look, I don't want to be a dick or anything, but we really need to move from here. So why don't you guys jump in and we'll hit the roads. We've got quite a drive ahead of us still."

"Sure, sure, sorry," Matthew says as he opens the door to the back seats. "Get in, lads."

Matthew takes his seat and looks out the window. Seeing the American flag on the back of a car, the reality starts to sink in. They've made it. Officially on American soil, and finally back on track to getting his daughter home. Matthew beams with pride.

"Okay, everyone strapped in?" Brennan asks.

"Yeah, mate," Phil replies.

"Right, let's get this show on the road, then," Brennan says as they pull out into the flow of traffic away from the airport.

"Alannah, you'll never guess what?" Matthew blurts out.

"What?"

"Just before we took off, I got a call from Eve."

"Are you kidding me?"

"Nope. It was her. I'd recognise that voice anywhere."

"Well, what did she say?"

"Well, she said 'Hello' and 'Father', and then something about it being true, and then the phone went down."

"Yeah, but tell her what you said before the phone went down," Phil chimes in.

"What?"

"You told her we're on our way to get her, and *then* the phone went down."

"Aye, you said you'd have done the same thing," Matthew says.

"Yeah, I would have. Of course, I would, but I mean, what if she has told you know who?"

"It doesn't matter if she has." Matthew replies sternly. "While you were sleeping, I figured it out: it turns out she cannot kill me. And I am the only one who can kill her."

"What the f—"

"Yeah, but if she is somehow successful in her takeover, then she has the power to kill me in any way she wants. That's right, isn't it Hermon?"

"Unfortunately it is, my friend."

"Well mate, I mean, if she wins, it's game over for all of us, cause I'm pretty sure she'll murder us in a heartbeat anyway," Phil says.

"I know, but my point is, she cannot kill me until that moment. So it's simple, I just have to make sure I get to her before she completes her transition and stab her heart with this." Matthew retrieves the crucifix from the inside pocket on his jacket.

Phil squirms in his seat. "Urgh, so you *do* have to stab her heart?"

"Yeah, and you know what? Now I know she can't kill me, I'm okay about it. I mean, I always wondered why she never came back and just killed me off. And now I know." Now he's saying his findings out loud, Matthew feels untouchable. "So, yeah, I'm ready for her. Put that bitch in front of me now and I'll ram this right into her chest." Matthew mimes stabbing the crucifix into her chest.

"So, we just have to get to her before she finishes the job," Phil says. "And God only knows when that's going to be."

"Well, not to alarm you or anything, gents, but have you taken a look at the sky recently?" Alannah says.

Matthew looks out of the window. Staring above the passing vehicles, he notices something out of the ordinary in the sky. He winds the window down, raises his phone and takes three pictures from different angles. Closing the window as it's letting in an almighty chill, Matthew looks at the first image.

"Wait, what is that?" Matthew says, baffled.

"I know, right," Alannah responds. "I mean, I'm not a rocket scientist or anything, but I know supernatural activity when I see it. And that ain't holy."

"Good Lord, it's happening," Hermon says.

Nervous as Hermon's predictions have never been wrong before, Matthew says, "Well it looks like we're going straight to the orphanage, then. Element of surprise."

"No, it won't happen in the daytime. She only strikes at night." Pushing his glasses back up the bridge of his nose, Hermon continues, "The scroll stated that—"

"Wait a minute," Matthew interrupts. "I get that, but don't we want to attack her *before* she strikes?"

"No. Not at all. She can easily capture you and keep you hostage until she's completed her takeover and then we're all going to be dead. We have to keep you well out of her way and get her while she is vulnerable."

"A vulnerable demon. Never heard of that one." Phil laughs.

"What do you mean, Hermon?" Alannah asks. "How will we know when she's going to be vulnerable?"

"I'm not sure, to be honest with you."

"Well, how do we find out?" Matthew says.

"I was hoping to conduct some more studying, but with the collapse of the tomb, the hospital visit, the shock of finding them and now ending up in America, I just haven't been able to get online to search for material."

"Might this help?" Alannah says as she reaches into her handbag and passes back the book Smashing of the Clay Pots.

"Dear God, where did you get this from?" Hermon says as he holds the precious ancient book. A look of astonishment spreads across his face.

"The New York Public Library. A girl named Julianna helped me find it."

"Huh, that's quite comical." Hermon chuckles.

"What is?" Phil asks.

"Well, the archangel sent by Jesus to help the disciples along their way was indeed called Julianna."

"You're kidding me?" Phil says.

"No, not at all, actually. I'm quite amused by this myself."

Looking extremely concerned, Alannah says, "So she was a ghost, then, is that what you're saying?"

"No, I'm not saying that. I'm just merely pointing out the connection. It's quite an encouraging sign."

"So if we're not going straight to the orphanage, then where are we going?" Matthew asks.

"Okay, so you know I told you Brennan has friends in the village where the orphanage is?"

"Yeah."

"Well, we're going to head over to their home and check in to see if they've been noticing anything supernatural or out of the ordinary taking place over the past few months. Obviously, you guys can't come with us, so we're going to drop you off at a B&B that we managed to book for you. I mean it might be a squeeze, but it's all we could get at such short notice. We just thought this way you could rest and freshen up while we gather all the information we can from Lisa and William. And, well, now it will give Hermon a chance to review the book."

"How close is it to the orphanage?" Matthew queries.

Biting her lips, Alannah says, "Hmm, I'm not sure, to be honest."

"It's around a twenty-minute drive. Give or take due to the holiday traffic," Brennan confirms.

"Mate, I think you better listen to Hermon on this one and not go near it," Phil says, looking worried. "If you're our only hope of defeating this bitch, then we better wait it out and go whenever the time is right."

Aware that his friend is right, Matthew submits, even though it is killing him inside. After such a long time, to be within reaching distance of his daughter and his granddaughter and not be able to run to their aid, Matthew feels a whole new level of frustration.

"I know. I promise, I'll be good," Matthew says. "I'll hang back until Hermon can figure out when the time is right. And, Alannah,

Brennan, thank you for all your help with this. From the bottom of my heart, I appreciate you both so much."

"Don't mention it," Alannah says. "She murdered my family, too. I want justice for my sisters and those children back where they belong, with me."

Turning back to the window, Matthew sees the people in other cars staring and pointing at the sky, looking equally as bewildered by the ever-changing colour of the clouds. Peering back up at the clouds himself, he sees the black element taking over the purity of each cloud, one fragment at a time. Shaking his head, Matthew hopes they're not too late.

"Please, God. Help us," he whispers.

Chapter Twenty-Eight

"He's here."

Seated in the rocking chair inside her room, Eve is wrapped up in a warm fuzzy blanket and is cradling Honey. Singing her a little song, she rocks back and forth in a rhythmic fashion. Her eyes are welling up. Fearful about what will happen over the course of the next eight hours, Eve is savouring the moment with her daughter. Unsure of their fate, but aware that Jezebel is confident of her plan and her successful reign over the universe, Eve feels a deep internal sadness. This outcome will seal Honey's fate and it's one she never wanted for her precious baby. Just the thought of handing over her own daughter's soul eats Eve up inside.

"My baby, I am so sorry I got us into this mess." Eve sobs. "I didn't know. I really didn't know. She had me fooled like everyone else, and now I don't know what to do. The sky is already transforming and the clock is ticking." Wiping her tears, Eve continues. "One thing I am certain of, my darling, my precious baby girl, is that I want you to know that no matter what, I will always love you, and I tried to fight for you and your purity for as long as I could."

"You've really taken to this role, haven't you?" Thomas says as he appears at her side.

"Goodness. Can't you knock or something?"

"Knock? Really?" He laughs.

"Well, you know what I mean. Warn me before you show up, or don't just show up behind me or at the side of me. I keep thinking it's *you-know-who*."

"Okay, I promise I will whisper your name before I appear next time, okay?"

"Okay." Eve says as she looks back at her daughter to admire her cuteness.

"Look at how gorgeous my niece is..." In a giggly tone, he continues. "Aren't you, aren't you just gorgeous and you know it. Yes, you do."

Smiling, Eve's body warms at the sight of her daughter's gummy grin at her uncle.

"Wait, she can see you?" Eve says, stunned.

"Yes, of course she can. Children are susceptible to different frequencies. They haven't been programmed yet to believe or disbelieve what is in front of them. And so anything they see, they believe." Returning to his giggly girlie tone, he leans in and strokes Honey's cheek as he says, "Don't you, my little chunky butt."

"It's over, Thomas," Eve blurts out. "There's nothing more I can do. She's going to win this war, and I have to accept that I've played a huge part in this destruction, and now I am powerless to stop it." Eve's eyes are bright red as she tries to hold back the tears. "I can't even save my own daughter, Thomas. I mean, what kind of mother am I?"

"Hey, you're the best mother there is, let me tell you. Honestly, Eve, that little girl is lucky to have you as a mummy. You're an inspiration."

"I'd hardly go that far. I've destroyed families, including my own." Standing, Eve walks across to Honey's crib and places her inside.

"Eve, it's not about what you have done wrong, it's about what you do to make it right."

"I can't do anything to make it right," Eve says as she marches across to the window. "Have you not seen the sky? She's already in transition. And I tried to reach out to my father, but I got too scared that she'd somehow hear me, or pick up the cell frequency radiating from my room, so I slammed the phone down and broke it into a million pieces."

"Did you hear what he said as you ended the call?"

"No. Just something about him never stopping looking for me."

"He said that he was on his way to get you. Father's here."

"What!" Eve exclaims.

"Yes, he landed in New York a few hours ago."

"How… I mean, what… where is he?" Eve seats herself in the rocking chair. Her legs feel weak.

"He'll be arriving at a local B&B any minute now."

Sobbing into her hands, Eve's overwhelmed.

"We might be able to win this thing, Eve. I just need you to work with me."

"Have you seen him?"

"Who… father?"

"Yeah."

"Yeah, I've seen him. He's a bit beaten up, but he's ready for the battle, and he seems to have a rather good team alongside him."

Wiping her face, Eve sniffles, "Team?"

Thomas makes his way towards Eve and kneels beside her. "Yeah, there's a few others who are helping him – you know, gather information, stay strong, all the usual stuff you need when you're about to fight the most dangerous and powerful demon ever known in existence."

"So, he knows how to defeat her?" Eve looks to Thomas, her eyes now puffy.

"Well, that's why I'm here. Father has a theory on how she is defeated and he's right about the majority of it. However, there are certain missing fundamentals that I need to discuss with you, as if all bridges are not burned correctly, then father will stand no chance, and she *will* be successful in her takeover. It's going to take a cunning combination of you and father for this to go to plan."

"I'm in," Eve replies.

"Wait, hang on a minute, you don't even know what's expected of you yet," Thomas protests.

"Is it going to save my daughter from being tainted by evil?"

"Yes."

"Then I'm in. I don't need to even think about it. Just tell me what I need to do, and I'll do it."

A desperate mother, Eve is willing to sacrifice anything she can to save her daughter from the clutches of evil. Standing from the chair she marches her way to the crib, reaching in she collects Honey and holds her tight.

"Mummy is going to make this right. I promise I will protect you."

It's time to make things right! Aware she must step up and remove Jezebel from her reign of terror, Eve's prepared to pay the price for her mistakes and misjudgements. She is ready and willing to do whatever Thomas requests of her to put an end to this destructive behaviour.

Chapter Twenty-Nine

"The Terrible Twosome!"

Holding the bag with presents inside it firmly in one hand, Alannah links arms with her husband with the other as they walk up the long pathway leading to Lisa and William's house, which looks more like an English manor. In absolute awe, Alannah can't believe just one family lives inside this ginormous home.

Surrounded by the winter wonderland on the lawn, Alannah's eyes light up. All that's missing from this magical creation is a real-life Santa, and some Elves tapping away making toys. Clearly Lisa and William have incredible taste and a love for Christmas.

Impressed by their efforts, Alannah says, "I can't wait for us to have a proper home, so we can dress it up like this."

"What's wrong with the apartment?" Brennan says sarcastically.

She rolls her eyes. They finally reach the door and Brennan rings the bell. Straightening her blouse and fluffing her hair, Alannah anxiously waits for Lisa or William to answer. Biting her bottom lip, she looks to Brennan.

"Just be calm. It's going to be alright," he says to her.

"I know."

Before she can say anything else, the front door is opened by a slender woman wearing a plum-coloured jumper, a black skirt and thick black tights, complimented by a reindeer antler headband.

"Merry Christmas, you two," she says, beaming. "Welcome to our home."

Noticing a gash across her face, Alannah is instantly taken aback.

Brennan gently nudges Alannah's arm before leaning in and giving the woman a hug. "Hey, Merry Christmas, Lisa. This is my wife, Alannah. I know you guys haven't met yet."

"Aww, Merry Christmas, Alannah, it's so great to finally meet you."

Deciding not to say anything about the laceration to her face, Alannah hugs her. "Merry Christmas to you and your family. And thank you so much for letting us call over on Christmas Day at such short notice. Here, it's not much but we got you all some gifts."

Taking the bag from Alannah, Lisa says, "That's too kind of you. You honestly didn't have to, but thanks, guys."

"Did I hear an Irish accent…?" William appears from behind Lisa wearing a rather embarrassing Christmas jumper with a flashing Rudolph nose.

"Hey, Merry Christmas, man," Brennan says, putting out his hand. Sharing a long overdue fraternity palm clasp and manly hug with his friend, Brennan continues, "Yeah, so this is Alannah, my super cool wife."

"Alannah, great to meet you," William says as he hugs her. "I mean, we were starting to think that this one had made you up from his fantasy list or something…"

"Aw, come on, man." Brennan smirks, his face going red. "We're not even in the house yet and you're already starting."

"I know, I know, I'm sorry. I'm just fooling around. Alannah, I apologise. It's just been a while since we've seen each other, and I've had a few beers." Stepping outside, he says, "Come in, come in."

"Thank you," Alannah replies as she steps into the house.

Looking up, William shouts, "Ew, look at that ugly fucking sky. What's going on with that?"

"Dude, I think you've had a few too many eggnogs." Brennan laughs. "It's early afternoon and you can't even stand up right."

"Eggnogs. Eggnogs." William laughs. "Not me, I'm on the beers and alcohol."

Shaking his head and rolling his eyes, Brennan chuckles. "Come, let's pour me one of whatever it is you're drinking."

"Yes, let's do that," William replies as he sets off swaying back inside the house.

Taking off her shoes, Alannah feels the warmth from the heated flooring. The house might be oversized, but it certainly is toasty. Alannah notices a black hair tie on her wrist and decides to fix her hair up high. Brushing the loose strands of her hair off her face, she tugs at her blouse to straighten it once more before following Lisa into the kitchen.

"Them two lunatics have gone into the living room. I think William wanted to show Brennan his baseball card collection. He's got it all laid out on the table. Driving me crazy, he is." Waving a bottle of red wine, Lisa asks, "Wine okay?"

"Erm, yeah, sure, why not. Just a small glass should be fine. We've got kind of a busy schedule, so I don't want a fuzzy head." Alannah laughs awkwardly. "You know, I never drank until recently, and now I always seem to make bad choices when I've had a few too many."

Laughing, Lisa replies, "Oh, I know that feeling all too well."

Scanning the kitchen, Alannah cannot believe how big it is. In fact, she's sure it's bigger than the kitchen they had in the nunnery and that was used to cater for every person living inside the convent. Organisation is clearly Lisa's speciality as there is not a single sign of Christmas chaos to be seen. In fact, Alannah spots that she's even prepped all the food for their Christmas dinner. Colourful vegetables have already been chopped perfectly and layered in the steamer on the side. The turkey has been basted and is resting on top of the oven. Neatly placed side by side are around five other silver tin dishes on the side, covered and ready to go in the oven. In awe of her ability to put all of this together and still look fabulous, Alannah smiles as she seats herself at the island in the centre.

"So, how are you finding living in America?" Lisa asks as she pours Alannah her drink. "You came over straight from Ireland, right?"

"Yeah, I did, that's correct. Oh, I love it here. It's a big transition, but I mean who doesn't love America, right?"

"Oh, for sure. Certainly is the land of dreams," Lisa replies as she raises her hands in a *look-at-what-I've-got* kind of way.

"Yeah, exactly. Well, you know first-hand with this beautiful home you live in."

"Aww, thank you so much. We designed the house ourselves. It took a while for completion, but honestly, don't tell my husband this because I drove him insane over it, but it was so worth the wait."

Looking around, Alannah jokes, "So how many butlers do you have?"

"Oh no, there's no butlers. I have a cleaning lady who comes twice a week and that's it. It's just me, William and the twins."

"That's nice. So, where are these handsome boys I've heard so much about?" Alannah asks.

"They're in their toy room."

"Aw, that's super sweet. I bet they've been excited all morning, what with Santa's arrival."

"Yeah. Sure."

"Well, I'd love to meet them."

Stopping dead in her tracks, Lisa doesn't respond to Alannah's request.

Alarmed by Lisa's reaction, Alannah says, "Sorry, did I say something wrong?"

Taking a deep breath in and passing Alannah her wine, Lisa remains silent.

Confused by the dramatic change in her energy, Alannah asks, "Erm, is everything okay?"

Again, no response.

"Oh dear, they haven't been naughty boys this morning, have they?"

Without turning her head, Lisa gives her a glancing look of fear. Now Alannah knows something isn't right.

"Lisa, you can talk to me, you know." She reaches her hand out to hold Lisa's. "Is everything okay with the boys?"

"I…" Lisa shakes her head. "I'm being silly, it's nothing, just forget it."

"Okay, but please just let me say one thing." Stretching out and placing her hands on Lisa's shoulders, Alannah looks her dead in the eye. "I'm not sure if Brennan told you, but I have been a loyal sister to a convent all my life. I trust unto God, and right now I'm getting all sorts of signals telling me that something isn't right with you."

Breaking eye contact, Lisa throws back the remainder of the wine in her glass and then immediately refills it. "Oh no, don't be silly," she says in her unconvincing tone, watching the wine splashing into the glass. "Everything is perfect."

Sceptical, Alannah plays along. "Perfect. Well, that's a relief. So, can I go and meet the boys? I'd like to give them their Christmas present."

Twiddling her fingers, Lisa reverts to staying quiet.

"I'd love to meet them."

"They're napping," Lisa says as she takes another huge gulp of wine from her glass. Turning her back to Alannah, Lisa walks away and stands by the kitchen sink. Looking out of the kitchen window, wine in hand, she says nothing further.

"You just said they were in their toy room."

"Oh no, I was wrong, that was earlier. They were playing just before you came."

"Oh, okay," Alannah says as she perches herself back up onto her seat by the kitchen island. Deciding to get off the subject, she says, "It's real nice having children around at this time of year. I'm sure you've all had a lot of fun this morning and that's why they're wiped out."

"You have children?"

"No, not biologically anyway. At the convent, we housed fifty orphaned children who I like to think of as close to my own. I'd do anything to protect them."

"How kind and unselfish of you all."

"Yes, I miss them all terribly. Tell me to shut up, it's none of my business, but that's one heck of a gash upon your face there. How did you get it?"

Closing her eyes, Lisa breathes deeply and says, "I... erm..." Struggling to speak, she again gulps her wine.

Becoming really concerned for this woman's safety, Alannah notices the wine in the glass sloshing around. Her hand is trembling.

Putting the wine glass on the side, Lisa says, "Oh, it was nothing, really. I tripped."

"You tripped."

"Yeah. I don't want to talk about it."

"Okay, that's fine. We don't have to talk about it, but you should know I could help you."

"I just...." Lisa cups her head in her hands. "Argh, I'm just being paranoid, for sure. I'm sorry, I shouldn't be speaking to you about this."

"Hey, hey, hey," Alannah says as she hops off the chair and rushes back to Lisa's side.

Alannah guides her to the nearest chair. Kneeling beside her, Alannah says, "Please, just tell me what's wrong. It's Christmas, for goodness sake, you shouldn't be shaking, you should be smiling, singing and playing with your family."

"I know, it's just so sad."

"What's sad? Please, tell me. Let me see if I can help you."

"So... the boys..."

"Yeah."

"They have been acting standoffish for a while now."

"Okay, what do you mean by standoffish?"

With sadness in her eyes, Lisa says, "I don't know, maybe it's just me they can't bear to be around."

"I'm sure that's not true."

Fidgeting in her chair, Lisa continues, "Well, they've been very aggressive recently at home. Hitting out. Spitting. Saying they no longer want to live with me or their dad. It's like they're filled with nothing but hate for us both and I don't know what we did wrong."

Alannah knows exactly what's happening in their home, but she doesn't want to scare Lisa, so she tries to play dumb. "Well, yes, that's a little strange. But I mean has anything changed in the household? Any dynamics, arguments or anything like that?"

"Nothing at all. Myself, William and the boys have always lived a very healthy and happy lifestyle. I mean, there is this one thing…"

"What is it?"

"The only thing I've noticed is a difference at night. I don't know why, but we're all suffering terrible nightmares together. And the boys have been calling out a lot."

"Sorry, you said *all* of you have been suffering from nightmares?"

"Yeah." Lisa pauses. "I'm sorry, you must think I'm mad. Why am I telling you all this, I've only just met you. Sorry, let's talk about you. So how did you and Brennan meet?"

"Lisa, listen, please calm down, I'm not here to judge anybody. All of my life I have helped people gain clarity and feel better by handing everything over to our Lord. It's natural for me to want to help you. I can see the pain in your eyes. Please, don't be concerned, I think I can really help you all if you'll just let me."

Pausing for a moment, Lisa looks to the ground. "Okay," she says. "They keep calling out for someone. I can't quite make out what the name is, but as soon as I go to wake them up, they seem almost as though they've been – now I know this is going to sound strange but please, just hear me out before you call me crazy."

"Lisa, you're in a safe space."

"They appear possessed. Like really possessed. I've been hit so many times. The other night, Ashley grabbed me by the throat when I woke him. It didn't seem like he was going to let go and his strength was unbelievable. If it wasn't for my husband hearing me scream before he gripped me, it doesn't even bear thinking about what might have happened."

"Is that how you've got that gash on your face?"

Lisa sobs. "I don't know. I had this nightmare that Ashley made his way into our room and attacked me while I lay in bed. It was like it never happened in my reality. I jumped up and there was no one in the room, so I went to the bathroom and splashed my face with some water because I was sweating and there it was. This huge disgusting gash on my face. I screamed and ran to William, and he said that his head was hurting because he'd had a nightmare, too. We went and checked on the boys together and they were sleeping."

"Have either you or your husband tried speaking to the boys?"

"Yes. They won't speak to us. It's like they suddenly decided to despise us overnight. This morning was horrific. They refused to open a single gift. They just kept saying this wasn't their home anymore and they wanted to go and live with their real family."

Tears start to fall down Lisa's face. Quickly wiping them away, she clears her throat. Alannah grabs the box of tissues and passes them to Lisa.

Wiping her face and blowing her nose, Lisa says, "Thank you. I just don't know what to do."

"Would you mind if I went and spoke to them? I am a religious sister, after all, and I have plenty of experience dealing with disobedient children. As you can imagine, orphaned children aren't always easy to care for."

"Baby, look what William's got," Brennan shouts as he rushes into the kitchen waving what appears to be a baseball card in his hand. "It's a PSA grade ten nineteen-fifty-two Topps Mickey Mantle. Do you even understand how much this is worth? And this clown just has it sitting in a box in his cabinet at home."

Nodding her head in the direction of Lisa, Alannah mouths, "She's upset."

"Oh shit, sorry. I didn't realise you two were having a moment."

"Sorry, Brennan," Lisa says, mid blowing her nose. "It's just been a tough morning with the boys, that's all."

"I was just saying I should go and have a chat with them. You know since I worked with disobedient troubled children for years at the convent."

"Yeah. You should let Alannah go speak with them. She's really compassionate and kids really like her. I'm sure she'll help you out."

"What you losers talking about?" William says as he enters the kitchen, throwing back the remainder of his bottle of beer.

"The boys," Lisa replies.

"Oh, those little shits. I've started calling them the terrible twosome, haven't I Lisa?" William laughs.

"It's not funny, William. We're in a mess. Alannah's going to have a word with them."

Huffing, William says, "Good luck to ya."

Standing up and placing the box of tissues back on the island, Lisa says, "It can't get much worse than it already is, so there's not an awful lot to lose. Come, I'll show you to their room."

Looking worried, Brennan says, "Maybe I should go with you."

"No, I'll be okay on my own," Alannah replies.

"Baby, let me go. You don't know what you'll be met with."

Alannah reaches into her blouse and pulls out the rosary beads she's wearing. Kissing Brennan on the cheek, she says, "I've got the protection of our Lord, I'll be okay."

"I love you. Shout me if there's any problems and I'll come running."

"I will. Love you, too." Alannah then follows Lisa out of the kitchen.

Walking out into the front entrance, Alannah stares up at the endless wooden spiral staircase. Hanging perfectly central is the largest crystal chandelier Alannah has ever seen in her life. Expensive items for a family with exquisite taste and a limitless about of money.

"The boys are inside the toy room on the top floor. Apologies, it's quite a walk."

"Oh, don't apologise. It's fine."

As they travel up the stairs, Alannah notices all the hooks on the wall are empty and the pictures are piled up on the floor. "Redecorating?" she asks.

"Huh…"

"The pictures on the floor."

"Oh, no. I think we might have had a mini earthquake last night because when we woke up the floor was covered in glass and all the frames had smashed to pieces."

"Oh… that's a shame."

"Just one of the many things to add to the list."

Feeling a little out of breath, Alannah's relieved to finally be at the top of the second staircase. She notices a significant difference in energy. This floor isn't as bright as the rest of the house. Seeing the dark oak wooden door with colourful letters that spell out Ashley and Kane's Toy Room upon it, Alannah reaches for her cross. Kissing it, she makes the sign of the cross.

Tapping on the door, Lisa says, "Boys, it's mommy and her friend, Alannah. She wanted to come and say hello to you."

Silence meets them both.

"Boys, it's mommy. Can you open the door for me, please?"

Alannah takes charge. "Watch out," she says to Lisa as she grabs the doorknob.

She twists it and pushes the door open to be met by a bizarre scene. Scanning the room, she sees the walls are covered in upside-down crosses. And it's very clear that the boys have drawn these as they go no further than their height. Standing at the door, Lisa breaks down crying.

Ashley and Kane are stood facing the wall. They haven't so much as flinched since Alannah's entrance into the room. Toys are spread out across the floor in a strangely organised fashion. Alannah slowly steps towards them, her cross in her hand. Now within touching distance of the boys, she can hear them chanting in a language unknown to her under their breath.

"Ashley, Kane, I've got a present for you both downstairs. Why don't you come and join us? It might be fun."

The pair don't acknowledge Alannah. Instead, they continue with their chanting. Realising it is going to take an almighty power to bring the boys back around, Alannah starts praying. "Dear Lord, please relieve both Ashley and Kane from any evil that may have manipulated its way into their purity."

As she prays, the boys chant louder.

"Remove any evil that may have invited itself within them. Return them back to their rightful owners. They are children of God. Lord, hand them back over to Lisa and William who love them dearly and deserve their love and loyalty. Bless and protect these boys with all that you have."

Chanting louder and louder, Ashley turns his head to face Alannah. Black veins are popping through his skin and his complexion is pale.

Remaining strong and showing no fear to the demon within him, Alannah continues, "Ashley, I know you can hear me, I denounce the evil within you. Rid yourself of the malevolent spirit that has intruded its way into your body. Come back to us, Ashley. It is not your time. Come back to us. By the power vested within me, I forbid you, demon, from taking him. Lord, save this boy."

As Alannah finishes, Ashley collapses to the floor.

"Lisa, quickly come get him."

As Lisa rushes into the room, Alannah turns her attention to Kane, who is now looking at her and snarling. Continuing with his chanting, Kane takes a step closer to Alannah. Looking down at his brother on the floor being cradled by his mother, Kane launches toward Lisa, his teeth bared.

Alannah places the cross on Kane's head and shouts, "Lord, you have saved Ashley, now it is time to rid Kane of the same vile entity that has invaded his body. He is your child. He is a child of God, not a child of evil."

Wailing, Kane tries to resist.

"Come back to us, Kane. Lord bring him back. Be gone, evil spirit. Rid yourself of this innocent boy! Be gone. By the power vested within me, I forbid you, demon, from taking this child. Lord save him."

With the final word spoken, much like his brother, Kane goes limp and falls. Alannah catches Kane and cradles him.

Out of breath, Alannah looks to Lisa and says, "Are you okay?"

"I think so." Lisa sobs, shaking from head to toe.

Hearing footsteps, Alannah looks to the door just as William and Brennan burst their way into the room.

"What's happened?" William shouts frantically.

"It's okay. It's going to be okay," Alannah says as she strokes Kane's soaking wet hair.

"Baby, what happened?"

"Brennan, you should have seen them. It was horrible. I've managed to rid them of her for now but I think she's that strong it won't be long before she's back. We've got to act fast."

"What's going on?" Lisa cries.

"Look, we can't tell you what's happening right now, but my advice to you, which is going to sound harsh, is that you need to restrict the boys before nightfall. You might even need to sedate them and put them somewhere secure and safe where they can't get out, like a panic room. Do you have one?"

"We have a tornado cellar in the basement."

"Perfect. It is imperative that you lock the boys in there as soon as you can."

"Wait, can't we stay with them?" William queries.

"No. It is you they're after. If you stay with them, the transition might take place and that will be the end for you both. It's as simple and serious as that."

"William, what's happening?" Lisa whimpers through her tears.

"I don't know, but we'll sort it," he replies. "Please, don't worry, our boys will be okay."

"I'm so sorry, we're going to have to leave," Alannah says. "We've got to try and stop this from happening to every child. Please, promise me you'll sedate them and put them safely in the secure hiding place?"

"We promise," William says.

"Brennan, come on. We have to go."

Grabbing Brennan by the arm, William says, "I don't know what you guys are up to, but please, be careful, man."

"I will."

Feeling faint, Alannah can't believe what has just happened. Her mind and body have gone into overload right now. Turning, she holds Brennan and says, "I was so scared."

"It's okay, baby. I got you," he replies as he carries her out of the house.

Chapter Thirty

"Midnight."

Matthew lies on the floral bedsheet with his arms tucked behind his head, deep in thought. He rotates his swollen ankles, imagining how blissful his life will be after the demise of the evil that has been taunting him for so long. He smiles as a vision unfolds in his mind. Being chased along the beach by Eve and his granddaughter, Matthew reaches down and splashes water in their direction. Embracing his imagination, Matthew chuckles. A playful family sharing laughter, love and smiles is all he's ever wanted, and now he's closer than ever to getting it back.

A sudden bang jolts him back to reality. Matthew winces as the door flings open and Alannah and Brennan burst into the room.

"Are you okay?" Matthew asks, jumping up. "Here, sit down."

"Sit down, baby," Brennan says as he places Alannah onto the bed. "Can we get her some water, please?"

"Sure," Phil says as he grabs a bottle of water out of the fridge and passes it to Alannah. Without speaking, she gulps it back.

"What happened?" Matthew asks.

Wiping the excess water from round her mouth, Alannah clears her throat before she says, "It was horrible." Tears fall down her face. "The boys were already possessed."

"What!" Matthew shouts.

"Yes. I had to denounce the evil and bring them back. It was terrifying. Those poor babies just looked horrific. And the parents, good Lord, the mother had been slashed by one of the boys. It's so lucky I was there with my blessed rosary beads because I don't think those two would have made it through the rest of the day."

"Wait, what… how… I mean…" Matthew's unable to find the words. "What the actual…"

"I know," Brennan says. "I only made it upstairs after she'd already rid them of the spirit. I was with William in the living area, and we heard a lot of shouting and screaming, so we ran upstairs, but by the time we'd arrived, she'd already saved the boys."

"Oh my goodness, Alannah, that is so brave of you."

"Thank you." She sniffles.

"You did amazing, baby. I'm so proud of you." Brennan says as he kisses her on the head.

"Where are they now?" Phil asks.

"I told them they needed to put the boys somewhere safe, and potentially sedate, and restrain them, as I wasn't certain that the possession wouldn't resurface."

"Shit," Phil says.

"Gents, we have to stop her. I've looked evil in the eye and it's scary. We're going to have to act fast," Alannah says.

"Well, Hermon's made another break though, thanks to the Smashing of the Clay Pots. Tell her, Hermon."

Pushing the glasses back up the bridge of his nose, Hermon says, "I'm sorry for what you have just been through, Alannah. I have researched this entity for many years now, so I am aware of its capabilities and powers, and I can imagine just how horrifying this encounter would have been for you. However, I am happy you have made it out unharmed."

"Thank you, Hermon. That means a lot."

Retrieving the book from the top of the small cabinet, Hermon flicks the pages before making his selection. "Here it is. Okay, so this entry states the following: *A time of chaos. Not a time of peace. A time to build. Not a time to release. Busy up high creating and not observing, this is when she will be seen. As the transition of time takes place, from one day to the next, get ready, as her eyes will not meet.*"

"I mean, I'm not being funny, but what does that mean in English?" Phil says with a dumbfounded look on his face.

"I believe this is basically stating that there will only be one available time slot in which she will be vulnerable. And I think it's going to be at midnight. What other time ticks from one day to the next?"

"Good spot, Hermon," Matthew says as he claps his hands together. "Right, what time is it now?"

"It's half past four."

"So, we've got… around seven and a half hours before kick-off. That's plenty of time."

"Matthew," Hermon says in a less than enthusiastic way.

"Yes, Hermon."

"Well, the time's just the easy bit. I think she's going to be up within the clouds. And I'm not sure how we're going to get up there."

"Fuck!" Matthew shouts. "Erm, what if we try and hire a helicopter?"

"On Christmas day. Is that a joke?" Phil laughs.

"Okay, what if we steal a helicopter?"

"Steal a helicopter? Now you are having a laugh. And I suppose you're going to propel into the sky like some action movie star!" Phil sets off belly laughing.

"Mate, stop laughing. This is serious."

Putting up his hand up, Brennan says, "I took flying lessons a while ago. I might be a bit rusty, but I should be able to fly a helicopter."

"I didn't know you had flying lessons," Alannah says smiling.

"Yes! Thank *you,* Brennan," Matthew says. "That's settled, then. We'll steal a helicopter from somewhere, and Brennan will fly me up." Clapping his hands together once more, Matthew shouts, "Right, what's the next challenge?"

Addressing the room, Hermon says, "We honestly have one shot at this, everybody. Precision and timing are going to mean everything. If we miss this window, we're screwed, basically."

"How long do I have to get to her and stab her heart?"

"Interesting you should ask, because I was wondering the same thing, so I carried on reading and found an interesting sentence." Scanning the page, Hermon continues, "Ah, here it is… so this bit reads: *A single strike for every number of the fallen angel shall suffice.*"

"Again, English please," Phil says.

"The fallen angel is the number six. I think we've got six minutes, maybe even six seconds to take her out. Either way, I don't think we have long."

"Six minutes or seconds, are you fucking kidding me? You never told me that when we spoke about it before," Matthew protests. "We might as well throw the towel in now, lads. Six minutes or seconds. How the bleeding hell am I going to jump from a helicopter and get to her heart in six minutes or seconds? Talk about setting me up to fail. Who made that fucking bullshit rule up?" Matthew punches the wall. "For fuck's sake! Shit! Shit! Shit!"

"It's going to be okay," Alannah whispers. "I believe in you. Everyone inside this room believes in you. You've been selected for a reason and you will achieve the right outcome. You've got us by your side." Alannah smiles. "And, if you go down, we all go down, so we might as well try and win this thing together."

Knowing Alannah's right doesn't calm Matthew down in the slightest. The fate of the world is resting on his shoulders and it's starting to feel heavy.

Looking to the group of misfits he has surrounding him, Matthew exhales deeply, "Midnight it is, then! Now let's go find a helicopter to steal and make a plan."

Chapter Thirty-One

"Showtime!"

The raven is flying over the Atlantic Ocean. She has travelled the globe in record time, gliding from country to country, leaving her trail of mass destruction behind. The fully formed mist is ready and waiting to pounce. Developing rapidly, this hungry element is desperate to take possession over every human body. It successfully deceives all those who encounter it. Its victims assume it is a regular thick fog on a cold winter's night, and walk into it, not knowing its true deadly nature. Embedded deep within is the Dark Empresses final implantation: molecules of her DNA filled with poison, just waiting to be ingested.

Proud of her evil accomplice, Jezebel has been waiting for her to arrive back at Moycullen, so she can reward her for her efforts. But the raven hasn't made it back just yet. Moments away from the birth of her empire, Jezebel looks out of the window and becomes engulfed by a huge sense of empowerment.

A true sight of beauty greets her eyes. Moycullen has been completely taken over by her precious suffocating mist. Seeping through the cracks, the ever so obedient mist creeps into Jezebel's room. Yanking her window open, Jezebel hangs her head outside. Inhaling the toxic haze, she closes her eyes and rolls her head back. The sweet, sweet poison circulates around her, sending orgasmic sensations throughout her black veins. Tilting her head as far back as it can go, Jezebel opens her eyes and stares at the beauty of her vortex. Jet-black and bubbling away, much like her subservient mist it waits for her command to activate its true power and potential.

Leaning back into the room, Jezebel slams the window shut and turns to her desk. Reaching inside the drawer, she removes another of her sacred possessions – the bulky black leather-coated worn-looking book with the silver upside-down cross on the front. Opening it, she flicks through the pages. Finding the entry she desires, Jezebel's senses kindle.

Raising her arm, she chants the following: "*In noctis tenebris et coepit eat. Effectum esse coepisset. Ut non debet dici potentia tua. Asserentes auctoritatem tuam. Capere. Capere. Capere!*"

As the thick black substance drips from her mouth onto the pages, Jezebel smears it into an upside-down cross and slams the book shut.

Eve is tucking Honey into her crib. Her daughter looks up and gives her a gummy grin. Smiling back, Eve's heart warms. But the unconditional love she holds for her daughter is only adding to her pain. Fighting back the tears, Eve is totally unaware of how this evening is going to pan out. A multitude of thoughts circulate inside her head. Honey lets out an innocent little chuckle and Eve chuckles back. Reaching inside the crib, Eve strokes Honey's curly hair and softly sings, "Princess, my baby princess, no matter where I might be. Princess, my baby princess, with you I will always be. Princess, my baby princess, my heart will always belong to thee. Princess, my baby princess, it's time to go to sleep."

Eve lowers the adjustable crib side and kneels on the floor. Resting her head against the pillow, next to her daughter, Eve whispers, "Everything I do, I'm doing for you and your future. Being your mother has been the best thing ever and I am lucky that I have you." She wants to tell her daughter exactly how she feels in the hopes that it is getting through to her in her dreams. "You see, before you came along, I had no clue what unconditional love was. I love your father, don't get me wrong, but there's something about having a little person that's part of you that creates a special kind of love, and I'm so grateful that I got to experience this with you."

Honey sucks in her little pink lips and her eyelashes flutter.

"You're so pretty." Kissing her on the cheek, she whispers in her tiny ear, "Baby girl, Uncle Thomas is going to look after you this evening as mummy has got a particularly important job to do, okay?"

Honey mumbles in her sleep.

"I'm going to take that as a yes!" Eve laughs. "Don't tell anyone, but Mummy has to help your granddaddy save the world. Yes, you have a granddaddy, who you will meet soon. From what I remember about him, he is kind, he is caring, and I know he is going to love you oh so much, Honey." Wiping the tears from her cheek and chin and desperately trying to compose herself, Eve continues, "Uncle Thomas is going to protect you and keep you safe while I'm gone. You will be taken care of, my princess." She kisses her on the head once more, her tears landing on Honey. "I will always love you, my baby girl. You will always be my first ever true, true love, no matter what. I just really want you to know that."

Smelling the fragrant scent of her hair for a final time, Eve stands and raises the crib side and locks it in place. Turning, Eve sees that the mist is seeping into her room, invading her space.

Panicking, she says, "Thomas…"

"I'm here, don't worry," he replies. He's sat in the rocking chair, rocking back and forth.

"Please come and protect her," Eve requests as she wipes her face yet again. "This mist cannot touch her skin, or she will become possessed instantly."

"Don't worry, she has a protection layer on her already." Pointing to the ceiling, he winks and says, "Had a chat with the big man upstairs before I came."

Eve relaxes a little and her posture slumps.

Standing, Thomas makes his way to Eve and places his hands on shoulders. "I'm more concerned about you. Are you sure about this?"

"Never been surer about anything," Eve says with her head high.

"And you remember exactly what you have to do and timings etcetera?"

"Yes. I've got it burned inside my mind."

"Have you told anyone?"

"Not a soul."

"Okay, then let's get this show on the road."

"Let's," she replies.

"Eve, I just want to say that what you're doing is truly admirable."

"I'm doing this for my daughter to have a future and nothing more, so please just promise me that you will protect her at all costs."

"I promise. And Eve…"

"Yes."

"Mother wanted me to tell you that she will be with you every step of the way and she's crazy proud of you."

Saying nothing, Eve looks to the clock. Clearing her throat, she says, "Right, it's almost time. I must go." As she walks towards the door, Eve looks back at the crib a final time before whispering, "Sweet dreams, my princess." She cleans her face off for a final time before opening the door and leaving the room.

Making her way to the main room, Eve is met on the middle landing by Elisabeth. The pair snarl at one another. Eve says nothing to her biggest rival. A deafening silence circulates around them. Entering the main room, Eve heads straight for Lewis, who is standing in his spot with his head low.

Hugging him, she whispers in his ear, "I love you. Thank you for always loving me and giving me the best gift ever."

"I love you so much and right back at ya. You, Honey, Freddie, Terrance, Rupert and Hope are my life."

Tickling the tip of her nose onto his, Eve smiles.

Hearing the rustling of feet, Eve looks to the door. The children slowly begin to fill the room. Led by Freddie, Terrance and Rupert, row after row of children fill the space. With their heads low, every child stands in their usual place. As the last child enters the room and takes up their position, a giggle travels round the room and echoes through Eve's eardrums. Looking up high, she smiles as she sees Hope whizzing across the ceiling. Another innocent baby she is going to help free from the sadistic shackles. *Thud. Thud. Thud.* The walls tremble. Eve knows this can only mean one thing. Jezebel is on her way.

"The orphanage is just over there," Matthew says to Phil and Hermon, who lie on the ground next to him in the forest overlooking the Delaware River.

"What, where those green lights are in the distance?"

"I think so. But to be honest, I'm not sure because this fog is throwing me off. I mean surely it is, right? Where else are you going to get green lighting inside?"

"True." Looking to his watch, Phil says, "Mate, we haven't got long. What are we going to do about the helicopter issue?"

"If Brennan doesn't turn up soon, I'm just going to have to jump in the deep end."

"What do you mean?"

"Well, it's all or nothing, right?"

"Oh gosh, mate, what you gonna do?"

"I'm thinking of catching her off guard as she's leaving."

"Leaving…"

"Yeah, if I can reach her before she starts rising, I might stand a chance of grabbing her on land. And then I'll just, you know, improvise by wrestling her to ground to complete the deed. I think I'll be strong enough, don't you?"

"Yeah mate. Sure," Phil says, sounding unconvinced.

"What other option do I have without a helicopter?"

"I know, mate. Right, well, if you're gonna do that, then I'm coming to help you."

"Thank you," Matthew says as he smiles at his friend's support.

"Do you have the crucifix, Matthew?" Hermon asks.

"Yeah, it's here," he replies as he pats his jacket.

Panicking, Matthew reaches inside his trouser pocket. He sighs with relief as he feels the outline of the heart-shaped locket. Matthew is ready to follow through with the commitment he made to himself. Aware that he will be faced with her any moment now, Matthew will finally have the ability of ramming this tainted item down the evil bitch's throat as she lies dying.

"How you feeling?" Hermon asks.

"I'm ready. And I just want to say thank you for everything. If it wasn't for you, we'd have no clue how to defeat her. I'm forever grateful."

"Don't mention it. I want the world rid of her, too."

Standing with Eve and Elisabeth on either side of her, Jezebel holds the worn-looking leather book firmly in her hand.

"It is time," she bellows. "Fear should be spread across this planet. We will take what is mine. What has always been mine. And you will exist under my ruling. Come, my children, show you true selves."

As soon as Jezebel has made her command, every individual in the room transforms. An almighty scream goes up as they appear to rejoice. Jezebel's eyes light up as she takes in the view before her. She's very aware that this is just the beginning. Shortly every child will officially join the empire created by her. And the best bit is they will remain a mirror reflection of her too. Raising her arms, Jezebel feels electrical forces accelerating around her body.

"Children of the world unite. Go! Ignite the evil within. Kill any living adult you can find. Snap their necks, rip out their hearts, slit their wrists, do what is needed to get the job done. Ensure that they are dead. Gather, my children of darkness, go! *Temimi. Temimi. Temimi.*" And just like that, almost everyone inside the room disappears.

Across the globe, children are levitating out of their beds, and adults are being restrained inside them. Adults who are awake are being taunted and choked, and the children are being empowered. The poisonous mist intertwines with their bodies and seeps into their every pore. Children of Japan, the United Kingdom, Australia, Africa, Europe, Brazil, Russia, Germany… the children of the world are all transitioning together under Jezebel's command! Every child around the world drags their bodies towards their parents' and any adult within their reach. Paralyzed, the adults are powerless. They can only move their eyes and endure watching their possessed children drag their way over to them, ready to devour their souls.

As she sees this unfold in her mind's eye, Jezebel's veins pump with electrical energy. Gaining more power than ever before, Jezebel believes she is now unstoppable.

She peers at Eve and Elisabeth. "You two, follow me."

"Yes, Dark Empress," they reply, bowing their heads.

"As soon as we leave, I will rise up and commence the next phase of the vortex. It is *imperative* that you guard me at all costs, do I make myself clear?"

"Yes, Dark Empress."

Content that Eve and Elisabeth will protect her, Jezebel drags her feet towards the door. Lugging her body, Jezebel twitches her head. As the door flings open, she's instantly met by a gust of the mist as it bursts through the open doorway.

"Retreat, my precious creation. Now that the children have accepted the evil, I need you to fill the sky and merge with my vortex to release the portal."

Exiting, the mist travels up and rests at the vortex. The two elements combine and sparks begin to fly. The vortex is now becoming a deep grey. As the ground clears, Jezebel steps outside. Peering at Eve and Elisabeth through the gap in her hair, Jezebel orders, "Protect me."

"Yes, Dark Empress."

Rolling her head back, Jezebel closes her eyes, reaches her arms out and chants, "*Surge sursus. Surge sursus. Surge sursus*!"

Turning her head, appearing suspicious, Elisabeth says, "I think I hear something behind that bush."

Putting out her arm, Eve says, "I will go. Protect her at all costs."

"Shit, shit, shit, shit, one of them is walking over, mate," Phil says. "Oh fuck, we're dead. We're dead. Get your fucking cross thingy – quick!"

"Calm down," Matthew says, his heart in his mouth. "Just stay still and be quiet."

"Oh shit, mate, she's already travelling into the sky. Good luck grabbing her legs now," Phil whispers. "We're so dead."

"Phil, seriously, you need to shut up and stay still," Matthew snaps.

Laying on the ground completely stiff, Matthew, Phil and Hermon try to hold their breath to minimise movement. The entity enters the forest and begins gliding through the trees. Matthew's heart pounds. Fear is travelling round his body at an insane rate. He's got to take action, he's come too far to lose now.

"Just breathe deeply. It's you or her, mate. It's you or her," Matthew mutters to himself. "Please, God, if you can hear me, now would be a real good time to help us out."

Matthew hears twigs snapping next to him. Just as he is psyching himself up to attack and tell Hermon and Phil to run and save themselves, he hears, "Father."

"What the f…" Phil mumbles.

Confused, Matthew goes to stand up.

Grabbing his arm, Phil says, "Mate, don't go out, it could be a trap."

"Father, it's me, Eve. Please, I'm here to help you, but I can't stay long."

"Let go of me, it's her. I know my daughter's voice when I hear it," Matthew says as he leaps up off the ground. "Eve," he cries out.

Transforming into her human form, Eve puts out her arms. "Father, it is true."

Matthew's sight has gone blurry through his tears. He stumbles over a branch, twisting his ankle. Not letting this stop him, Matthew hobbles his way over to his daughter and leaps into her arms. Matthew holds her close. Tears stream down his face. The whole moment feels as if it is going in slow motion. Brushing her hair back off her face and kissing her on the head, Matthew sobs.

"Darling, oh my, I haven't stopped looking for you. All this time, my princess. I knew I'd find you."

Crying uncontrollably, he sees Phil and Hermon appear at the side of him. "It's her. It's really her."

Phil's eyes well up with tears.

"Eve, darling, this is…"

"Phil, Lewis's father," Eve says, still tucked into her father's arms. "I know. Hi, Mr Parkinson."

"Come here, you," Phil says as he joins the duo and squeezes them tight.

"And that is Hermon. He's helped us work out how to defeat her."

"Hi Hermon," Eve says.

"Hi, young lady. I've heard so many things about you."

Matthew holds Eve by the shoulders to get a good look at her. "I can't believe it. Darling, you're coming home." Throwing his arms around her once more, Matthew doesn't want to ever let her go again in his life.

"Father, I don't have long," Eve whispers. "Elisabeth will come looking soon if I don't go back. Listen to me, you cannot defeat her alone."

"Yes I can, I just have to stab her heart with this," Matthew says as he shows her the crucifix.

"Father, you are mistaken, you have to stab the silver heart that hangs around her neck. There is no way for you to get close, so I will have to go and snatch it from her."

"No way!" Matthew protests. "There's not a chance that I'm letting you near that evil bitch again. You will stay here, and I will go and do it."

"Father, please, just listen to me. There is no way you can get up to her, it would take a miracle, and how often do they come around?"

"Often enough for me to know that I'm not sending my daughter to do my dirty work. I brought her into our lives, I'm going to be the one that finishes this."

"Mate, I think you should hear her out. She's the only one who can get close to her without raising concern."

"Would you send your daughter up there?" Matthew shouts at Phil.

"Father, please. I really need you to be on board with this as I'm running out of time. She will soon have infused the two elements and the portal will arrive. Then it's game over for mankind."

Giving in, Matthew says, "Fine. We'll try it your way, but I'm not happy about it."

"Thank you. Okay, so I will shoot up, snatch the heart from around her neck as she is reaching her climax and then I will bring this to you. Father, you must combine the crucifix with the locket immediately, do you understand?"

"Yeah, I mean that sounds easy in comparison to what we thought we had to do."

"Father, by any chance do you have the matching locket?"

"Yes, it's here, look..." Matthew says as he retrieves the tainted item from his trouser pocket.

Matthew's hands tremble. The pair stare each other dead in the eye.

"Promise me, you will do everything I ask of you?" Eve says.

"I promise."

"I love you so much, Father. Thank you for not giving up on me."

"You're my daughter, Evelyn Jade, I would do anything for you," Matthew says as he tucks the loose strand of hair behind her ear.

"I get a feeling that you would." Eve smiles. "Right, stay here and wait for my signal. Once I shout, you come and retrieve the locket from me."

Unable to stop himself, Matthew grabs her a final time and holds her tight. "I have never stopped loving you," he cries.

"I have to go," Eve says, wiping the tears that have fallen from her eyes.

Letting go of her as she turns, Matthew falls to the ground and cups his head in his hands.

"Mate, we need to go and hide," Phil says.

"How can I have been so stupid and just let her go like that? I've only just got her back. I've just made a huge mistake, I have to get her back," Matthew says as he goes to chase after her.

Holding him back, Phil shouts, "Mate, you have to let her go. She's grown now. Please, you don't want to get her or the rest of us killed, just come and hide behind this tree."

Dragging Matthew away from the direction of the chaos, the threesome retreat into the forest out of sight.

Looking high, Eve sees Jezebel summoning the portal. The sky is dark grey, with a huge whirlpool forming. Huge bolts of electricity are surging at a rapid rate through the sky and are crashing down on the ground. Transforming back into her evil form, Eve leaves the forest.

"What took you so long?" Elisabeth shouts.

"It was a false alarm. An animal was rushing around, and I had to take care of it to ensure it doesn't cause any chaos."

Seeing Elisabeth staring at her with a sceptical eye, Eve barks, "Check over there, will you." She points in the opposite direction of where her father and his friends are. "Make yourself useful."

Staring up high, Eve hears Jezebel chanting. She knows the words. If she is going to do this, she will need to act fast, as there's about two minutes left before the takeover is complete. Leaping off the ground, Eve takes off. Flying up over the orphanage, as she peers down, Eve sees the reality. There are people screaming and running around everywhere. Possessed children of all ages are wreaking havoc across the streets.

"It's time to put an end to this," she shouts.

As she shoots towards Jezebel at full speed, a huge bolt of electricity shoots past her body, narrowly missing her head. Fighting against the wind that is circling at an unnatural rate, Eve pushes through the pain. She's almost there. Feeling a tug on her leg, Eve doesn't even bother to look back. She stays focused on her mission. She can't let her daughter down, she has to do this for her. Pushing one a final time, Eve reaches Jezebel. Releasing her razor-sharp nails, Eve slashes through the back of the chain and rips it off her neck.

Plummeting back down, Eve turns to ensure Jezebel isn't coming after her. Thankfully she is locked inside her transition trance. Her eyes are not open, and she is not present, as all her power travels around the globe rapidly. However, Eve does see Elisabeth, and she's hot on her tail. The clock is ticking. Jezebel will be stuck for at least the next ninety seconds. Trying to push harder, Eve struggles against the force of the vortex, which is now pulling her back up. Believing she's going to make it, all of a sudden Eve feels a hand grip her leg. Looking over her shoulder, she sees it's Elisabeth!

"You're going to die!"

As the pair spin out of control, Eve drops the locket. Floating down, she is unable to catch it as Elisabeth tugs on her, trying to fight her mid-air.

Seeing a woman's face appear, Eve hears, "Do it for your daughter. I am so proud of you, my darling. I believe in you."

Eve knows this is her mother. "Noooo!" she screams.

Determination fills her body. Eve is ready to end Elisabeth. No one is going to get in the way of her saving her daughter. Surges of electricity blast past the pair. Eve reaches for Elisabeth's eyes and presses them back inside her head. Eve's face suddenly burns as Elisabeth gashes it with her nails. Eve pushes her eyeballs deeper into their sockets, and Elisabeth finally let's go of her grip. Regaining her balance, Eve launches her body back down through the sky to the ground. The locket is still drifting back down. Around sixty seconds left. Eve's heart is racing.

Now millimetres away from grabbing the chain, Eve shouts, "Father, now!"

Seeing Matthew run from out of the forest, Eve grabs the chain and throws it in his direction. He reaches up high and catches it. Stumbling back, he trips and lands on his back. Finally, reaching the ground, Eve rushes to his aid. Just ten seconds are remaining.

"Did you catch it?"

"Yes," Matthew replies. His hands shaking, he pulls the other locket and the crucifix from his trouser pocket. As she's about to give Matthew the next instructions, Eve gets a sudden chill down her spine. "Oh no."

"What?" Matthew replies as he looks up. Peering over Eve's shoulder, Matthew's eyes widen.

"Eve, please!" Lewis bellows from afar.

"Come here…" Jezebel turns to him and says.

"Please, just do as she asks," Lewis pleads as he approaches.

No longer in control of her body, Eve turns, and with her head low, she makes her way to Jezebel. Eve's heart skips a beat as she sees Jezebel has her arm around Lewis's head and her bladed nail to his throat.

"Please, don't hurt him," she begs. "I'll do anything."

"Oh, now you want to do as you're told," Jezebel taunts. "Didn't think I'd have a backup plan to your defiance. This one came running as soon as I summonsed him. So obedient," Jezebel says as she licks his face with her grey coarse tongue.

"Please, Dark Empress. Do not punish Lewis for my rebellious behaviour." Crying, Eve pleads a final time. "Please. Take me instead."

"Where's the fun in that?" she replies as she lets out an almighty laugh and slits his throat. She throws him to the ground.

"Nooo!" Eve cries as she falls to her knees.

Lewis has transitioned back to his human form. "Eve," he gasps, holding his bleeding throat.

"No… Lewis!" Phil shouts as he charges towards Jezebel. "My boy. Not my boy."

Suddenly, a whirring sound in the distance distracts Jezebel.

"Father now! Stab the hearts now!"

"But I don't know which one it is," Matthew says, looking panicked.

Tears are gushing down Eve's face. "Please, you have to stab them both."

"But you'll die!" Matthew cries.

"I have to go, dad. Please, you have to let me go."

"No way, Eve, I'm not losing you again. You're coming home with me."

"Father, please, you have to save my daughter."

"No, Eve, I can't. I won't lose you again. Please, I can't do this." Matthew's face is covered in tears and his nose is gushing.

"You have to let me go. I have to die with her, it's the only way. We are one. I promise I'll be okay. Mother and Thomas are waiting for me. Please, I will do anything to save my daughter. Just take good care of her."

Matthew freezes.

Jezebel approaches. Phil jumps up, but is instantly slashed across the face. He lies on the ground bleeding heavily. She reaches out to inflict more pain upon him.

The clock has almost ticked its final tock. The vortex is now almost at full sustainability. Matthew needs to act fast! There is rustling from all directions. Hundreds of demonic children appear, all on their way towards Matthew.

"Father, please, let me go!" Eve shouts.

"Matthew, you have to do something fast," Hermon says.

Tears are gushing down Matthew's face. "I love you so much, Evelyn Jade. Tell your mum I'm sorry I couldn't protect you both!"

"Father, I promise, just please do it. You have to, for my daughter."

"I'm so sorry, Eve. I will always love you!"

"I will always love you too, father."

Screaming, Matthew raises his arm. He stabs the hearts together onto the crucifix. A bright beam of light bursts from the centre, accompanied by a powerful force. Matthew drops the lockets and crucifix and is thrown back. He hits his head on a rock and is knocked out cold.

THE FINAL CHAPTER!

The day is bright, breezy and full of hope. Standing in the living room of his luxury three-storey home, Matthew Honey gazes out at the beautiful serenity of the small English beach. He's wearing pale blue chinos, a white t-shirt, and his wrist is filled with tatty cotton friendship bracelets of every colour. It's a more chilled-out, laid-back look for Matthew. Even his hairstyle is more relaxed.

Standing with his back to the white living room door that's now covered with children's drawings, Matthew continues to stare peacefully out of the window at the sea. He looks up to the piercing blue crystal-clear sky and watches as delicate white clouds drift gracefully by, a subtle reminder that the world is continually passing with ease.

A gentle smile begins to form on Matthew's face. "Good morning, my family," he whispers.

Hearing a stampede of footsteps coming from behind him, Matthew turns.

"There you are, Granddaddy!"

Matthew beams from ear to ear as he sees his precious granddaughter Honey looking all angelic in her birthday dress holding Gregg in her hand. Swooping down, he collects her from off the ground. Twirling her around, he says, "There's my birthday girl."

Letting out a deep tummy tickle giggle, Honey says, "Granddaddy, I'm going to get dizzy in a minute."

Stopping, Matthew holds her in his arms, and as he looks her in the eye, he says, "I cannot believe you're six already. I'm going to have to charge you rent soon, missy."

Honey sets off giggling again. "No, Granddaddy, I can't pay rent, I'm too little."

"What, you're too little with these beanpole legs?" Matthew jokes.

Admiring his granddaughter's toothless grin, Matthew sees his own daughter in her, he sees Eve. Welling up with tears and not wanting to cry in front of Honey, Matthew puts her down and says, "Oh would you look at that, it's almost time to go. Have you got your balloons?"

"Yep," Honey says as she skips out the door.

Patting down his pockets, Matthew feels for his phone.

Seeing Honey entering the room again, wrestling with the five oversized heart-shaped helium balloons, Matthew chuckles. "Come here, princess, let me help you."

Laughing, Honey counts them as she passes them to him. "One for Mummy. One for Daddy. One for Uncle Thomas. One for Grandma Lauren. And one for Grandma Alice."

"You're so clever." Kissing her on the head, Matthew says, "Right, let's go."

"Yay, let's go beach."

"Okay, I'll hold the balloons so that they don't escape and fly off, and I'll pass them to you when it's time to let them go."

"Okay, Granddaddy."

Matthew and Honey walk across the road hand in hand to the beach. As soon as the sand touches her toes, Honey removes her sandals and runs off. Doing cartwheels and rolling around, Honey is having the best time.

"Hey, princess, look, who's that over there?"

"Where?" Honey shouts, stroking the hair out of her eyes and spitting the sand out of her mouth.

"There." Matthew points straight ahead.

"Grandpops!" Honey shouts.

Beaming, Matthew's heart warms as he sees her running through the sand towards Phil, Selena, Hope, Freddie, Terence and Rupert.

Throwing his arms out, Phil shouts, "Happy sixth birthday, peanut!"

"Thank you, Grandpops," Honey says as she leaps in for a cuddle.

Feeling his phone vibrate, Matthew retrieves it from his trouser pocket with his spare hand. Seeing Alannah's face flashing on the screen, he smiles as he answers the video call. "Hey you."

"I haven't missed it, have I?"

"No, we've just got here now."

"I'm so sorry, it's been crazy at the orphanage this morning. We've got so many children here."

"Hey, Rita," Matthew says as he sees her little face peeping up behind Alannah.

Shying away, Rita doesn't reply.

"So, where's the birthday girl?" Alannah asks.

"Hold on one second, she's just with her grandpops."

"Oh, that's too cute."

Brennan's face appears. "Hey, Matthew."

"Hey man, how you doing?"

"Yeah, I'm all good. We haven't missed it, have we?" Brennan asks.

"No, we've just got to the beach now."

"Great."

"Honey, looks who's on the phone for you."

"Lana and Bren Bren. Hi, it's my birthday today."

"We know, beautiful girlie," the pair say.

"Happy sixth birthday, you big girl," Alannah says as she blows her a kiss.

"Where's Lizzie?" Honey asks.

"She's going to be here any second now," Brennan says. "Oh, look, as if by magic, here she is."

"Lizzie," Honey shouts. "Lizzie, it's my birthday."

Smiling on the screen of the phone is Elisabeth. "I know, little princess. I'm so happy I got to see you. Happy birthday."

"Thank you."

"We haven't missed it, have we?" Elisabeth asks.

"No, we've just got to the beach now," Matthew replies. "Just one second, guys. We'll get started in just a second."

As they hug one another, Phil says to Matthew, "Can you believe she's six already?"

"No, not at all. Time goes too fast, my friend." Seeing his friend's wife standing next to him, Matthew reaches over to Selena. "Hey, beautiful. Thanks for coming."

"Oh, you know I wouldn't miss this for the world," Selena replies.

"Hey guys," Matthew says to the rest of the Parkinson gang.

Seeing a familiar face in the distance holding a giant pink box with a silky ribbon around it, Matthew shouts, "What time do you call this? Last one as always!"

"Hey, what, I had to go get this one the biggest gift I could find, didn't I?" Terry shouts.

"Hey man, how you doing?" Matthew asks as he reaches round and gives Terry a hug.

"All good. Can't complain. Finally got my retirement through last week."

"Aw, congrats Terry," Phil says.

"I know. Looking forward to enjoying some time with the wife."

"Uncle Terry!" Honey shouts as she comes rushing over. "It's my birthday today."

"Really, I didn't know," Terry says as he hugs her. "I suppose it's lucky I walk around with spare presents then, isn't it, just in case it's a certain little girl's sixth birthday."

"That's how many I am, Uncle Terry."

"Well, I guess this must be yours, then."

"Princess, you can open that in a minute, okay," Matthew says. "Let's just get this started. Can you all gather round for me, please!"

"Come here, peanut," Phil says as he holds Honey close.

"Selena, can you just hold the phone up for me please, so Alannah, Brennan and Elisabeth can see."

"And me." Rita's little voice echoes through the speaker.

"And Rita."

"Sure. Of course."

Taking his position at the front, Matthew says, "Okay, I just wanted to say thank you so much for coming together today to celebrate our precious little Honey's birthday. As you all know, there are some people who can't be here in body." Matthew pauses as he tries to hold back his tears. "But these five are definitely here in spirit. Five incredibly special people who will always hold a place within our hearts. We love you all." Matthew says as he looks up high. "Every year, we come together and celebrate the life of our precious little blessing, that is Honey. We celebrate together as a unit under the watchful supervision of those who live in the sky."

"That's where my Mummy, Daddy, Uncle Thomas, Grandma Lauren and Grandma Alice live," Honey says.

"Yes, princess," Matthew replies. "Birthday girl, come here."

Stepping forward, Honey collects the balloons from her granddaddy.

"Happy sixth birthday, princess, from us all."

Kissing each of the balloons, Honey shouts, "I love you, Mummy, Daddy, Uncle Thomas, Grandma Lauren and Grandma Alice." She lets go of all the balloons.

Picking her up, Matthew cuddles Honey and holds her tight as he watches the balloons take off high. As tears trickle down his face, Honey wipes them.

"Don't cry, Granddaddy," she says. "We'll always have each other."

"We will, darling."

Coming together, the group wrap their arms round one another as they watch the balloons rise up high, swirling off together side by side in the sky. The greatest sacrifices are made for the ones we love. And no matter what, the children will always be the innocent ones!

About the Author

A.L. Frances is a thirty-three-year-old British author.

The Broken IV – Vengeance is the final book of a four-part series and marks A.L. Frances' debut in literary fiction.

Born in Wythenshawe, South Manchester, she is the product of a broken home. Her formal education was cut short before she could gain any qualifications and she became a mother to three children by the time she was just twenty years old. At twenty-one A.L. Frances suddenly finds herself cast in the role of a single parent, destined to repeat the cycle of her own difficult upbringing.

Determined to give her children a better start in life, she moved to the countryside village of Hollingworth, and eventually settled into a career in law. It was during this transition that she found herself on a journey of self-discovery. Attending multiple mindset enhancing seminars in England, America and Canada, she was exposed to the tutelage of inspirational speakers such as Bob Proctor, Tony Robbins, and Mel Robbins among others. A.L. Frances was eventually introduced to Peggy McColl, a New York Times Best Selling Author. Standing on the stage, Peggy said the words that would inspire her into action. Peggy said, "Everyone has a book in them." as she pointed into the crowd. It was at this point that A.L. Frances fell in love with the idea of writing her own book and telling her own story; one that would address one of her biggest fears: the vulnerabilities of broken homes.

At the age of twenty-nine, A.L. Frances decided it was time to start the next chapter of her life.

What follows is the start of her journey…